nw

Pages of STACKS
Promise

★ NUMBER SIX IN THE AMERICAN CENTURY SERIES ★

Pages of Promise

GILBERT MORRIS

Revell

Grand Rapids, Michigan

© 1998 by Gilbert Morris

Published by Fleming H. Revell
a division of Baker Publishing Group
P.O. Box 6287, Grand Rapids, MI 49516-6287

New paperback edition published 2007

Previously published in 1998 under the title *A Time To Build*

Printed in the United States of America

Library of Congress Cataloging-in-Publication Data
Morris, Gilbert.
    [Time to build]
    Pages of promise / Gilbert Morris.
       p.   cm. — (American century series : bk. 6)
    Originally published: A time to build, c1998.
    ISBN 10: 0-8007-3220-0 (pbk.)
    ISBN 978-0-8007-3220-2 (pbk.)
    I. United States—History—1945–1953—Fiction. 2. United States—History—1953–1961—Fiction. 3. Family—United States—Fiction. I. Title.
PS3563.O8742T55   2007
813'.54—dc22   2007027719

Scripture is taken from the King James Version of the Bible.

To Jimmy Jordan, my favorite cousin

I think often of the days when we were young
and am very grateful for them, Jimmy.
May the Lord bless you richly in these latter days.

CONTENTS

PART FOUR   QUIET TIMES

THE STUART FAMILY

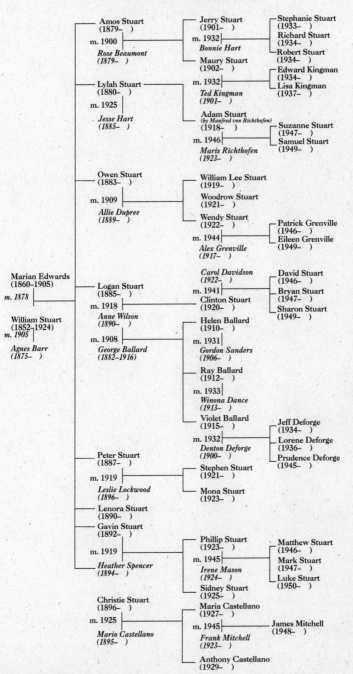

Marian Edwards
(1860–1905)

m. 1878

William Stuart
(1852–1924)
m. 1905
*Agnes Barr
(1875–)*

Amos Stuart
(1879–)
m. 1900
*Rose Beaumont
(1879–)*

Jerry Stuart
(1901–)
m. 1932
Bonnie Hart

Stephanie Stuart
(1933–)
Richard Stuart
(1934–)
Robert Stuart
(1934–)

Maury Stuart
(1902–)
m. 1932
*Ted Kingman
(1901–)*

Edward Kingman
(1934–)
Lisa Kingman
(1937–)

Lylah Stuart
(1880–)
m. 1925
*Jesse Hart
(1885–)*

Adam Stuart
(by Manfred von Richthofen)
(1918–)
m. 1946
*Maris Richthofen
(1923–)*

Suzanne Stuart
(1947–)
Samuel Stuart
(1949–)

Owen Stuart
(1883–)
m. 1909
*Allie Dupree
(1889–)*

William Lee Stuart
(1919–)

Woodrow Stuart
(1921–)

Wendy Stuart
(1922–)
m. 1944
*Alex Grenville
(1917–)*

Patrick Grenville
(1946–)
Eileen Grenville
(1949–)

Logan Stuart
(1885–)
m. 1918
*Anne Wilson
(1890–)*
m. 1908
*George Ballard
(1882–1916)*

*Carol Davidson
(1922–)*
m. 1941
Clinton Stuart
(1920–)

David Stuart
(1946–)
Bryan Stuart
(1947–)
Sharon Stuart
(1949–)

Helen Ballard
(1910–)
m. 1931
*Gordon Sanders
(1906–)*

Ray Ballard
(1912–)
m. 1933
*Winona Dance
(1913–)*

Violet Ballard
(1915–)
m. 1932
*Denton Deforge
(1900–)*

Jeff Deforge
(1934–)
Lorene Deforge
(1936–)
Prudence Deforge
(1945–)

Peter Stuart
(1887–)
m. 1919
*Leslie Lockwood
(1896–)*

Stephen Stuart
(1921–)

Mona Stuart
(1923–)

Lenora Stuart
(1890–)

Gavin Stuart
(1892–)
m. 1919
*Heather Spencer
(1894–)*

Phillip Stuart
(1923–)
m. 1945
*Irene Mason
(1924–)*

Matthew Stuart
(1946–)
Mark Stuart
(1947–)
Luke Stuart
(1950–)

Sidney Stuart
(1925–)

Christie Stuart
(1896–)
m. 1925
*Mario Castellano
(1895–)*

Maria Castellano
(1927–)
m. 1945
*Frank Mitchell
(1923–)*

James Mitchell
(1948–)

Anthony Castellano
(1929–)

Part 1
Wartime

PROLOGUE

Elvis Presley and Pat Boone and bobby-soxers and hula hoops are standard symbols of the 1950s in America. It was a postwar era, "peacetime," generally. But turbulence on a smaller scale characterized the postwar world. The Soviet Union under Joseph Stalin strengthened its control over vast areas of Eastern Europe—Bulgaria, Czechoslovakia, East Germany, Hungary, Poland, Romania. Stalin had promised civil liberties, free elections, and representative governments, but Soviet-trained political leaders, supported by military force, gained power. Anti-Communists were soon in jail, in exile—or dead.

This aggressive demeanor in Europe prompted the formation of the North Atlantic Treaty Organization (NATO) in 1949, a mutual-defense pact between Canada, the U.S., and most countries of Western Europe. Throughout the fifties, NATO increased in military strength and emphasized maintaining the "balance of power" in Europe between East and West. A "cold" war was under way that often seemed near the flashpoint, it was feared, of World War III—of all-out nuclear war. It was an era of competition, tension, and conflict between East and West, Communism and capitalism, national self-determination and totalitarianism.

In many places in the world the Cold War did indeed flash into hot wars, not directly between the "superpowers" but between factions aligned with one side or the other—war by proxy, it was called.

The stage had been set for Asia in 1945 at the Yalta conference between Stalin, Roosevelt, and Churchill. Stalin agreed to enter the war against Japan after the defeat of Germany. The Soviets fought no battles, but by the time Japan surrendered, the Soviet army had moved into northern Korea and much of Manchuria to accept the surrender of Japanese forces there. The Soviets sealed off the Korean border at the thirty-eighth parallel and set up a government run by Soviet-trained Communists. They refused to participate in free elections under UN supervision for one government for the nation, so South Korea elected a separate government. Soviet forces withdrew from North Korea in 1948, leaving behind an entrenched Communist regime and a well-trained and equipped army. Reunification of Korea by force was the goal of the war begun in 1950 by the North Koreans.

In the United States the postwar years were boom years, an era of full employment and peak production, although occasional brief periods of recession and high unemployment occurred. Those who had lived through the privations of a depression and a war were immersed in a sea of newfound economic comfort. People were happily buying new cars, new homes, and television sets.

But prosperity was marred by racial unrest and by fear of Communism at home and abroad. In 1949, eleven leaders of the Communist party were convicted of conspiring to advocate the overthrow of the U.S. government by force.

Senator Joseph R. McCarthy's sweeping accusations against "Communist sympathizers" in the government were opposed as early as June 1950 by Senator Margaret Chase Smith and other members of McCarthy's party, but it was 1954 before he was censured by the full senate.

Prosperity shifted the focus in American family life. People who didn't have to worry about subsistence placed children and family life at the top of their priority lists, according to polls. The postwar baby boom was under way, and parents felt their destiny was to make the world better for their children. They were determined that their offspring would not suffer hard times as they had. Some sociologists define the fifties as a "filiarchy"—society was not ruled by the willful demands of the young but by indulgent, sacrificing parents. "Do it for the kids" was heard on every hand.

But middle-class conformity and social stability were also challenged, by swaggering antiheroes such as James Dean and Marlon Brando, by the nonconforming beatniks, then, from 1956 on, by Elvis "the Pelvis" Presley and the beginnings of rock and roll music.

In a world of prosperity and in turmoil, the grandchildren and great grandchildren of Will and Marian Stuart looked for a peace that is complete and enduring.

1

GROWING UP

A street-model hot rod screeched to a stop in front of the split-level suburban house, and the sound of loud, laughing voices broke the silence of the neighborhood. Across the street, Mr. Gunderson opened his window and stared out for a moment, then slammed it shut.

A shadowy form separated itself from the automobile. There were raucous calls, and a female voice cried out, "Be good, Bobby! Don't do anything I wouldn't do!"

The car roared off with a screech and the smell of burning rubber. Two people in the house moved away from the window. The knob turned, and the door was opened slowly, as if to keep the sound down. Sixteen-year-old Bobby Stuart entered—then stopped stock-still when he saw his parents waiting for him. Shock ran across his face, but his devil-may-care air seldom deserted him. He stood in the open doorway and saluted his father, saying, "Private Bobby Stuart reporting for duty, Sir." He squinted his eyes and grinned. "What are you two doing up so late? Don't you have to fly tomorrow, Dad? Mom, you *never* stay up this late!"

Bobby's sister, Stephanie, a year older, had sneaked down to the landing. She could not restrain a grin—she was glad that her parents could not see it. There was something irresistible about Bobby, and even though he was constantly in and out of trouble, there was a cavalier air about him, a bubbling exuberance for life that made it hard for anyone to be angry with him for long.

17

His father did not have that difficulty, however. "Young man, do you know what time it is?"

Bobby peered at his watch, holding it close to his face. "I believe it's twenty minutes till two—or to look at it in a little better light, Dad, it's one forty. I'm a little bit late," he said cheerfully. "But I just forgot the time."

Something about the way his son pronounced his words and the way he stood alerted Jerry. Bobby was speaking very carefully, pronouncing each syllable. *That's the way drunks do*, Jerry thought grimly. He stepped forward and—sure enough—holding his face a foot away from Bobby's he said, "No point holding your breath! I can smell that liquor on you! You smell like a distillery!"

"Dad, I just had one or two drinks." Bobby shrugged and grinned.

That grin was his undoing. Jerry slammed the door shut and shoved his son backward against it. He had never been very physical in disciplining his children—had rarely ever spanked them—so his action caught Bobby completely by surprise. Bonnie, Bobby's mother, gasped and stepped back from them.

With his eyes barely two inches from his son's as he held him against the door, Jerry spoke with careful emphasis through clenched teeth. "Don't you ever again come in late and drunk. Never again! Is that clear?"

Bobby's grin was gone. So was the alcoholic blear from his eyes. For a moment he'd believed his father might hit him. "Yes, Dad," he said. But in the second before Jerry released him something else showed in Bobby's eyes—resentment and an anger of his own.

Stephanie quietly slipped back upstairs. Richard, Bobby's twin, was listening in the dark hall outside his room to the commotion downstairs. Stephanie paused outside her bedroom door and whispered, "He's going to get it this time."

"No he won't. Mom will talk Dad out of it. She always does."

"You couldn't see from here. Dad nearly hit him! You wait
and see, Richard, he'll be grounded til the century's over!"

Bonnie had not interfered in the confrontation between
father and son. But as she and Jerry lay in bed later, they
talked about what had occurred.

"I knew I should have stuck with keeping him grounded,
but you said, 'Oh, he's only young once. Don't make him miss
out.' I think he needs to miss out. Maybe it would get his
attention," grumbled Jerry, still angry.

"How could you attack him like that? I was afraid you were
about to punch him!"

"I was afraid so, too." Jerry seemed to finally regain his
composure. "I'm sorry I frightened you. But, honey, I've had
it with him and his carousing friends. He has a terrific musical
ability, just like my granddad. But there's more to life than
music."

"You do realize, don't you, that he's just like you?" Bonnie's voice sounded harsh in the darkness.

"He's not like me at all."

"Well, maybe you don't remember your Cara Gilmore
days, but I do." She was angry—miffed at any rate—and
turned away from him, emphatically ending the conversation.

Bonnie had rarely thrown Jerry's wild youth in his face.
Her doing so told him how deeply distressed she was. He lay
staring at the ceiling and drifted off with painful memories
of the beautiful, the exciting Cara who had so captivated
him.

The next morning the household awakened to the sound
of Jerry Stuart's raised voice laying down the law to the now-
sober Bobby. Jerry delivered a stern lecture not-so-privately,
then announced at breakfast, "Bobby's not driving the car
until I give the okay." Bonnie said little, but she looked upset
and tired.

The three siblings went to school in the '36 Ford that the boys had resurrected and owned equal shares in. Richard and Robert were twins, but they didn't look all that much alike. Bobby's hair was auburn rather than black like the rest of his family, and no one in his family had eyes like his, either, a cornflower blue.

The twins' sister, Stephanie, was tall, a little over five feet nine inches, with the lean, athletic, California-girl look. She had the blackest possible hair, with enough curl so that she could try different styles. Her eyes were blue-green, or gray-green, or sometimes just blue or green, for they changed, like a chameleon, depending on what she put on. This pleased her, for in this respect she was unlike the girls that she grew up with.

Richard was driving, and taking his eyes off the road, he glanced at Stephanie, then at his twin, who was whistling carefully and appeared not to have a care in the world. Richard said, "Well, you're grounded, are you?"

Bobby shrugged. "Aw, Mom and Dad are a little strait-laced, but it'll blow over." He then proceeded to tell them about the party. "We had a real good time. I played guitar, and Tim Roberts played the piano, and Hick Seastrum was on the drums. It was a real knockout!"

As they pulled into the lot in front of the high school, a tall, brick structure, Stephanie stared at the building with distaste. "Only another month and I'll be out of this place!" They got out of the car and made their way up the steps. Inside, they separated, going to their classes, and none of them believed that Bobby would be grounded for long.

Stephanie's much longed for graduation came and quickly was over. She'd attended the parties and events associated with it happily enough since they signaled the end of school. She hoped she'd like college better, but mostly she tried not to think about it. The family had its own celebration, in spite of the ongoing verbal conflicts between her father and her brother Bobby. Her grandparents, Amos and Rose Stuart, flew out from Chicago for a vacation to attend. They'd flown home a week ago.

A wide spot in the creek that lay past the rough dunes a half mile from their house had always formed a swimming pool for the three young Stuarts. Today Richard and Stephanie came in the midafternoon, without Bobby, and plunged in, splashing gleefully. For half an hour they swam and splashed water at each other, and Richard pursued Stephanie, threatening to dunk her, but she was a better swimmer than he. The pool was thirty feet wide and at the deepest part over six or seven feet deep.

Stephanie thought she saw a snake and squealed, scrambling out on the bank, but then Richard held up a piece of vine and laughed at her cheerfully, saying, "This is a bad old snake all right!"

Finally the two came out and lay down on the blanket, drying off quickly in the late June sun. Stephanie put on her sunglasses and put her hands under her head. She was wearing a black one-piece bathing suit. She murmured, "What day is it, today? The date I mean."

"The twenty-fourth."

"Saturday, June 24. More than a month since graduation. I'm so glad it's all over."

Richard was wearing a pair of faded tan cutoffs. He rolled over, rested his chin on his arm, and said, "You going to Chicago to work for Grandpa?"

"Oh, he'll never give me a job. He wants me to go to college. I'd rather work for him, though."

Richard flopped on his back, shaded his eyes with his hands, his fingers laced. The sun soaked into him, and he dozed off. He awakened sometime later when he heard Stephanie say something. "What did you say?" he muttered.

Stephanie was sitting up combing her hair. "I said, are you going to go to college?"

Richard sat up, rubbed his eyes, and blinked like an owl emerging from its tree. "Man, it's hot today!" He thought about her question for a moment. "I don't know, Steph."

She smiled at him affectionately. "Is this Streak Stuart I hear talking, sought after by half the colleges in the country?" She called him by the nickname his friends often used, for he had run the fastest hundred-yard dash in a California high school that year. He had received several offers of track scholarships for college, but all the time he had said very little.

"Still a year away," he muttered. He stood up, stretched, and said, "You know what I'd really like to do?"

She looked up and admired the lean, muscular form of her brother. He was just an inch under six feet and looked like a sprinter, although taller than most. "What?" she asked, putting her comb into her bag and rising to face him.

"I'd like to do what Superman does." He laughed, a little embarrassed, and said, "You know, keep the world safe for democracy."

"You idiot!" she said, affectionately. "I mean, what are you going to do for a living? That job doesn't pay much. Besides, Superman's already got it sewed up."

"Don't forget Captain Marvel, and now there's Wonder Woman and Batgirl. You women are always trying to help save the world. What I wish you'd do is learn to cook."

"Well, you be Superman, and I'll be Lois Lane, girl reporter. Lois doesn't have to cook." They grinned at each other, for they had always been very close. They piled into the Ford and made their way back to the house.

Richard took his shower first, while Stephanie stayed downstairs and helped her mother prepare supper. Bonnie Stuart had black hair, like Stephanie, and it hung like a waterfall down her back, without any curls. She had enormous dark blue eyes and an olive complexion, a legacy of her Spanish mother.

Stephanie had just come downstairs after her shower and Richard was setting the table when their father came in the front door. Jerry Stuart was a tall man of forty-nine with dark hair going silver at the temples and eyes the same blue-green as his daughter's. He had a quick spirit about him, which was as it should be in a flyer. He had piloted fighters in World War II, and he'd stayed in the military for a while after the war trying to make a career of the air force. But military life was too structured and restrictive for someone of his personality, especially someone who'd flown daredevil aerobatics in an air circus. He'd tried commercial aviation for a while, but that, too, had grown more and more restrictive. With his father's financial help, he'd bought two surplus military C-47 cargo planes and started a business hauling freight. He didn't fly aerobatics any more, but he was the boss.

"Just in time, Dad," Stephanie said. "We've got your favorite—" She looked at his face more carefully and said, "What's wrong?"

"Haven't you heard the radio?" He looked over at Bonnie, who came in wearing a white apron over her dress. His voice was oddly tense as he said, "The North Koreans have invaded South Korea."

Richard asked quickly, "What does that mean, Dad?"

Jerry tossed his hat on a side table. "It means there's going to be a war," he said.

"Oh, no, Jerry! Maybe not!" Bonnie spoke with a touch of fear threading her voice.

"I think it'll have to be."

Bobby came home in time for supper and heard the news. After supper they watched grainy images flicker across the television screen of North Korean soldiers wearing rumpled, bulky uniforms and odd-looking hats. Then the newscasters began to interpret it, and Jerry listened, his face stiff and serious. It was already Sunday the twenty-fifth in Korea. The attack had come in the early morning hours.

"Will there really be a war, Dad?" Richard asked.

"I'm afraid it's likely."

Richard was quiet for some time, then he said, "I want to join up."

Bobby's head swiveled almost comically. "You're only sixteen years old!" he said in disgust. "It's against the law for you to join the army, isn't it, Dad?" he said, turning to Jerry. Bobby and his father had hardly spoken a civil word to each other in weeks, but this was an extraordinary event, and a truce was in force.

"Bobby's right. You're not old enough, Son."

"I'll be seventeen next year. That's not too young."

Stephanie watched her parents exchange glances. They seemed to have some language, unspoken, that they used at times like this. Her glance went to Richard's face, and a fear seized her. *He's too young to go!* She thought of him out on a muddy battlefield, shot and bleeding—and dying. She had a very vivid imagination, Stephanie did. Their father, she knew, had been through some hard times during World War II but had come out intact. She remembered when he'd come home from overseas. But no one had attacked America—she didn't understand this war. It had exploded like a land mine beneath them and it frightened her. She went over and sat beside her father, leaning against him as if for some sort of assurance. He turned to smile at her affectionately. He smoothed her curly black hair where it had fallen across her forehead and said, "We'll just have to trust the Lord, like we always have to do."

2

An Old Soldier Gets a Call

Adam Stuart sat on the couch, slumping comfortably into the small canyon his body had made in it through many years of use. No more than five foot ten, Stuart was still at thirty-two almost as trim and fit as he had been at twenty. He had a square face and rather cold blue eyes that could light up with warmth at times. He was good-looking enough that fawning starlets would flirt with him even if he wasn't a movie producer. He looked over at Maris, his German-born wife, who was sitting beside him with a new book she was reading, *Common Sense Book of Baby and Child Care*, written by Dr. Benjamin Spock. Mischief brightened Adam's eyes, and he reached over and shut the book, remarking, "You don't need that book. You know how to raise kids."

Maris turned to look at him with surprise. She was tall, with ash-blonde hair, blue eyes, and an oval face. Her birth name was von Richthofen, and her father had been a distant cousin of the famous Red Baron, World War I ace Manfred von Richthofen. None except the immediate family knew that Adam was the illegitimate son of the famous German flyer. When Adam was shot down over Germany during World War II, he encountered Maris, and they had fallen in love. She and her family helped him get back to England, and as soon as he could after the war, he went back to Germany to find her, and they married. He brought her to the United States, and now every day of his life he thanked God for such

25

a wife. "Almost time for *Howdy Doody*," he said. "We couldn't miss that."

Maris moved over closer to him, and they held hands. She had made a place for herself in America, although her speech betrayed her German birth. They had returned to Germany twice since the war to visit family there.

She looked down at the two children on the floor. Suzanne, age three, with blonde hair and blue eyes, and one-year-old Samuel were, for once, sitting still watching the image on the television.

A black-haired, broad-faced man with a wide grin appeared on the screen holding a puppet with freckles and also with a wide grin and large ears. Buffalo Bob Smith smiled at the "peanut gallery," the audience of young children in the studio, and called out, "Hey, kids! What time is it?"

A chorus of voices sounded out, and Suzanne joined them. "It's Howdy Doody time!"

"I don't like this one as much as *Hopalong Cassidy*," Adam remarked, squeezing Maris's hand.

"Well, I don't like it as well as *Kukla, Fran, and Ollie*, but Suzie does."

"When Samuel gets a little older, we men will have *Hopalong Cassidy*."

Maris shushed him, and they watched the program. Afterward, it was time for the news, and Suzie pouted but finally contented herself by playing with Samuel. She treated him like a big doll, although she was barely able to pick him up. The two of them were engaged in some sort of argument in the corner of the room when the news came on.

The announcer spoke in a solemn voice directly into the camera. "The powerful American war machine," he said, "has been strengthened as President Truman authorizes a broad military buildup for the fighting in Korea and grants the military the power to wage war.

"Today, the president ordered the mobilization of marine corps and national guard troops, bringing into service 114,000

American men, with another 100,000 soon to swell the military ranks by way of the Selective Service System. With increasing manpower, Truman also boosted funding to meet the challenges of Communist aggression made more apparent by the Korean War. Congress approved his request of $1.2 billion to continue the mutual defense assistance program, which aids nations combating Communism. . . ."

Maris asked, "What does it all mean, Adam? Are we losing the war?"

"We are right now. The North Koreans have swept down through most of South Korea, and so far we haven't been able to stop them."

"What about the South Koreans?"

"They're overwhelmed. They're under UN command now." Adam shook his head grimly and added, "The troops made a good stand north of Taejon, but eventually they had to pull back south of the Kum River."

"General MacArthur's in command. He will win."

"A commander's only as good as the troops, the planes, the tanks he's got—and til now he hasn't had much."

There was an eruption in the corner, and Maris got up to settle the argument. Looking over Suzie's head, she asked Adam, "Can't you help? You always want to play, but you never want to discipline."

"Yes, dear. Come on, you two, let's get ready for bed!"

Lylah Stuart Hart sat in her office listening to phonograph records that were playing songs at least twenty years old. A wave of grief suddenly engulfed her. She murmured, "Jesse—!" At seventy, Lylah was still a lovely woman, although more fragile since Jesse's death. Her auburn hair had turned silver, and her large violet eyes, deep set and wide spaced, had not lost their luster. She leaned back in her chair. Jesse had been dead for two years, but every day Lylah had to make the adjustment to being alone—to being a widow. She looked at the papers piled on her desk but had no inclination to go through them.

Lylah started when the phone rang beside her hand. She picked it up to hear her secretary say, "You have a call from Mona Stuart, Miss Lylah."

"Put her on," she responded, willing herself to composure.

Lylah waited until a voice said, "Hello? Is this you, Aunt Lylah?"

"Yes. Hello, Mona. Where are you?"

"At Mom and Dad's, in Oklahoma City. The play in New York closed after only a few weeks. I came home to consider my options and, of course, to see Mom and Dad and Stephen. And I'd like to come and see you, if you don't mind."

"Why, of course, dear. When would you like to come?"

"There's a flight out this afternoon, late. I could come in and spend the night and meet you tomorrow morning, if you're not too busy."

"Why, that will be fine. Will you be coming alone?"

"Yes, Stephen would like to see you, too, and, of course, the folks, but that'll have to wait, I guess. Will tomorrow be all right?"

"Call me as soon as you get in town."

"I will, Aunt Lylah. Good-bye. See you tomorrow."

Lylah replaced the phone in the cradle and leaned back, her thoughts going to her niece. Lylah's brother Peter and his wife, Leslie, lived in Oklahoma City where they were in the oil business. Their son, Stephen, was in business there, too, but Mona led a different kind of existence. She had been active in the USO in World War II, longing to be an actress. She had fallen in love with a second-rate leading man, and Lylah suspected she'd had an affair with him. Since the war Mona had not been able to find her way. She had been in several second-class theatrical productions but hadn't had much success. *Mona is not a young woman anymore, at least not to me*, Lylah thought as she leaned back. *Let's see, she's twenty-seven—no longer able to take just any role that comes along.*

Restlessly Lylah rose and went to look out the window. Her eyes went to the pictures of Jesse on the wall, and she wished to hear his cheerful voice, to feel his arms go around her, and his kiss—but that was gone. She and Jesse had made Monarch Productions the best of the smaller studios in Hollywood. It would never be as large as MGM or Columbia, but the quality of the pictures it turned out was the equal of anything the larger studios did, and they worked hard at keeping pace with the innovations ever changing the movie industry.

Lylah moved back to the desk and started wading through the papers that called for her attention. Her staff shielded her from all except the most critical and pressing items. When her son, Adam, had come back from the war he had thrown himself into the workings of Monarch Studios, until, since Jesse's death, she felt no qualms about letting him take the reins.

Her eyes went again to the pictures of Jesse, and her heart ached. She knew that Mona was unhappy, and for Peter's sake she hoped she could help. But it was hard to help young people these days.

Mona's brother, Stephen, arrived to take her to the airport. He was wearing an off-white shirt with long sleeves, its pointed collar open at the neck, a brown checked sport jacket, brown narrow-legged trousers with cuffs turned up at the bottom, and two-tone suede shoes with crepe soles. He looked tan and healthy. "Better hurry up, Sis!" he said. "The plane leaves in an hour."

"I'm all ready." Mona had dressed for her flight in a green rayon dress with a rounded shoulder line, a scooped neck, three-quarter-length sleeves, a calf-length narrow wrap-over skirt with a wide inset panel that buttoned on the side, and a pair of low-heeled black shoes. She was carrying a large suitcase and a smaller one with her cosmetics. Stephen took the large suitcase, and the two made their way out to his car, a maroon 1951 Cadillac convertible just off the assembly line. Tossing the bags into the backseat, Stephen opened the door and grinned. "First class, eh?"

"Beautiful car. How much did it cost?"

"Twice as much as it was worth," Stephen quipped. He wore no hat, and his tawny hair ruffled in the breeze, his gray eyes keeping a sharp look on the traffic. "You never did tell me why you're going to see Aunt Lylah."

"I'm going to ask her to give me a part in a movie."

"Hey, now, that's a good idea. I don't know why you haven't done it before." Stephen swerved sharply and cut around a motorcycle rider, then slapped the Cadillac's dashboard. The car's action was smooth and effortless. He glanced at her. "Why *haven't* you asked her for a job before?"

"I suppose I wanted to make it on my own," Mona said. Her hair was blowing in the wind, and she put up her hand in an effort to hold it down. "Does this thing have a top on it?"

"Why spend all that extra money for a convertible then leave the top up?" Stephen grinned brashly. He had a practical side to him, and those who went up against him in business deals found his toughness, also. But he was amiable and willing to help any of his many friends and even those who were not his friends. He hadn't married yet, and, at twenty-nine, good-looking and well off, he was the prime target of many a woman's eye.

They were about to part at the airport, and a sudden thought came to Mona. She asked, "Stephen, will you have to go into the army?"

"The army? Why, no!"

"But they're going to be drafting men, and you're not married, and you don't have any of the other deferments."

Stephen's teeth were white against his tan as he chuckled deep in his chest. "That's no problem, Sis. I'm an essential part of the war effort. My plants are making electronic parts for planes and subs and tanks. Can't win a war without those," he said cheerfully. Then he shrugged and said more seriously, "You know, Mona, this war's a bad thing, and I wish it weren't happening—but I'm going to make a lot of money out of it. Doesn't seem right, getting rich off a war, but somebody's going to make the parts, and it might as well be me." He leaned over and kissed her, saying, "Have a good time in Hollywood. Don't fall for any of those phony leading men. They're all pansies."

The next morning at her hotel, Mona rose early, feeling refreshed, and donned a new outfit, a dark blue linen suit with a fitted jacket and a high collar worn buttoned so that no blouse was showing, a belt around the waist of the jacket, a narrow skirt, and black high-heeled shoes; a large black handbag completed her attire. She had breakfast in the hotel's spacious restaurant—California orange juice, cereal, and eggs Benedict. She drank her coffee slowly, trying to get the things she wanted to say to Lylah clearly in her mind.

When Mona arrived at Monarch Studios and gave her name at the gate, the guard smiled and said, "Yes, ma'am, Miss Lylah is expecting you. Go right on in. Do you know the way to her office?"

"Yes, I know it. Thank you."

Miss Lesley was a cheerful, sweet-faced woman of fifty who had been Lylah's assistant for many years. She greeted Mona, then said, "Your aunt said to show you in as soon as you arrived. Adam is with her."

Mona entered the office and was greeted at once by Adam, who came over and gave her a hug. "I have a bad habit of hugging pretty girls," he said, kissing her on the cheek. "And Hollywood folks always kiss everybody, even total strangers. It's one of the good things about the place—or maybe it isn't. I have to kiss ugly people, too."

"Adam, you shouldn't say that!" She loved this cousin, five

years her senior, and admired him greatly. Turning to Lylah, she said, "Aunt Lylah, you're looking beautiful as usual."

"And you're talking Hollywood talk as usual." Lylah smiled as Mona came over and kissed her. "Sit down. We'll make some coffee, or do you prefer something cold? I made a cake last night. Not a very good attempt, though. I miss Jesse's cooking. He was the best cook I ever saw. He spoiled me, I'm afraid."

Mona saw the grief in her aunt's eyes but said nothing. She knew that Lylah and Jesse had been closer than most married couples, and she had always admired and envied them a little for that. Sitting down, Mona accepted coffee and tasted the cake, and although it was not very good, she bragged on it with enthusiasm.

They talked about the family, and it was a large family, the Stuarts, scattered all the way from the hills of Arkansas to the skyscrapers of Chicago and the sandy beaches of Los Angeles.

Mona finally sensed the right moment and said, "I feel like a beggar with a hand out coming to you two, but I stayed away as long as I could."

Quickly Lylah said, "You don't have to feel that way, Mona. What is it? I think I already suspect."

"You're probably both more than suspicious," Mona said wryly. "I want a part in one of your pictures." She had planned it this way, to say only the bare fundamentals. No begging, no pleading, just a simple, straightforward request. Now that she had made it, she picked up her coffee and waited for their response.

Adam at once said, "What sort of picture do you have in mind, Mona?"

"I'm not very particular. I don't think I can afford to be. I'm a little tired of the theater and haven't done well there. I thought I might do well in films. Can you two give me some tests, and perhaps you've got a project that I can do something in?" She added, "Oh, I'm not asking for a starring part, of course, and I know that making feature films is different from the stage, but I'd like to try something. This is what I've been thinking of for a long time."

Lylah spoke. "I don't see any problem. You're a fine actress, Mona, although I haven't seen the latest things you've done. I don't think you've been fortunate in your choice of vehicles. There's a great deal more flexibility in the world of motion pictures. I think we need to find what you do best."

"Well, I'm past the age of playing ingenues," Mona shrugged, "but I'll try anything to get a start—even put on a long dress and bonnet and be in a cowboy movie."

Adam and Lylah both laughed at this, and it was Adam who said with a grin, "Well, that shows you're ready for anything. Let me set up some tests with Frank Haviland. I'll tell him to use his own judgment, and he's the best at that sort of thing I know of. We'll find something," he said warmly.

Mona felt relief wash over her. "I can't—I can't tell you how much I thank you. Both of you. It was so hard for me to come here and ask for a favor."

"You're not getting a favor," Lylah said. "It's a business proposition, and I'll say right now, Mona, that if Frank and Adam don't come up with the right project, I'm afraid we'll have to say no thanks."

"That's all I want. Just a chance," Mona said quickly. A warm feeling went through her as she looked at these two members of her family. Adam took her on a tour of the studio and introduced her to Frank Haviland, who was his right hand at Monarch. Haviland was tall and thin, with a shock of iron gray hair and sharp black eyes. He listened carefully as Adam explained, then he turned his gaze to Mona. "Be here tomorrow at eight o'clock."

"Do you have some scripts I could look at?"

"I'll sort through what we've got and send them over to you by messenger. Are you at a hotel?"

"Why, yes." She gave her hotel and room number.

"They'll be there sometime this afternoon."

"I'll study them tonight, Mr. Haviland."

"Just Frank." He grinned and then said, "Get a good night's sleep. They say I'm a hard taskmaster."

Adam put Mona in one of the studio limousines and sent her back to the hotel, then returned to his mother's office. He and Lylah talked for some time about the possibilities of finding a role for Mona.

"I haven't really seen enough of her to know if she can make it or not," Lylah said quietly. "People think making movies is easy, but it's worn out more people than any profession I know of."

"Well, we'll have a better idea after tomorrow," Adam said. He was standing with his back against the wall, his arms crossed, studying his mother. He had noticed the signs of age were more apparent, and he knew she missed Jesse with a fierce grief. He considered what he had to say next, knowing that it would add to her burden, but there was no way to avoid the subject.

"Mother," he said quietly, coming over to stand beside her, "I've got something to tell you."

Lylah caught the tone of his voice and turned swiftly to face him. She stood up and asked, "What is it, Adam?"

"I'm being recalled to active duty." He saw that the news hit her hard and said, "I won't be in combat. You don't have to worry about that. They're establishing a training section just outside Los Angeles for bomber pilots, and I guess they think I've still got something to offer." He watched her face, saying, "I know this is difficult."

"It's not so bad. Not as long as you won't be going to Korea."

"There's no chance of that, and the good part is I'll be right here in L.A. and able to divide my time."

"Have you told Maris yet?"

"No, I'll face that job this evening."

"She won't like it, I'm afraid." Lylah put her hands on his cheeks and pulled his face down and kissed him. "You're a good son, Adam, and you're the best thing that's ever happened to me."

Adam said, hoarsely, "Well, that's sweet of you to say so. You're the best thing that ever happened to me, too. Why, I wouldn't be here if it weren't for you." He grinned at her.

Lylah asked, "Do you ever think of your father?"

"The Red Baron, you mean? Of course. Quite a bit. But Jesse was the father I knew and loved. He's the one I miss."

Lylah thought back to her brief, passionate romance with Baron Manfred von Richthofen. "Manfred was a strange man," she whispered. "The most lonely man I've ever seen in my life. I think if he had outlived the war, he would have been the most unhappy man in the world—but he would have been so proud of you, Adam, just as Jesse was."

Maris was aware all during dinner that something was on Adam's mind, although he played with the children as usual. He went through the ceremonies of putting them to bed—which included making a parade through the house with Suzanne on his shoulders and Samuel in his arms. They marched through all the rooms singing "Howdy Doody Time," then he put them in bed, saying a prayer over each of them.

When he came back from the nursery, he sat down at the kitchen table where Maris had coffee poured, and after he had tasted his, she said quietly, "You're thinking about something. Is it trouble at the studio?"

"No, things are going well," he said slowly. "Mona came in today. She wants to get into pictures."

"Do you think she has a chance?"

"A very good chance. She's a beautiful woman, and she's got some good experience on the stage. She's got a good voice, too. Frank Haviland is working on some tests for her. We'll know pretty soon." He swirled the coffee around, then said, "You know me pretty well, don't you?"

"Pretty well. I've made a close study of you." Maris smiled over her cup but was troubled. "What is it, Adam?"

"I've got a notice from the air force."

Apprehension leaped into Maris's eyes. "You have to go back into the service?"

"Just as an instructor. I won't be seeing any combat this time, and it'll be right here in Los Angeles. I won't even have to leave home. I'll just get up, and instead of going to the studio, I'll go out to the air base to train bomber pilots."

Maris smiled in relief. "I've been expecting something like this, but I thought you'd have to go to Korea."

"No. I'm just an old soldier answering the call," he commented. "It'll be hard on Mother, but Frank's coming along so fast that he can do my job as well as I can."

They went into the living room. The television was still on and Jack Benny was talking with Rochester; they listened for a time, and when the program was over, Adam got up and turned the set off. He came back, put his arms around Maris, and kissed her with more ardor than usual. She said, "I'm glad you'll be out of the clutches of all those beautiful women for a while. I won't have to worry so much about looking matronly."

He smiled. "Matronly! I feel sorry," he said softly, "for all the men in the world that didn't marry you. They don't know what they're missing."

3

TRUMAN WAS RIGHT

1950 ended badly for America, at least in Korea. For a time in September, the troops were successful in containing the North Koreans. On the sixteenth, UN forces launched a counterattack. MacArthur liberated Seoul before the end of the month, and it appeared that the war might be over quickly. President Truman went out to Wake Island in mid-October and the two men discussed strategy. MacArthur, always the old war horse, assured the president that he would take Pyongyang, the North Korean capital, within days.

United Nations forces did so on October 19 and reached the Chinese border, having captured most of North Korea. But on November 3, China threw its massive military weight into the conflict, engaging U.S. forces at Unsan, and the United States was on the verge of a full-fledged war with the Chinese Communists. Military leaders were shocked to discover that two Chinese divisions were fighting in the northwestern part of the country, while another five divisions had massed in Manchuria on the north side of the Yalu River—three hundred thousand combat-proven Communist troops overwhelmed the Eighth Army and X Corps, which withdrew by land and by sea. Regiments of the First Marine Division were surrounded far inland at the Chosin Reservoir. They reached the coast, fifty miles away, in thirteen days of heavy engagement that has been called one of the great fighting retreats of history.

Stunned by the upsets in Korea, President Truman de-

clared a state of emergency in the United States and urged
all Americans to join the battle against Communist imperial-
ism. A few weeks earlier, complete victory seemed at hand,
but with the entrance of China, America faced a new and
determined challenge by a fanatic enemy.

It had been Jerry's idea to invite the relatives living in the
L.A. area to join in a night out to celebrate the New Year,
even though he and Bonnie faced 1951 with apprehension—
Richard and Robert would celebrate their seventeenth birthday, and Richard had announced firmly that he was dropping
out of school and joining the marines. Nothing his parents
said would dissuade him. He had signed all the papers, and
his parents yielded. Richard was scheduled to leave for boot
camp on February 2, but the marine corps delayed his induc-
tion until two days after his high school graduation in May.

The L.A. Stuarts made a sizeable party for New Year's.
The cousins all came—Gavin's two grown children, Phillip
and Sidney; Adam, with Maris; and Mona. Lylah opted for a
quiet evening at home. But Gavin and Heather came, and all
three of Jerry's children were there, even Stephanie, home
from college for the holidays. They all gathered in the Sky-
light Room, the ballroom of the Delmonico Hotel, at nine
o'clock. Jerry went at once to shake hands with his uncle
Gavin. Gavin Stuart had flown Sopwith Camels, British-built
fighters, in World War I against von Richthofen's "flying circus." After the war he had done everything a pilot can do,
including flying in the first airmail service and organizing an
acrobatic flying circus. He had been Jerry's mentor in flying.
Gavin now worked as a consultant to Lockheed and other
large companies. At fifty-eight, he was still trim and fit, and
his hair was dark except for the white streaks at his temples.
For this occasion he was wearing an evening tail suit that
consisted of narrow gray trousers, a gray cutaway jacket, a
white silk shirt with wing collar, a white-and-gray-striped
waistcoat, and a black bow tie.

"You look great, Gavin," Jerry said. "If you drop dead, we won't have to do a thing to you."

"What an awful thing to say, Jerry!" Heather, Gavin's wife, still retained a trace of her British accent. Her hair was blonde, and her blue eyes were as large and brilliant as ever, and she looked ten years younger than her fifty-six years.

Phillip Stuart was twenty-seven and looked like his mother. He had blonde hair, blue eyes, and was very tall, six feet two. His wife, Irene, was a small, dark-haired woman, and the two of them had produced three sons whom they had named Matthew, Mark, and Luke. Phillip joked that he wanted to name them after the twelve apostles but Irene felt that was too ambitious. Phillip's sister, Sidney, was two years younger than he. She was a very attractive woman, with her father's dark hair. Sidney was engaged to her college sweetheart, Nolan Cameron, a tall, handsome blonde who was in medical school. They planned to get married next year. Gavin was particularly proud of Sidney—she was the first of the Stuarts to graduate from college.

Phillip was wearing an air force uniform and had first-lieutenant's bars on his shoulders. Jerry turned to him with surprise and said, "The air force doesn't seem to care who flies their airplanes. When did all this happen, Phil?"

"Well, since I've always been a flier, when I volunteered, they snapped me up. I guess they're raking the bottom of the barrel." He stepped across and put his hand out to Richard saying, "I hear you're gung ho for the marines, Streak."

"Yes, sir, Phil. I don't leave til after graduation, though."

"You picked a rough outfit," Phil shrugged, "but those are the fellows that get the job done on the ground. Good luck at boot camp. I hear you'll need it."

Stephanie was wearing a sapphire blue taffeta evening gown that had long sleeves and a sweetheart neckline. It cut in tight at the waist, and the long full skirt fell nearly to the floor, where blue satin slippers peeked out. Phil stepped forward. "If my wife will look the other way, I'm going to dance with a beautiful young lady."

"Why, I'll be happy to entertain the troops." Stephanie smiled back and drifted off in his arms. She was a fine dancer and so was Lieutenant Stuart.

"You're worried about your brother, I suppose."

"Yes, I am, Phil. It's not just that he's going into the service but into the marines. You know what they do. They're always the first ones to hit the beaches."

"I know," Phil said soberly. He shook his head. "He's so young. It seems like just yesterday he was collecting baseball cards and excited about a new bicycle. Now he's going out to do the roughest job in the world."

Across the room, Jerry was dancing with Bonnie. He regarded her dress with a lifted eyebrow. "That dress ought to be illegal."

"Oh, hush! I'm forty-five years old!"

"Why, Grandma, what big eyes you have," Jerry grinned. He held her closer and tried to do a fancy turn and managed to get his feet tangled up.

Bonnie laughed aloud, her eyes sparkling. "You can't dance any better than you ever could. I thought pilots were supposed to have balance, and you fall over your own feet!"

Jerry ignored her comment. "Your beauty drives me mad," he said calmly and pulled her closer.

"Don't hold me so tight."

"You shouldn't smell so nice and feel so good." He kissed her hair and said, "Do you realize that in a few years, we'll be grandma and grandpa? Does that make you feel old?"

"I'm looking forward to it," Bonnie said. "I hate it that Stephanie's gone, Richard is about to leave, and Bobby's hardly ever home. Nothing would make me happier than to have a bunch of young Stuarts crawling around getting into everything."

They danced for a while, keeping to themselves. The band played "Younger Than Springtime," and Jerry whispered, "That's an old one." Then they started with "Far-Away Places." He kissed her again and said, "That's the first tune we danced to. Do you remember?"

"Of course I do. Only it wasn't that one. It was 'I'll Be Seeing You in All the Old Familiar Places.'"

"That one, too," Jerry said with a smirk.

Across the room, Richard was approached by his cousin Mona, who walked right up and said, "If you're going to be a marine, you've got to become more aggressive. You're just standing here. Ask me to dance."

Richard grinned abruptly. "Be glad to. May I have this dance, Mona?" He was a bit dazzled by this beautiful older cousin's attention.

The two moved out on the floor, and Mona made light talk for some time, then she raised her large eyes and said, "You're awfully young, Richard. Why didn't you wait a while? This war may be over by the time you're a little older."

"I've got to do my part. All the Stuarts have fought when they had a chance."

Mona shook her head. "They certainly have; even the women have served. Did you know our cousin Wendy and I toured with the USO? And now you join the marines and Phil runs off to the air force!"

The music picked up as the band started playing "Don't Sit under the Apple Tree," and Mona laughed. "That's a little bit too fast for me!"

"Let's go get some refreshments," Richard suggested. He put his hand on her arm, and they made their way to a long table.

After that song, the musicians took a break, so Richard and Mona sat down and chatted. As they sipped on colas, Richard asked, "Are you feeling like a Hollywood native yet?"

"Do people ever feel like they really belong here?"

"I grew up here in L.A., close to Hollywood but not part of it. It's home to me. Dad mentioned you're working on a movie for Aunt Lylah. What's that like?"

Richard hadn't been around the movie business and was interested in what Mona told him about the process.

"My dad did some flying in a movie once," he said. "That's all I've ever heard about it."

"There's so much competition for parts—that's difficult and makes it hard to have friends in the business."

"Don't you feel like you've made friends here, Mona?" Richard asked, looking directly at her.

"Not real friends. But I've never been good at making friends anywhere."

Richard frowned. He always wanted to fix things—and people—and his impulse was to give Mona advice about how to make friends. But as he looked at her he had another thought and said, "I bet they're all jealous because you're the prettiest."

His comment surprised her, and she reached out and put her hand on his arm. "Why, Richard, what a sweet thing to say!" The admiration Mona had always had from men had been a barrier in her friendships—girlfriends were always afraid she'd take their boyfriends, and she had certainly done so on a few occasions. But there was something so matter-of-fact about Richard's statement. It wasn't made with any hidden agenda. As they sat talking, she found herself pouring out her frustrations with her lack of success in, it seemed, every area of her life. She felt like a second-rate actress; in her relationships with men she felt she was never seen for her real self—just for her beauty.

The young man listening to her felt overwhelmed by all of these adult revelations, but he looked at her and said, "Mona, I can't do anything about any of this, but I can be your friend."

She put one arm around him and hugged him. "That's a lot to do, Richard. Thank you. I'll hold you to that." By now the musicians were returning. "I guess we should get back to the party." Adam was coming over to ask her to dance.

When the party broke up, soon after midnight, Mona made

a point of saying good-bye to Richard. "Keep safe, Cousin," she said, "I need all the friends I can get." She kissed his cheek, and they parted.

"What was that all about, Streak?" asked Bobby. "Something going on between you and the movie star?" He grinned at his brother and winked.

Richard elbowed him and said, "You're just jealous 'cause you wish it was you!"

Mona lay awake into the early morning hours. She hadn't faced a lot of things about her life, about how unhappy she was, how lonely, how disappointed. Thinking about another new year made her feel depressed, and it had gushed out in her conversation with Richard. She smiled, through tears, thinking how she must have shocked the poor kid.

Darkness was just giving way to early morning light when she fell asleep, saying, like a mantra, "I'm a Stuart. We never give up."

Richard's concern that the war would be over before he could get to Korea was clearly unfounded in the early months of 1951. The Communists reoccupied Seoul on January 4. United Nations air forces continually attacked communication centers and airfields north of the battle line. Seoul was retaken on March 14. On April 11, Truman relieved General MacArthur of command of the UN forces for publicly disputing administration policies and replaced him with General Matthew B. Ridgway.

Soon after, fresh Communist troops launched a general offensive toward Seoul. By April 30, although UN lines had been pushed back south, they held three miles north of Seoul.

On May 16, Chinese Communist divisions launched an attack down the center of the Korean peninsula along a seventy-five-mile front, but by May 20, the day after Richard and Bobby's graduation, the attack had been contained, the Communists suffering heavy casualties.

Entering the marine corps recruit depot at San Diego was like stepping into another universe. All comfort was left behind, and the intangible mystique of the marines began to work. Richard and some other boots had been picked up at the bus station by truck. Their marine driver shouted, "No _____ talking! No _____ smoking! No _____ gum chewing! Sit up straight!" They dismounted from the jolting truck and formed a motley rank in front of a sand-colored receiving building. The base's buildings were a hacienda style with wide archways and flat or red-shingled roofs.

A drill instructor greeted them with a piercing scream and turned the air full of more profanity, then shouted, "Fall in!" Gunnery Sergeant Sterken, one of their three drill instructors, was a southerner with a contempt for anyone not born in Dixie. He considered California part of the North since it had not been part of the Confederacy. Sterken was a huge man, some six feet four inches and 230 pounds, and his voice was even bigger.

Private Richard Stuart stumbled along in clumsy civilian fashion to the mess hall, to a breakfast of bologna and cold lima beans.

The boots began to lose their individuality at the quartermaster's, where they had to strip naked. When not a stitch or a thread was left, each was given underwear, socks, a bill cap that came down over their ears, green pants, and a yellow T-shirt with the emblem of the marine corps in red. They mailed their civilian clothes home. The discard of the garments meant the death of the old life. Looking over at another recruit, Jack Smith, Richard said, "A man doesn't have much personality when he's naked, does he?"

Smith, a tall, black-haired man of about twenty, shook his head. "And I hear the fun's just beginning."

As Richard emerged from the quartermaster's building,

he thought, *Twenty minutes ago I was a human being sur-rounded by sixty other human beings. Now I'm just a number—193153 USMC.*

The next stop was the barber's, and the cry "You'll be sorry!" began to greet them. The barber made five strokes; as the last one completed a circle, he said, "That's all, Private."

Richard laughed as the barber asked Smith, the next in line, "Would you like to keep your hair?"

"Sure would," Smith answered quickly.

"Then you better get a sack." A laugh went up for the old joke, and Smith's head was as bald as the other recruits when he stepped out of the chair.

As day followed day, Streak Stuart forgot that he had any life outside of the marines. The boots were insulted, shouted at, pushed down with their faces in the mud while they did push-ups, and, endlessly, they drilled. Always the marching, always the running. Station parade every Friday. March to the mess hall, march to the sick bay, run to draw rifles, run to the obstacle course. March and run. Feet slapping cement, treading the ground. Always the voices of the drill instructors, "Column right, march. . . . Forward, march. . . . Left oblique, march. . . . Platoon halt."

It seemed like madness, but it was a discipline. A recruit couldn't address a drill instructor without a "military" rea-son. Sergeant Sterken was a strict man and was capable of commanding a boot to clean out the head with a toothbrush because he called his rifle a gun. "Stuart, you burr-headed idiot," he bellowed once to Richard, with a grim smile, "you are the most fiddle-footed excuse for a private I ever saw! You'll shoot yourself in the foot before you get out of here, clown!"

Quonset huts served as barracks. The boots were allowed no radios and got a newspaper only on Sunday. They couldn't smoke except at times permitted by the drill instructors. Richard and his squad stuck close together and laughed at each other when the drill instructors were not around. While there was the camaraderie of suffering among the boots, Richard made no close friends, for everyone was aware that the unit would be broken up as soon as boot camp was over.

The war rolled on while they trained. In June, the Soviets put out a statement considered a "peace feeler," and a long summer of wrangling and negotiations got peace talks haltingly under way. But the boots were barely conscious of it.

Richard grew hardened to the profanity. It was in the air like oxygen, and though he himself never swore, almost everyone else did. The talk was much about women, and on this also Richard had nothing to say. This didn't pass unnoticed, and he acquired a nickname of "Preacher," which did not stick long, for he made no protest. He was known as Streak to everyone, and in the dashes that they were commanded to make with full field packs, he so far outdistanced his nearest competitor that even the drill instructor had a good word for him. "Make sure you're runnin' toward the fight instead of away from it, Stuart," he snarled.

The hikes were grueling. Once one of the socks Richard used to pad the straps of his pack slipped out of place, but his whole body was so numb he didn't feel the strap cutting into his shoulder until, back at the barracks, someone told him he was bleeding.

The recruits spent three weeks at Camp Matthews living in tents, learning to shoot. Marines are above all things infantry, and it was the goal of every recruit to qualify with the M-1 rifle. All of the southerners could shoot, Richard noticed. Try as he might, he could never equal them. Still, he qualified as a sharpshooter. An expert rifleman's badge is to shooting what the Medal of Honor is to bravery. It even brought five dollars a month extra pay, not an inconsiderable sum to one earning only twenty-one dollars.

Painfully, Richard became a marine. He spoke of soldiers as dog faces and sailors as swab jockeys and referred scathingly to West Point as "that boys' school on the Hudson." After twelve weeks of boot camp, he was sent to Camp Pendleton for four more weeks of training in weaponry and small-unit tactics. The war seemed very far away, and it was sometimes difficult for Richard to keep his mind on the voice of the gunnery sergeant.

B Company was like a clan or a tribe, of which the squad was the important unit, the family group. Like families, each squad differed from the others because its members were different. Richard observed with some interest that no racial or religious bigotry existed, and the squad in no way resembled the movies put together by Hollywood where each squad had a cross section composed of Catholic, Protestant, and Jew, rich boy, middle boy, good boy, white, black, Asian. His squad looked more like an all-American football team.

Mona approached Lylah and Adam on the set. "I'd like to talk to you when you have time. It's about an idea I have."

"All right. Now is a good time," Adam said. "We were just going up to the office. Come on up."

Once in the office, Mona said, "I know what you two need most is some amateur telling you how to run Monarch Studios." She saw them both smile, and she shrugged, "I know you get that all the time."

"Good ideas sometimes come from the ranks," Lylah said. "What is it, Mona?"

"Have you thought of doing a war picture?"

"We've done several," Adam said, a puzzled look on his face. "What did you have in mind?"

"As far as I know, there are no movies out about the war in Korea. They're not even calling it a war," she said in disgust, "but it is, isn't it?"

"It certainly is." Adam nodded grimly. He looked over at Lylah and said, "Have you thought about this, Mother?"

"No, I haven't. Not yet."

"But if you make one now while the war's still on, you'd be the first," Mona said.

48   Pages of Promise

Lylah suddenly smiled at her. "You didn't have any idea of starring in it, did you, Mona?"

Caught off guard, Mona flushed, then faced Lylah. "I'm available," she said, "but I'm not asking for anything more than just a chance."

"You know, I think she's got a good idea," Adam said. "I don't know why it is that movies about wars always come out afterwards. There were very few good movies about World War II until the war was almost over." He cocked his head and looked at Mona and said, "I'm pretty busy teaching those fellas how to fly airplanes. Why don't you and Frank Haviland get together on this?"

"He wouldn't listen to me."

"Frank always listens to good ideas. If it's no good, he'll shoot it down, but you won't know until you try."

"Thanks, Adam," Mona said. "I'll do that."

"And I'll tell you, Stephen, Frank is really excited about the idea. He thinks it has real possibilities."

Stephen had come to see Mona on one of his business trips to Los Angeles. He smiled. "Sounds like a good idea." They were having lunch at a fine restaurant. Just then some men Stephen knew entered and were seated nearby, and he introduced them to her.

Stephen and Mona finished their lunch. "I've talked myself dry," she said. "What do you think, Stephen?"

"I don't know anything about the motion picture business," he said, "but I know the fella that gets in first has an advantage. I think you did the right thing." He excused himself, saying, "I'll be right back. I need to call the office and check in."

Mona waited for him, thinking about the film, but she came to herself when she heard the name Stuart used by one of the men in the group. He evidently had just joined them, for she had not met him, but she heard him say, "Stephen

Stuart is going to get into trouble. He's cutting too many corners."

Mona rose from her table at once, touched the man on the arm, and when he turned around she said, "Stephen Stuart is my brother. What did you mean by what you just said?"

"Your brother?" The man was short and pudgy but had direct gray eyes and a stubborn look around his lips. "I didn't intend for you to hear it, but I don't mind saying it again. I've said it to him."

"What do you think he's doing?" Mona demanded.

"He's shorting quality on government contracts," the man said, "and he's going to get into trouble sooner or later with the government. And maybe there's more."

At that moment Stephen appeared and, taking one look at the man, said, "Hello, Ben. You still giving me a bad name?" Without waiting for an answer he said, "Come on, Sis. Let's go."

When they were in his car and headed back to Mona's apartment, she said, "What did that man mean? He said you were cutting corners on government contracts."

"He's sore because he lost some business to me. His name's Ben Morrow. He's a whiner," Stephen said carelessly.

"You're not doing that, are you?"

"Look, I'm in business, Mona. I've got to make the best product I can for the least amount of money. If I can see a way to save two cents on a part that works just as well, then I'll take it." He leaned over and smiled. "Don't worry about it. Your big brother's able to take care of himself."

There was an assurance about him and success in every feature. When Mona got out of the car, she put the matter out of her mind, thinking, *Stephen's smart, and he wouldn't do anything really wrong.* Then her mind was filled up again with thoughts of starring in a movie, and she hummed to herself as she went up the stairs to her apartment.

4

STEPHANIE GOES
TO A BALL GAME

mos Stuart leaned back against the enormous walnut tree that shaded the white frame house from the blazing heat of the sun. He had come back to Arkansas to the home place, the house where he had been born. He looked across at his brother Logan, who sat on a cane-bottom chair, teetering perilously, whittling on a piece of cedar. Amos knew the knife would be a Barlow, for it was all Logan admitted to having the qualities that a knife ought to have. Long, curling shavings fell from the stick and formed a pile at Logan's feet.

"If you had taken up wood carving, you'd be rich by now," Amos remarked, brushing a fly away from his face. He was the oldest of the clan at the age of seventy-two. He had been five foot ten when he was young but knew that he had shrunk an inch, and he was considerably overweight. His ash-blonde hair was streaked with gray, but his dark blue eyes were still alive, and there was a youthful force in him that one finds in elderly people sometimes. He had become famous as a writer and as an editor for the Hearst newspapers, and for years he had carried on a weekly radio program that was immensely popular. He was a friend of presidents and, beginning with Theodore Roosevelt, had known them all. Now he sat back, sweat gathering under his white shirt and his gray trousers wrinkling at the knees from the heat of late spring.

"I'm glad you could come, Amos. I get a little bit lonesome for my folks. The Stuarts are scattered all over creation now."

Logan, at sixty-six, still retained mostly auburn hair and had the Stuart dark blue eyes. He was thin and wiry and not tall, and he had been one of the best farmers in the Ozarks in his time. These days, however, his son Clinton and his son-in-law Dent did much of the work. As he shaved the paper-thin shavings from the cedar, he proceeded to bring Amos up to date on his host of descendants, some of them with the last name of Ballard, for Logan had married a widow with three children. His grandchildren were the pride and joy of his life.

"How's the newspaper business, Amos?"

"Going to perdition in a bucket," Amos snapped. "Most of the stuff that's written is lies and poorly written lies at that!" He went on giving newspaper writers a hard time, and then he saw Logan grinning at him.

"You ought to give it all up and come back here on the farm. You never was much of a farmer, but I could teach you a few things."

Amos smiled. "I'd never get Rosie to do that. She's a city girl." He looked over the house and out at the barn that was propped up on one side by thick saplings. "That old barn's still standing," he muttered. A grin came across him and he said, "I remember just before Lylah first went away to Bible school. Owen and I caught her out there smoking ciga-rettes."

"Boy, she set that Bible college on its ear, didn't she, Amos?"

"She set lots of folks on their ears. She's doing real well, but she's missing Jesse like I never saw a woman miss a man." Amos shook his head and said, "I reckon she's about ready to go on and be with him, although she's doing well with that motion picture business of hers. Adam's doing a lot of it now."

"What about this here war? What's going to happen to it?" Logan asked.

"We're gonna win it!"

"Why did President Truman yank MacArthur out of there?" Logan asked. His older brother was, in his mind, the smartest man who had ever lived.

"Well, it comes down to this. Russia is hooked up to the North Koreans, ever since the end of World War II. That means we're really fighting Russia already—like Truman says, the Russians are fighting a war by proxy. So MacArthur wanted to cross over the thirty-eighth parallel that cuts Korea in half and just go all the way to China to stop the Chinese from coming into North Korea. Well, that would have brought direct confrontation with China and probably Russia too, and Truman is a smart enough man to know we don't want to fight World War III. So he yanked MacArthur."

"I always liked General Mac," Logan observed easily. "He's a fightin' man."

"He is; he's a military man. He didn't have to worry about the whole country like President Truman does."

"I like Truman," Logan nodded. "You always know where you stand."

"He's never been anything but a small town businessman. He's not sharp and foxy like Roosevelt, but people like him because, as you say, Logan, he always means what he says."

Logan reached into the bib pocket of his overalls and pulled forth a small package. "Want some gum?" he said.

"No. These store-bought teeth don't take to gum." Amos grinned. He watched as Logan undid the paper and pulled out a small card. "What's that?" he inquired.

"Baseball pictures," Logan said, handing it over. "This one's Ty Cobb. Might be worth a little bit some of these days."

"Yeah, baseball cards have been around as long as I can remember. I used to have a pretty good collection myself."

"Well, that grandson of mine, Jeff, I think he knows every

baseball player that's ever lived. He's always pestering me to buy more gum. I've chewed," he said humorously, "until my jaws ache. He says I got to find one of Honus Wagner."

"Why, I guess he *would* like that one. Wagner is probably the greatest ballplayer ever."

"That's what Jeff says. Well, anyhow, he claims that anyone could get a heap of money for a card with Honus Wagner on it—an old one, that is."

Amos handed the card back and said, "I'll send you my old collection. You can give 'em to Jeff for a Christmas present or a birthday maybe."

"Well, now. Won't that be fine?" Logan smiled broadly, and his eyes twinkled. "Now be sure you don't go through there and take all them out that's worth money."

"Oh, I wouldn't do that!" Amos protested.

"I don't know. You Yankees from Chicago will do about anything, I reckon. Tell me what else is going on in the world."

"Well, they keep testing atom bombs out around Las Vegas. The biggest one, the flash was seen 250 miles south of the Mexican border—500 miles from Las Vegas! Some reports said they're ones designed to be carried by soldiers on the battlefield."

"You don't tell me!"

"I'm afraid so. And we have to keep on with developing all these weapons because we keep hearing about the Russians making atomic weapons. Like with these riots in Egypt against Britain and all this turmoil over the Suez Canal. If things get out of hand, we'll need to be able to protect ourselves and our allies. And same thing with this war in Korea."

"Yeah," Logan said, "I heard one speech when President Truman said that the only true road to peace is to face up to them Russians with force—the defense of Europe is the defense of the U.S. is what he said."

"And he wants taxes to be raised to do it. You won't believe all the zeros in the amount of money it's gonna cost you and me, Brother, us taxpayers," said Amos. "Never mind about all that. Tell me what's happening on the farm here."

Logan spoke slowly in his flat Arkansas drawl, which had never changed. He gave a roll call of old friends who had died, marriages, births. Amos had forgotten most of them, but he enjoyed listening to Logan talk. Logan said, "I got one thing I really don't understand. Over there in the bend of the river, that land that used to belong to the Cartwrights? Well, some young folks bought it. I don't know who they are. I met 'em a few times. Seem pleasant enough, but they're kind of odd."

"What's odd about 'em?"

"Well, all the men got beards, most of 'em anyway, and the women all wear long dresses, just like Ma used to wear. Looks like they're trying to step back in time."

"What are they doing over there?"

"Oh, they say they want to farm the land. They don't know much about it though. Most of 'em are from big cities back East. One of 'em," he said with a smirk, "planted some corn in the shade of the trees. Said it was too hot in the sun. Didn't get much of a crop, that fella didn't."

Amos laughed and shook his head. "They'll never get rich on that land."

"They don't intend to get rich. They just want to live their own way, I reckon. They dry a lot of their food, and they built 'em a bomb shelter in case the bomb drops on us here in Arkansas." Logan chuckled at that idea. "Nice young folks, but their morals, I think, are a little bit lackin'. Some of 'em livin' together without bein' married, so the talk goes."

"Well, if you get to where you can't get along with Anne, I reckon you could leave and go join up with 'em."

This idea, too, tickled Logan, who snapped his knife shut and slipped it into his overall pocket. "Come along," he said. "Let's go get some buttermilk. Maybe after a while I'll drive you over there and you can write a story on them young folks—and give me half the money for it," he added slyly.

Amos returned to Chicago on June 7 and the next morning was working at his desk when he looked up and saw his granddaughter Stephanie weaving her way through the newsroom. She saw him watching and flashed a charming smile at him. He was surprised and delighted to see her. Amos felt particularly flattered by the interest Stephanie had shown in the career that meant so much to him. She'd been telling him since she was about eight that she wanted to be a "newspaperman" just like him when she grew up. "Hello, Grandpa," she said as she entered his office. "Are you busy?"

"Never too busy for a good-looking girl," he said. He got up, went around, and took her hug. She kissed his smooth cheek, then took a seat. "That's a man-catchin' outfit you got on," he said eyeing her dress. The dress was nutmeg brown and had a V neck and a short, pleated skirt. A short bolero jacket, trimmed in dark brown, with three-quarter-length sleeves, covered the top of the dress, and a wide V-shaped belt in dark brown cinched in the waist. Amos shook his head. "How old are you now? Fifteen?"

"Oh, Grandpa, you know better than that! You came to my high school graduation a year ago."

"Well, I guess I forgot. How's college?"

"I made straight A's."

"It's a good thing you did. I'd have tanned your hide if you'd done anything else—after your daddy got through with you. How are your mom and dad?"

"Mom's fretting because she's got no kids to take care of, and we're all a little bit worried now that Richard's gone into the marines."

"Well, he's like some of the other Stuarts, I guess. If there's a fight, he's got to get into it."

"Well, you know what's happening over there. The marines have been in the thick of it."

Amos nodded, and he knew she was exactly right. The First Marine Division had fallen into some of the hardest fighting in the war. They had advanced on the "punch bowl," a volcanic crater lying about twenty-five miles north of In-chon. Fighting had congealed into a fierce slugging match, and the First had taken heavy losses. Amos was apprehensive about his grandson joining up so young, and he said as kindly as he could, "I'm sure God'll take care of him. He's got lots of prayers going up. I got a phone call from Lenora yesterday, and she said she's fasting and praying for Richard even now while he's in basic training."

"Dear Aunt Lenora!" Lenora Stuart had been crippled in a riding accident in her youth, but from her wheelchair she practically ran the Salvation Army unit in Chicago. "I'll go by and see her."

Amos leaned back and said, "I know you didn't come just to chat. What is it you want, Stephanie?"

"I want to go to work for you, Grandpa," Stephanie said instantly. "I want to go to Korea as a war correspondent."

Amos laughed, his face wrinkling and his belly quivering. After all, the Hearst organization was one of the largest in the business, and for an eighteen-year-old to walk in off the street—"Well, I'll give this to you, you'll never go wanting for lack of gall!"

"I'm serious, Grandpa. I don't want to go through three more years of college. I want to go to work now. I want to be where the action is." Her eyes sparkled, and she leaned forward, making a most attractive picture. For some time she argued, but her heart sank when her grandfather simply shook his head. Then Stephanie grew indignant. Standing to her feet she said, "All right! I'll go across town and go to work for your competition!"

This threat startled Amos, and he shook his head and held up his hand. "Now wait a minute! Don't fly off the handle." He looked at her fondly and said, "You're just like I was when I was your age. I had to have my own way right when I wanted it. I mostly didn't get it, though," he said. "All right, Grand-daughter. I'll give you a try." A thought passed through his mind, and a wicked light of amusement touched his eyes. "You won't last long, though."

"I will, too!"

"No, you won't. I'm putting you with the toughest reporter I have. He's got no use for women. Well, not exactly. He likes women a little *too* well—good-looking ones, that is. It's just that he doesn't like female reporters."

Stephanie smiled brilliantly. "Thank you, Grandpa." She came over and kissed him again, which pleased him inordinately.

"You always were an affectionate girl, but don't be kissing around on Jake Taylor."

"Who's Jake Taylor?"

"He's your new boss. Come along. I'll introduce you to him."

He got up out of his chair stiffly, for he had rheumatism in his knees, and led her through the outer office into a narrow hallway. There were four doors there, and he moved to the last one. Opening it without knocking, he stepped through and held the door for Stephanie, who came in and saw a man sitting behind a desk, a hat shoved far back on his head.

"Jake, this is my granddaughter, Stephanie Stuart. She's come and pestered me for a job as a reporter, so I'm giving her to you. You have my permission to run her off if she can't handle it. You two get acquainted. Afterward, Stephanie, you're comin' home with me for dinner. I assume you'll be staying with your grandma and me at least for a while?" He stepped out and shut the door and chuckled. *Jake's mighty mean—but that granddaughter of mine, she has a mighty firm look in her eye!*

Stephanie waited for Taylor to speak. She could tell, even though he was seated, that he was very tall and was strongly built. He wore a gray sport coat with a maroon tie, but his collar was pulled open. He had reddish-brown hair and sharp brown eyes, and they took her in critically. There were scars around his eyes, and one of his ears was puffy.

When he didn't speak, she said, "I see you're a prize-fighter."

Taylor's eyes opened fully then, with surprise. "You noticed that, did you? All these scars and my cauliflower ear? Well, I used to be." He motioned with his head to a picture hanging among others. "That's me when I was eighteen; I was going to be the next heavyweight champion of the world."

Stephanie moved over to the wall and studied the picture. It was a younger Taylor wearing trunks and holding his fists up for a publicity picture. His curly hair was down in his eyes, and he was unmarked at the time. She turned back and said, "Why did you decide to give up fighting?"

"I got my brains beat out in my third professional fight," he said, laughing. He had a dimple in his right cheek, and she thought he looked like a rough-hewn Clark Gable.

He was appraising her, as well. She said, "This must be awful for you, for your boss to shove a novice into your lap." He grinned suddenly and she flushed. "I didn't mean that literally."

Taylor's eyebrows went up, and he straightened in his chair and patted his thighs. "Any time you need a father confessor, my lap is available."

"I had enough of that sort of talk in junior high school, Mr. Taylor," she said. "Now, let's get one thing straight. This is a business arrangement."

"Right," Taylor said, assuming a stern frown. "I don't want you making any advances toward me, Miss Stuart! I know how you young women are, always after older men." Taylor looked to be twenty-five, and there was a light of humor in his eyes as he leaned back and locked his fingers behind his head. "Sit down and tell me why you think you can be a reporter," he demanded.

For the next twenty minutes, Stephanie talked. "I've always wanted to be like my granddad. He's gone everywhere, he knows all sorts of people, he's had an exciting life. That's what I want," she began. "I want to see the Casbah, to live in London or Paris, to travel to Korea and Japan, to learn about life, and to write about it." Taylor prodded her with sharp, probing questions. He was a reporter, all right, and by the time the interview was over Stephanie felt drained. "Well, are you satisfied?" she said.

"Nope. This is all talk. We'll find out if you can write." He leaned forward, shuffled through a bunch of papers, and handed her some. "Write this up," he directed.

Taking the wrinkled papers, Stephanie squinted her eyes. "Why, this writing is terrible!"

"It's mine!" Taylor answered cheerfully. "I just jotted down the general facts. Now, you put it all together. You know, the where, the who, the how, the why, and so forth."

"You mean—in here?"

"Oh, no. Come along. The office next door is empty. A fellow named Hatton had it until yesterday morning."

"Well, won't he care?"

"He doesn't work here anymore. I fired him. Come along." When he stood up she saw that he was at least six feet two and had the heavy shoulders of a boxer. She followed him as he ambled out and moved to the door next to his and opened it. "Here's your kingdom," he said. "All you need. A desk, a phone, and a typewriter. When you get through, bring it back to me. Let's see what you can do."

Stephanie was startled by the suddenness of it all. The door closed behind her, and she approached the desk, which was a scarred oak model that had seen much service. The chair that she sat in was on rollers, but one was missing so she had to keep it balanced. A battered Underwood typewriter was the only thing on the desk, and, feeling vastly intimidated, she began to examine the scribbling. For over two hours she worked, having difficulty interpreting some of Taylor's notes, and she typed several drafts before she was satisfied. She pulled the last sheet of paper out of the typewriter and stood up. Her back ached, and she had the feeling that what she had done was worthless. Nevertheless, she marched out of her new office, knocked on Taylor's door, and entered when he commanded. "Here it is, Mr. Taylor."

"First names go better around here. You're Stephanie and I'm Jake."

"All right. That suits me fine." Stephanie watched as he scanned the pages and she waited with dread for his verdict. She fully expected him to tear to shreds what she had written and was surprised when he looked up smiling.

"This is pretty good," he nodded. "Sit down, and I'll show you a few things that the paper demands from everybody. Basically you've done a good job. I didn't think anyone could read my scribbling. I can't read it myself half the time."

A wave of relief swept through Stephanie, and she sat down, her knees weak. She listened as he pointed out some of the standard policies of the paper, and when he handed the article back, marked up carelessly, she took it and said, "I'll make these changes right away—Jake."

"We'll be leaving right after lunch," he said pleasantly. "We're going to cover a ball game. You follow baseball?"

"Not very much."

"You will. Game starts at one, but we can be a little bit late."

She completed the changes and excitedly showed Amos what she'd been doing. He showed her around the building some and had sandwiches and Cokes brought in from a place across the street. They were still eating them in his office when Jake appeared and motioned to Stephanie from the far side of the newsroom that it was time to go.

She went outside with Jake and got into his battered Pontiac, which started reluctantly. They reached Wrigley Field and entered. She had only been to two or three ball games in her life, and none of them were major league. Both Bobby and Richard were avid baseball fans, and she had picked up a little from them, but all she could remember were some stars of the game, names like Jackie Robinson, Ted Williams, and Stan Musial. She did not know a single Cub player and wondered if she could deceive Taylor into thinking she knew more than she did.

He led her to the press box and snapped out the names of the reporters—all men—who grinned at her. One of them asked Stephanie, "How does a nice lady like you get to run around with a thug like Taylor?"

"Just lucky, I guess," Stephanie answered, and a laugh went up from the reporters.

"We'll watch the game from up here," Taylor said, finding a chair and pulling it up to the table. "Best seats in the house."

Stephanie watched the game, speaking only when spoken to and desperately trying to pick up as much as she could. The Cubs lost by a score of eight to one, and the reporters all groaned as they got up to leave. "Come on, Steph," said Jake, "I'll take you down to meet some of the players."

She followed him through the crowd fighting its way out at the exit, and they came to a sign that said Dressing Room. Jake opened the door and waited, but Stephanie stood staring at him.

"What's the matter? Come on!"

"I–I can't go into the locker room!"

Taylor cocked his head to one side. "How am I going to introduce you to the players if you won't go into the locker room?"

"Well," she said firmly, "you bring one of them out here."

Taylor laughed abruptly. "I was hoping I could get you inside. It'd be quite a treat for the boys. All right. Tell you what I'll do. I'll get the losing pitcher out here, and you can write a story on how it feels to be a loser."

"Thanks, Jake," Stephanie said. She waited outside, and soon the pitcher came out looking dejected. His eyes narrowed when he saw her, and he said, "You ain't the reporter that Taylor wants me to talk to?"

"I'm afraid so."

The pitcher had a huge wad of tobacco in his mouth. He spat expertly to his left, then shrugged. "I ain't never been interviewed by a female reporter."

"Well, I've never interviewed a baseball player either, so it'll be a first for both of us."

The interview went well, for the pitcher seemed to be pleased at finding a sympathetic listener. He gave a long list of reasons why the Cubs had lost, and none of them were his fault. When it was over, he said, "I hope you do me right in the newspaper."

"I will. Look for it," Stephanie promised. She closed her notebook and found Jake, talking to one of the players.

He came over to her at once and said, "Did you get the stuff?"

"Yes."

"Okay, when we get back to the paper, type it up and have it on my desk in an hour. Then call it a day."

Later when she handed him the article, he glanced over it quickly, then said, "See you tomorrow, Stephanie."

"All right, Jake." She stopped long enough to say, "Thanks for being so nice."

"Oh, I'm nice. Everybody knows that." He smiled then turned back to his work.

Stephanie collected her belongings and took a taxi to her grandparents' home. Amos had called Rose, who greeted her at the door with hugs and kisses and seemed as excited about her getting the job at the paper as Stephanie was herself. "Oh, Grandma, I can do this job," she said. "I know I can!" Later she chattered about the baseball game through supper with Amos and Rose, relating every detail she could about the reporters in the press box, the players, the field, the fans, the sounds, the smells. *Maybe*, thought Amos, *just maybe she has the moxie for this business—at least til she falls in love and decides to get married*. Stephanie went upstairs and finished unpacking, then went to bed looking forward to her first full day at work on a newspaper.

Boot camp was over. All assignments were made, and Richard and Smith were both assigned to the same company, attached to the First Marine Division in Korea.

"Well, we're going to be together it looks like, Streak," Smith said, lighting up a cigar as the two parted for a final leave. "Don't get run over by a taxi or something. I need you to watch my back when we hit the beaches."

"Same for you, Jack."

The two separated, and Richard boarded a bus and made his way to Los Angeles. He was scheduled to leave on a ship for Korea from San Diego on September 20.

School had just started and Richard enjoyed the adulation of his former schoolmates. He went by the high school, and the girls with penny loafers and ponytails who swarmed about him seemed to be about ten years old. But he spent most of the time with his family. He went fishing with his father— both of them loved to fish—and it had been a good day for them. The sun sparkled on the green water. They anchored their boat over a coral reef, and the fish were biting. The boat rocked gently with the breeze. Jerry asked about Richard's training.

"Was it as hard as you thought it would be?"

"A lot harder, Dad, but that's the marine way. They figure to strip everything away and then build the marine on top of you."

"You're proud of being a marine, aren't you?"

"Yes, I am." The answer was quick and definite. Richard was wearing a T-shirt, and the firm muscles of his upper body bulged as tribute to the strictness of the training. His hair was cut in a crew cut, and he looked hard and tough, but there was no cruelty in his eyes.

When they turned toward shore, they'd caught enough red

snappers to eat for six months. That afternoon after the fish had been cleaned, Richard and Stephanie, who had come home from Chicago to see him, went down to the swimming hole. They invited Bobby, but he had a piano lesson.

They splashed and laughed and finally came out and sat down, and as Stephanie dried her hair, she said, "You look like one of those muscle men on the covers of magazines in the drugstore—*Muscles and Health* or something like that."

"All I need is an *S* on my chest." Richard grinned. "How did you manage to get a job working for Gramps?"

"I'm so glad not to be going back to college. I despised every minute of it!" Stephanie pronounced venomously. "I made him give me a job. I just turned on the old charm." She turned her shoulders bewitchingly and gave Richard a brilliant smile.

"Hey, don't turn that thing loose on me! Why, it could make a man keel over at fifty paces!"

"It's like Davy Crockett. He said he didn't have to shoot raccoons, he just grinned 'em out of the trees." She laughed and added, "He said one time he missed and knocked the top off an elm tree a hundred feet high!"

"Well, that's the kind of smile you got, Sis. Atomic power! Be careful. You don't want to maim too many poor devils chasing around after you."

"No danger of that. I've got a lot of plans." She ran the comb through her wet curls and said, "I'm going to be a war correspondent and travel all over the world. Then I'm going to write articles for *National Geographic*. You're going to be proud of me, Streak."

"I'm proud of you now, Steph."

Stephanie turned to him and reached out her free hand. "I'm proud of you, too, Richard. I'm scared about you going to Korea, but there's no point in telling you to be careful."

"I don't remember the sergeant giving us any instructions on that," Richard joked.

"Well, you've got Mom and Dad's prayers, and they're pretty potent. You've got mine, too," she said softly.

"Thanks, Sis."

The two sat talking for a long time. He asked, "How do Dad and Bobby seem to be getting along? Have there been any flare-ups lately?"

"I haven't heard anything. I think you joining up has made Dad go easier on Bobby. Like he's thinking he could lose you, so somehow Bobby's behavior doesn't seem so serious a problem."

"What do you think Bobby's going to do? He'll be eligible for the draft if he's not in college in another year."

"Oh, he talks some about going to college, but he's just treading water. He really wants to be a musician, a singer. He travels all over on weekends doing what he calls 'gigs.' Plays the piano like Paderewski."

"Or Leo Durocher?"

"No, you idiot!" She laughed.

"Wouldn't it be something if he got to be famous like Snooky Lanson?"

"He'll have to change his name. Bobby Stuart is not dramatic enough."

Richard pretended to think and said, "What about Hoagie Decarmo?"

This struck Stephanie as being very funny, and she continued to giggle as they threw their clothes on over their wet bathing suits and made their way home.

As they walked up the driveway Stephanie said, "Whose car is that?"

"Don't know. Let's find out."

They entered the house and were delighted to find their great-uncle Owen sitting in the living room talking with their father. Owen rose at once. He was sixty-eight but still athletic and strong. He had been a prizefighter in his youth and had lost his right hand in World War I. He put his left hand forward and turned it over to squeeze Richard's and nearly crushed it. "How's the marine?" he asked with a smile.

"Fine, Uncle Owen. I'm glad to see you."

"I had a meeting over in San Diego, so I thought I'd come over and say good-bye." Owen Stuart had been an evangelist for years, crossing the country and speaking in large auditoriums and in brush arbors all the way from Georgia to California, from Louisiana to Maine.

"I won't be here long. I'm shipping out day after tomorrow," Richard said.

"Well, we'll have some time to talk."

After supper Owen asked Richard to show him the ocean, so they drove to a beach a few miles away.

"I stopped in and stayed a day with Lylah," Owen said, speaking of his older sister. "You know, it's a marvel. Out of our whole family, we're all still living. Not many families have lived through two wars and have all the brothers and sisters still alive."

They were walking along the beach, and the water wrinkled and flashed at their feet catching the glints of the late sun. Seagulls followed them, circling, crying harshly. A majestic great blue heron crossed their path with precise steps. It turned one eye toward them, considered their approach, then made a few steps and took to the air, sailing away to light on top of a scraggly tree above the beach.

Owen stopped walking and turned to face Richard. "How do you feel about going out to kill people, Richard?"

The question was so abrupt that Richard could not answer for a moment. He picked up a starfish, sent it sailing into the water, then turned to face Owen. "They gave us a lot of lectures about that in training. How did you feel about it when you went to war, Uncle Owen?"

"I didn't like it. None of us did. Well, there were a few that seemed to. I always thought it was abnormal."

"We had some of those. They don't seem to think of the enemy as human beings."

"Men never do in war. We called our enemy 'Krauts' and to us they were all devils wearing spiked helmets. They had bayoneted babies in Belgium and had neither honor nor decency. At least that's what we were told, and I guess some of it came through."

"Well, that's what they've tried to tell us, but I've got a feeling that when I see one I'll see him as a man just like me."

"That reminds me of a poem I heard. I don't memorize much poetry, but I memorized this one."

He began to speak softly. Owen had a loud, powerful voice when he needed it, filling whole auditoriums, but it was quiet and almost gentle as he spoke the words:

> "Had he and I but met
> By some old ancient inn,
>   We should have sat us down to wet
> Right many a nipperkin!
>
> "But ranged as infantry,
> And staring face to face,
>   I shot at him as he at me,
> And killed him in his place.
>
> "I shot him dead because—
> Because he was my foe,
>   Just so! my foe of course he was:
> That's clear enough; although
>
> "He thought he'd enlist, perhaps,
> Off-hand like—just as I—
>   Was out of work—had sold his traps—
> No other reason why.
>
> "Yes; quaint and curious war is!
> You shoot a fellow down
>   You'd treat if met where any bar is,
> Or help to half a crown.

"I guess that's about the way it is," Owen said. "When you take the uniforms off, we're all just men. Creatures of God." He turned and said, "Do you have faith, Richard?"

"Why, yes. I was baptized when I was thirteen years old."

"That's good, but there's got to be more than that, especially where you're going. Being put under the water doesn't give you what you need in your heart." Owen continued to speak for some time of the soldier's need of God. He said, "You've heard all this before from your parents. They've given you a good foundation, but when you get out there in Korea and face the blood and the filth and the awfulness of it, don't lose it, Richard. Hang on to your faith in Jesus."

"I'll do my best, Uncle Owen."

Two days later, Richard stood on the dock, his bag at his feet. His family had come, and he said good-bye to each one, and it was hard. He could tell his mother was keeping tears back only by an effort, and he whispered, "Don't worry, Mom."

He embraced Stephanie, and she whispered, "I love you, Richard," then turned away quickly.

Bobby also had a paleness in his face that was not usual. He lost all of his cockiness with the stark reality upon him of Richard's going to war. He cleared his throat twice and said, "I wish you didn't have to go. Take care of yourself, buddy."

"You watch yourself, Bobby. You're too good a man to do anything except what's right."

Bobby looked at his twin with surprise and shock in his eyes; nodding, he said huskily, "Okay."

He and his dad hugged, and Jerry held him a long time, unable to speak. Then Richard picked up his bag, shouldered it, and joined the group of marines walking up the gangplank. On board the ship, he paused at the rail and saw them still standing huddled close together. He smiled and waved, and they waved back; then he made his way down the rail. He found his quarters, came back, and saw that they were still there. As he waved again, sailors cast off the lines, the ship shuddered and began to move, gathering speed slowly. Richard stood at the rail waving and smiling, and when the ship swung, cutting them off from view, he turned and, feeling slightly sick, walked to the prow where he watched the water as it curled around the sharp, cutting edge of the transport. It bubbled, green and white and gray, and he looked up and strained his eyes as if he could see all the way across the sea to Korea.

5

DEATH AT HIGH NOON

Corporal Richard Stuart and Lance Corporal Keller were on their way to pick up supplies from a truck a mile behind the line. Keller was following Richard at a little distance. Richard's rifle was in the sling over his shoulder, and he smiled to himself. *It's been so quiet nobody would even know there's a war on,* he thought. Information was that the enemy units had pulled back, and for several days there had been no fighting. As he descended a slight slope, he was momentarily out of Keller's sight.

Suddenly he was face-to-face with a North Korean soldier, barely twenty feet away, who obviously was expecting trouble no more than Richard was. The enemy, too, had his rifle slung over his shoulder. It was too late to run, there was no place to hide, and both of them grasped at their rifle straps frantically, knowing that the first man to get off a shot would live—and the other would die. Richard's rifle fell into his hands in the familiar position, but he did not raise it, only fired from the hip. The shot took the North Korean in the chest and knocked him backwards, his rifle flying in the air and landing in the dirt. Looking first to see if the man was alone, Richard went to him. Keller was running up by now, rifle at the ready. Kneeling over the fallen soldier, Richard saw that he was only a boy, probably not over fifteen. His eyes were fluttering and his chest was a bloody blossom. Then he looked up at Richard and smiled.

Richard woke with a start. *Why did he smile?* He had no idea what day of the week it was. It was September 1952, he knew that, but for a long time he lay half awake, tugging his filthy blanket around him for warmth, thinking about that soldier, who had died without saying a word. In the boy's pocket had been pictures of two older people, probably his parents. There were letters written in the language that Richard could not understand, and he had kept them for a while and then wondered, *What would I do with them? Write and say "I killed your son"?* He had thrown them away, but the incident was engraved on his mind. He'd relived it frequently in his dreams.

The sun struck him in the face, and with a groan he rolled out of his sodden blanket and poked through his pack for dry socks. Dry socks were almost all the religion he had left. He found a pair of gray socks worn thin by many washings, stripped off his old ones, and pulled the dry ones on over his dirty feet, noting he had no infection or trench foot. As soon as he pulled his boots on and laced them up, he began thinking immediately of a way to wash his extra socks. He would wait until noon, find a muddy stream somewhere, and use the sliver of soap that he hoarded as if it were gold; then he would dry the socks on a rock in the midday sun and have them ready for the next morning.

Standing to his feet, he saw men stirring, groaning, but too weary to do more than that. He shrugged into his overcoat, and the dried mud cracked and fell to the frozen ground. Buttoning it up, he picked up his rifle and automatically searched the low-lying hills to the north. He saw campfires still there that, a couple of hours before first light, had looked like the eyes of some terrible, evil monster as they flickered and glowed. He pulled out his canteen and drank some of the cold water—it tasted bitter from the chemicals he added to it every day—and then put the top back on and hooked it on his belt. The rifle and the canteen, these were always at his side, and the dry socks. That was what the war was about. The newspapers might say other things, and the politicians might make glowing speeches, but here in the mud of Korea, it was the rifle, the canteen, and the dry socks that a man thought about.

"What time is it, Streak?"

Richard looked over to see Smith coming out of his bedroll. He reminded Richard, in his gyrations, of some sort of insect emerging from a cocoon. Smith had obtained a sleeping bag with a zipper on it, and once he was inside each night, he managed to zip it almost all the way up. He stuffed his clothes into the remaining crevice so that he was sealed off from the world. Despite Richard's misery, a smile creased his lips, and as he watched the marine struggle out he said, "Some of these days you're going to come out of that cocoon and find yourself facing a Chinese or a North Korean."

Not answering, Smith pulled himself free and lit a cigarette and began puffing at it, shivering in the cold morning wind. "Well," he muttered, staring across to the north with half-shut eyes, "any business today?"

"Not so far."

"That's a miracle."

"Come on. Let's go back and see if we can negotiate some breakfast."

"All right."

Smith picked up his rifle and shook his canteen; the two men then started toward the rear, their feet breaking through the crust of frozen mud. "I wish it'd either freeze hard enough to hold us up or it would get warm enough to thaw everything out." It was a frequent wish on Smith's part, and he crunched along beside Richard, limping slightly. He had taken a minor wound in the leg, and the medic had offered to report it, telling him he'd get a purple heart. Smith had simply grinned at him toughly, saying, "Give me a Baby Ruth, and pass the medal on to somebody else."

Richard thought Smith was a great marine. He complained and griped, as they all did, but when the fighting started, he was the one you wanted at your back, the best shot in Baker company, Richard figured. In the eleven months they'd served in combat together, he had seen Smith's deadly fire.

They approached the trucks and saw the smoke of cook fires rising into the air like wisps of gray ghosts. The two marines joined the line, and each was issued reconstituted powdered eggs, a hunk of cheese, and a canteen cup full of hot soup. They each got a brimming cup of black, scalding coffee and sat down on the log of a blasted tree. They ate mechanically at first, then hungrily, then went back for seconds on the eggs.

"So these things are eggs?" Jack grinned at his companion. "The eggs of *what*, I wonder?"

"Crocodiles," Richard grunted. "Don't ask questions."

"When I get home and marry Molly," Smith said, "I'm never going to eat an egg again. Nothing but pancakes. That girl makes the best pancakes in Michigan." He went on extolling Molly's virtues, sipping the scalding coffee between speeches. He carried a picture of her, folded carefully in soft leather. Using one hand, he managed to pull it out and remove the cover. Staring at it fondly, he said, "Well, Molly, old girl, here's another day I've got to spend away from you. Wait until I get back, sweetheart," he said, kissing the picture. "You won't get rid of me then."

Richard had grown accustomed to Smith's habit of talking to the picture and kissing it. They all had developed little behaviors that kept their minds from the misery of the life they led.

When they finished their meal, Richard said, "We better get back and let the other guys come and get some of these crocodile eggs."

They traipsed back, relieved two men, and replaced them in the trenches. From time to time, Richard glanced over to see Smith, about fifty yards away, but mostly he scanned the horizon. No one knew when the next attack was coming, but, wearily, they knew it *would* come. The marines had taken

Siberia and Bunker Hills in mid-August, and the fighting had hardly let up since then.

Hearing a noise behind him, Richard turned quickly, not really expecting trouble but ready for it. He smiled when he saw the chaplain, Captain Prejean, strolling along through the mud as if he were back on his farm in Louisiana. Prejean was an educated man, like all the chaplains, but he had a Cajun accent thick enough to cut with a knife. He was a slight man with a dark-complected face enlivened by gray-black eyes. "How you are today, marine?"

"Fine, padre. Get down before you get shot."

"I'm not gonna get shot, me," the chaplain said. He stood bolt upright and stared placidly across the open plain broken by hummocks and gullies. "I think we're gonna have a good sun in two or three hours," he observed. "You want a candy bar? I got a Snickers."

"A Snickers bar? Give it to me, padre. That's a gift from heaven."

"No, that's a gift from me. Heaven gives different kind of gifts." The chaplain smiled, squatted down, and fished the candy bar out of an inside pocket. It was crushed and pushed out of shape, but Richard didn't care. He tore the wrapper off, took a bite, and chewed it, closing his eyes in ecstasy. "That's as close to heaven as I've been lately."

"You ain't been very close, have you? Not you." The chaplain smiled, and his white teeth gleamed against his dark skin. "You a good Christian boy?"

"I don't reckon I am. I oughta be. My folks taught me the Bible."

"You better listen to your folks."

"They're a long way away."

"But the Lord God, he's not far. Not him. He's right here in the mud."

"God in the mud. Doesn't sound right somehow." Richard ate the candy bar in small bites, crunching the nuts between his teeth and enjoying it as he had not enjoyed anything in weeks. "I oughta take part of this to my buddy," he said.

"Where is he? I got another one just like."

"Over there. See?"

"Oh, yeah. Well, I'll go in a minute. Anything I can do for you?"

Richard grunted. He looked up at the chaplain and said, "What's the use of it all, padre?" He swallowed the last morsel of candy bar, licked his finger, and shook his head with disgust. "We chase these birds up north, and they get reinforcements and chase us back south. Every time we play that little game and dance that little waltz, we lose good men. They lose more than we do, but that doesn't help me any. I don't see any sense in it."

"It doesn't look so good, does it? But I tell you, we're only seeing what happens in this one little place. I mean, when they came at us yesterday that was all any of us could think about, especially you men up on the frontline. That line coming across there, and the tanks that would be right behind 'em, and the planes coming down to strike us. That's the whole world, isn't that right?"

"You got that right, padre."

"Well, no way to get out of that. When we got a toothache, all we can think about is that toothache. A hundred thousand people might die of starvation in India, but our toothache is what we think about, not those people dying." He settled down on his heels and spoke quietly. He had a classroom air about him, and Richard suspected he had been a teacher, a professor, at some time. "What's happening in the big picture?" Prejean asked rhetorically. "Simple. You know what the sign of the Communist party is?"

"A red star."

"That's right, you. It's red because of blood, which means they'll shed all the blood they have to, and that star's got five points. That stands for the five continents of the world. The Communists have vowed to take the world."

"My dad says something like that. And he says you have to whip the Communists where they are or you'll have to whip 'em in your own backyard."

"Your dad's a smart man, him. That's why we're fighting here, and if we can't see nothin' but this square acre of ground, you and me we got to believe that we're really fighting for the good ol' U. S. of A."

Richard liked the chaplain, always had, but Richard's faith was small, and he thought of the boy soldier that he had killed. "What about the killing?" he said harshly. "That village we came to three days ago, some women and children got killed there, and maybe some of them not by accident."

Chaplain Prejean shook his head sadly. "No answer for that, marine. In a war men are away from home. None of their people are watching 'em. They been taught to kill the enemy, and there's no little switch on a man that he throws to make a difference. Men do things in a war that they'd be put in jail for back home." He fixed his eyes on Richard's face, and he spoke quietly. "You noticed that, I think. Men do crazy things here that they'd never do back in Ohio or Virginia."

Richard had a quick memory of Smith talking to a photograph and smiled faintly. "I guess you're right there, padre."

From far off came the rumble of artillery, and the two men turned in that direction. But both of them had learned to judge the sound of cannon fire, the distance, and this was too far away to hurt them. "They're hurtin' somebody," Prejean said, "but not us. There, you see? As long as it's not me, I don't worry—not me."

"Padre, would Jesus have been a marine if he lived in our time?"

The question caught the chaplain off guard. "You ask funny questions, you," he said.

"Well, would he?"

Prejean thought about it. "When Jesus Christ came to this world, he didn't come to be a marine. He came for something worse than that. He came to die on a cross." He continued to speak of Jesus and his death, and the chaplain's voice became earnest and his eyes half-slitted. "Don't make any mistake. We're fighting against flesh and blood, but Jesus said, 'My kingdom is not of this world' and he fought against principalities and powers, and he won his war." An exultant smile came, and the chaplain's eyes lit up. "That's why we can face the worst thing the world has, 'cause Jesus won."

"I'm all mixed up, chaplain."

Prejean leaned over and tapped Richard's shoulder. "We're not at the end yet. That's why there's still war and killing. But I'd like to think that you're holding back the powers of darkness a little bit. The Communists are godless people, the leaders anyway. They're determined to stamp out Jesus Christ and the cross. What town you come from?"

"Los Angeles."

"Imagine that the Communists were in Los Angeles. First thing they'd do is kill all the Christians. That'd probably be your folks—your family and you." He stood up then and said, "I wish I had a sack full of Snickers bars."

"Thanks for stopping by, chaplain. It was a help."

"You keep looking to the Lord Jesus. Put your faith in him."

The chaplain turned and strolled away. Richard watched as he went over and stooped down to give Smith the candy bar, and he thought, *That's some fella, that chaplain. I wish they were all like him.*

For two days after Chaplain Prejean's visit Richard thought about what he'd said. He even dug the New Testament out of his pocket, but his mind was too fuzzy to make much sense out of it. He spoke with Smith about the chaplain, and they agreed that he was a real man. Smith said, "You know, when Molly and me get married, I'd like to have that chaplain come and do the marrying." He grinned, saying, "But if he ain't around, I'll grab anybody that's legal." He pulled the picture out of his pocket, delivered his usual flowery speech, kissed it, then put it back. "You don't have a girl back home?"

"Nope. Not like you do."

"Too bad. You go back and find one. A man's only half a man without a woman."

The attack came at almost high noon, which caught the company off guard. Usually the Communist troops launched their attacks at night or in the early dawn. This time the sun had come out, the men were sitting around, some of them playing cards, others napping. When the alarm came, Sergeant Johnston came scrambling back. "Here they come! They got us surrounded on three sides! We got to hold 'em off, marines!"

It was as bitter and vicious a fight as any of them remembered. The enemy kept coming in fresh waves, but Richard fought coolly. He held his fire until he saw a good target. Jack turned and punched his shoulder. "You're earning that sharpshooter's money today, boy." Jack fought calmly, and the two men held the position until the attack was driven back.

Lieutenant Porterfield came along the line, crouched low. "We're pulling out," he said. "Fall back, but keep your heads. Go back fifty yards, stop, and cover the men you pass. Keep your heads now, marines."

They began their slow retreat, and Richard and Jack got separated. By 2 o'clock the marines had covered almost a mile.

Richard heard a tremendous rattle of fire over to his right and turned quickly. "What's that?"

"Some of our fellas got pinned down over there under that hill. Look! There's the enemy along that line." Richard looked where the lieutenant pointed.

"We got to get 'em out!" Richard whispered tersely.

"How? We don't have support to march up those hills."

Richard was searching the terrain. "There's a little gully over there that runs near the base of that hill," he said. "Maybe we can take a squad and get behind them."

The lieutenant was a large man with fair hair and light blue eyes. "You willin' to try, Stuart?"

"Let's go!"

Porterfield quickly gathered six others, and they faded along a ridge that concealed them from the enemy. The rapid fire continued and Porterfield cursed. "They've got automatic weapons! All we have is rifles!"

"They'll kill a man as quick as a machine gun, Lieutenant," Richard said. They advanced almost a quarter of a mile, and then suddenly the lieutenant's face turned purple. He grasped his chest and fell to his knees, saying, "Can't—make it. Something's wrong in my chest."

Richard glanced at the others and said quickly, "You two, Evans and Barker, get the lieutenant back."

"We can't carry him."

Stuart said, "Gimme your rifles." He grabbed the two M-1s and said, "Now you can carry him. Get going." Evans and Barker each took one of the lieutenant's arms and hoisted the man between them and started back.

Richard said to the others, "Look, we're almost there. If we get up that ridge, I think we'll be able to spot 'em."

"We got to cross that open ground," one of the marines protested. He shook his head. "That's suicide, Streak!"

"Well, we'll just have to outrun those bullets, won't we?" Richard said. He started, and the four marines followed him. They crossed the open space without drawing fire and all piled into a heap in the shallow gully at the base of the ridge, gasping for breath. Only then did automatic weapons begin to kick up dust around them.

"They got us spotted!" one of the marines said, as he flattened out.

"I'm going up and across to that rock over there. If I can get there, they can't get much of a shot uphill at me."

"You'll never make it, Streak!"

"You watch me, Keller!"

Richard left the cover of the gully, with the two extra rifles still slung at his back, and ran a zigzag pattern. Keller and the others did their best to lay down covering fire. Richard thought to himself, *You're the hundred-yard-dash man. Come on now. They don't call you Streak for nothin', do they?* Bullets chewed up the ground around him, and he felt one of them touch the small of his back, leaving a burning sensation. He zigzagged, stopping and falling and rolling, and heard the screams of the enemy.

The last ten yards, he simply made a running dive. He felt something strike his boot, and when he rolled over he saw that the heel had been shot away.

He sprawled behind the small rock—which seemed even smaller now that he was using it for cover—and threw a shell into the chamber of his rifle. He already knew what he wanted to do. Just pop up, take a shot, and pull back down.

He crouched, then with one motion rose up and flung his rifle steady. The scene below came clearly in view, and he saw a number of enemy soldiers, some of them looking up at him. One of them started to raise his machine gun. In one motion, Richard pulled his rifle down into position and fired. He saw the man knocked backwards, and he ducked down. Bullets dug in around him, splintering rocks, but he slithered left and about ten feet down the hill to another rock, popped up, and fired again. This was the game he played. Moving up and down, left and right along the ridge, taking whatever cover he could, he outguessed them. And meanwhile Keller's group took every opportunity to add their fire from the flank, plus the enemy was still taking fire from the marines they'd pinned down. Soon Richard heard cries of anger and despair, and without wasting time reloading his rifle, he grabbed one of the spares. This time he popped up and took four shots, each one knocking down an enemy soldier. There was return fire, but it was spasmodic.

Richard never knew how long this went on, but finally he heard commands, the firing from below subsided, and the enemy pulled back along the base of the ridge on the side away from where Keller's men were still firing. Richard, too, fired until they were all gone, then seeing that the way was clear, scrambled back to the others. After grins and slaps on the back all around, they regrouped and found Lieutenant Porterfield with a medic. His color had grown better. "I think you just won yourself a medal, son," Porterfield said after the others told him what had happened.

"I just need to get this boot heel fixed. Come on, Keller, let's let the lieutenant get rested up. We'll go see about the rest of the boys," said Richard.

The marines who had been pinned down were moving to rejoin the company. One of the first men Richard saw was Smith. "Think they're gone?"

"I think so." Richard looked toward the line of distant hills.

The men began their retreat again. The lieutenant did some talking, and soon word was out how Richard had thrown himself against the enemy to save the rest of them.

Smith said, "I thank you, and Molly thanks you."

"Keep the change, Jack."

They continued the withdrawal for thirty minutes, and the enemy seemed to have broken off the pursuit. A strange silence fell over the broken fields, and Richard and Jack stopped simultaneously and looked at each other. "The quiet sounds funny," Smith observed.

Richard turned and looked back over the hills. A flock of small birds was silhouetted against the sky, flying low. They lit on the ground twenty feet away and began pecking industriously in their search for food. "I sure would like to see—"

He never finished the sentence. He felt something strike his left side and thought that Jack had poked him with his rifle butt. It was in his mind to turn, but then the flock of small birds disappeared. Not so much that they just vanished, but they were suddenly covered by a cloud of dust. At the same time, a dull thud ripped his ears and the ground under him seemed to heave. He felt himself strike the earth, and in one instant, a flash of insight, he realized that a shell had exploded. At the same time he became aware of a terrible pain in his side, and as he was rolled over twice, he thought, *I'm being killed!*

He lost consciousness for a few seconds. When he awoke, his face was in the dirt, his nose clogged with it. He opened his eyes and tried to sit up, and pain made him gasp. He pushed himself up on one elbow and pulled his sleeve across his face. The acrid smell of cordite was in his nostrils, and he could not see for a moment for the white smoke. Then it cleared, and he saw bodies lying like bundles of old clothes around him.

"Jack!" he cried out. "Are you hit bad?" He forced himself into an upright position; looking down, he saw that the left side of his uniform was quickly soaking with bright, crimson blood. Ignoring it, he dragged himself to the body that lay closest to him.

Smith was lying face down, and when Richard pulled him over with his right hand, he saw that Smith's eyes were open. There was a slight upward turn to his lips, as if he had heard something that amused him secretly. Richard touched Smith's face, and the features did not move. The pain in Richard's side struck him then, and he collapsed, half sitting, beside the dead marine. He could see Keller and Evans nearby, both dead, and Sergeant Johnston, too, a little farther away.

The enemy artillery boomed, and there were geysers of dirt and mud further on down. The American artillery began to answer, and in the middle of this duel, Richard Stuart lay in the mud holding a dead man's hand.

Reaching over painfully with his wounded left arm, Richard took the picture of Molly from Smith's pocket. He opened its soft leather cover and looked from the picture to the smile on the dead man's lips. "You won't see Molly now," he whispered. He thought he would cry, but the tears would not come, and he felt himself passing out.

6

THE VINE

I n October 1952, Truman declared drought-stricken Oklahoma a disaster area, and in music, *Billboard* magazine picked "You Belong to Me," by Pee Wee King, as the most popular song. Gary Cooper starred in the western *High Noon*, which was destined to become a classic and to win Cooper another best actor Oscar.

On November 8, the Republicans won the White House for the first time in twenty years. General "Ike" Eisenhower, a World War II hero and the first commander of NATO's military, was elected president of the United States, with Richard M. Nixon as his vice-presidential running mate. Adlai Stevenson was defeated in a landslide vote. During that same election, John F. Kennedy upset Henry Cabot Lodge in Massachusetts and began his career in the U. S. Senate.

There was a spirit of hope in America. The war appeared to be winding down. It was a time of plenty. Wages had never been higher, employment was at an all-time high, and people came to the Christmas season happy and looking forward to a rosy future.

Merle Baxter, proprietor of the Delight Hotel in Mountain View, a small town settled in the heights of the Ozarks, never worried about Christmas business. For years his entire establishment, which included fifteen rooms and the restaurant, was bought out by the Stuart family. Merle said to his wife, Arlene, early on the morning of the twenty-fourth, "I wish we had more folks like them Stuarts." He spat a stream of tobacco juice toward the glass cuspidor and made a direct hit, then grinned. "They's enough of 'em got money, and they don't mind spending it at least once a year."

The Stuarts had already begun arriving, and by midday the hotel was swarming like an anthill. Cars with plates from states as far away as California were pulled up in front of the Delight, and the extra help that Baxter had hired to put on the big dinner and serve at the table were already busy.

Stephanie flew in from Chicago almost at the last minute, with Jake Taylor. They rented a car at Fort Smith, Arkansas, and drove over the frozen roads that wound up through the foothills and into the highlands of the Ozarks. As they talked, she was, as always, amazed that this tough-looking man was so well-read. He was telling her now about a newly published book by Hemingway called *The Old Man and the Sea*, and his sharp brown eyes glowed with excitement. He told about a sad episode in the book, and to her amazement she saw tears fill his eyes.

Amazed, she said, "Why, Jake, you're crying."

"Something in my eye," he growled. He changed the subject at once, but it revealed a side that she had noticed about Taylor. He was extremely sentimental and emotional, and he fought like a tiger to keep it concealed from the world. In order to do this, he had cultivated his reputation as a sharp, hard-bitten man with few illusions.

Stephanie reached over and put her hand over his. "It's all right to cry," she said gently. "My father cries sometimes, and he's one of the toughest men I've ever known."

"Does he really?"

"Yes, and he's not ashamed of it either."

"Well, if I ever cried, I'd be ashamed of it."

She laughed at him. "You're a fraud, Jake Taylor!"

Stephanie was delighted at the snow that had fallen, and they stopped on a rise and looked down at the small town of

Mountain View nestled in the valley. "Isn't it beautiful! Just like a calendar, isn't it, Jake?"

"Mighty pretty." He eased the car down, for the roads were a little icy. As they drove into town, he took in its one street with a line of one-story buildings on each side. When he got to the Delight he broke into laughter. "Look at that!" he said. The sign outside said: Delight Hotel—Mountain View's Tallest Skyscraper. Since the hotel was only two stories high, Jake found this amusing. "They've got a sense of humor around here."

"You better watch out, though. They don't take to Yankees. Try to talk southern if you can."

"Yes, ma'am. Y'all—shucks—grits," Jake spun off the list. "How's that?"

"Just terrible! Come on. Oh, look! There's Uncle Owen!"

Stephanie got out and ran forward to greet Owen, who hugged her, then she introduced him to Jake, and he shook hands with his odd left-handed shake—he turned his hand over because most people were right-handed. He looked the tall man in the eye. "Glad to meet you, Jake," he said. "I hear you're teaching this young woman how to be a reporter."

Jake smiled crookedly. "Well, Mr. Stuart, she's practically a veteran by now."

As they walked on, Stephanie said, "Somebody ought to write a book about Owen. He won the congressional Medal of Honor. That's how he lost his hand—in the First World War. He's done everything. Been a prizefighter, like you, and an evangelist."

"Maybe you should write it," Jake responded. "Fine-looking man. He looks you straight in the eye, doesn't he? Made me feel like he knew all about me."

Stephanie giggled. "I hope he didn't. He'd probably run you off with a shotgun."

Jake turned and looked at her directly. "Now, Steph," he said, "we've worked together for a year and a half, and in all that time have I ever made a pass at you?" He was wearing a camel's hair overcoat and a brown felt hat. There was something fiercely masculine about him. "Well, have I?"

"No, you haven't." She studied him for a moment, then her eyes twinkled, and her lips broke into a grin. "I have to look in my mirror once in a while to be sure I haven't turned into a hag."

Studying her curly black hair, which came out around her shoulders from under the green tam, and the blue-green eyes that he had learned more and more to admire, Jake said simply, "You're not a hag, Stephanie."

Stephanie's face flushed at his solemn reply, and she said, "Come on. You've got to meet everyone. We ought to wear name tags, but we never do. You'll just have to remember. We'll start right here." Stephanie stopped him in front of a cheerful-looking woman in a wheelchair, who was talking with an especially beautiful and well-coifed younger woman. "Hello, Aunt Lenora! Lenora Stuart, this is Jake Taylor, a reporter that I work with. Jake, this is my great-aunt I told you about who's in the Salvation Army."

"Nice to meet you, Miss Stuart."

Lenora extended her hand to him. "Please call me Lenora, Jake. I'm glad to meet you, too. My brother Amos mentions you, so it's nice to put a face with the name. And this is Stephanie's cousin Mona. You may have heard of her."

After more greetings and small talk, Stephanie and Jake moved on. Lenora and Mona resumed their conversation. They only saw each other at the Christmas reunions, but they usually found time for a friendly talk. Lenora said, "I'm sorry you never knew your grandmother. You were just a baby when your granddad died, and Mother had been gone many years already by then. I was only fifteen myself when she died."

Mona enjoyed talking about the family history with Lenora. Names always popped up that she couldn't place, and Lenora filled her in. Lenora seemed such a kind and—well— spiritual soul. She was always urging Mona to visit her in

Chicago, but Mona could never quite envision herself walking into the Salvation Army headquarters.

The dinner took place in the restaurant of the Delight, and the room was packed. In one corner of the dining room a fifteen-foot cedar tree stood covered with ornaments, silver ropes, and lights that the children and young people had worked on all afternoon. The tables were loaded with the traditional southern-style Christmas dinner—turkey, cornbread dressing, sweet potatoes, ham and greens. For dessert, pies, cobblers, and cakes filled one special table.

Amos sat at the head of a table, next to his wife, Rose. They were both seventy-three, and Rose had the beauty that remains in old age. She whispered, "I don't think we've ever had so many people here, Amos."

"Yes, it's a good crowd, but there's more Stuarts as the years go by, remember." Amos looked across at Jerry and Bonnie and murmured, "They're a fine-looking couple, aren't they? And I'm glad Richard got back from Korea in time to be here. He looks good, doesn't he?"

"I don't know. A little bit too pale maybe, but his wound's healing all right, isn't it?"

"Yes, he'll be fine."

Amos's eyes went around the room, finding where Owen sat with his wife, Allie. Amos stood up and tapped on a glass, and when the room grew quiet he said, "We're going to eat first and have the speechifying later, and some music. So, eat all you can hold, but don't get stupefied. Owen, I guess you can ask the blessing. Don't use the same one you used the last five years running. And let's keep it short."

Owen rose, grinning, and a laugh went around the room. He bowed his head and said, "Father, thank you for this food. Thank you even more for our family, for the young and for the old. You said in your Word that you put the solitary in families. Lord, I love that verse. You've put us into a family

88 Pages of Promise

so that we don't have to be alone. In the name of Jesus." He looked up and smiled. "Was that short enough, Amos?"

"About right. About right. Now, y'all lay your ears back and go at it," Amos said.

His wife laughed. "When you come to Arkansas, you start talkin' like the hillbilly you were sixty years ago."

"Not a bad way to be," Amos said.

Jake took a slice each of ham and turkey breast, some cornbread dressing, cranberry sauce, and sweet potatoes, then piled on celery stuffed with pimento cheese and olives; finally he had to draw the line. "If I get around this, I won't be able to walk much!" he said. He began eating but between bites said, "I liked what the preacher said about setting the solitary in families. I never had family, not really." He looked around the room and said, "It must be wonderful to grow up with uncles and aunts and grandparents and cousins. I never had anybody."

From Jake Taylor, this was the equivalent to another man breaking down and squalling. There was a sadness in his brown eyes, and he had stopped eating. Stephanie reached over and put her hand on his and squeezed it. "I'll share my family with you. They'll be glad to have you."

"A Yankee like me?"

"Yankee or not, they'll have to if I say so. That's the way we Stuarts are."

Jake's eyes crinkled, and the scars around his eyes seemed to intensify. He touched his puffed ear and said, "Even a beat-up thug like me?"

"Yes. You do have your moments," Stephanie said.

After the family had stuffed the last of the pies and cakes down their throats, Amos stood up and said, "Now for some singin', and we got a professional here. Bobby Stuart, I reckon this is where you let your light shine."

Bobby felt his father nudge him in the ribs and heard him whisper, "Go to it. Let's have some real music out of you, boy."

Bobby rose and went over to the piano and sat down. He said nothing but began playing "Jingle Bells" and singing in his clear tenor voice. Everyone joined in, and for fifteen minutes, they sang the old favorites. When he played "I'm Dreaming of a White Christmas" there was something in the way he phrased the words, something in his eyes as he looked out over the crowd. Everyone stopped singing to hear him.

Although Jerry had heard Bobby many times, he had never realized what a power this young man had over people when he sang or played. "I guess we didn't waste money on those music lessons, did we?" he asked Bonnie, who squeezed his hand. He turned and saw the tears in her eyes, and when he turned back to look at his son, there was a wonder in his own eyes.

Bobby came to the end of "White Christmas," then laughed. He suddenly kicked the piano stool back and said, "Folks, as Al Jolson used to say, 'You ain't heard nothin' yet!'" He began playing some of the same songs but with a beat that most of them had never heard. It was jazz, it was partly the blues of New Orleans, and even when he played "Rudolph the Red-Nosed Reindeer" it was different. He thundered the bass, his left hand carrying on a steady beat so that everyone in the room began swaying back and forth. He threw his head back, standing at the piano, sometimes his hair falling down in his face, and the powerful beat seemed to rock the old hotel.

Looking around, Amos saw that all of the help had come from the kitchen, and they were swaying and smiling with all their might. "Don't know what that boy's got," he whispered to Rose, "but it's something."

Finally Bobby ran his hand up the keyboard and up in the air with a sensational flourish. "Merry Christmas, and God bless us, every one!"

They all got to their feet clapping and crying, "God bless us, every one!" and Jake put his arm around Stephanie and drew her close. She looked up at him, surprised. "This is

some family you've got, sweetheart," he said. "I'd sure like
to be a part of it!"

The day after Christmas saw the Delight cleared out.
Stephanie and Jake drove back to Chicago with Amos and
Rose. The Los Angeles contingent included Lylah, Adam
and his family, and Mona. They had all gotten the same flight
out of Fort Smith. Around the old home place only Jerry,
Bonnie, and the twins remained.

Logan felt concerned about Richard, who made some effort to join in the celebration, but there was a stillness in him
that troubled some of the family. Logan talked to Jerry, who
merely said that since Richard had come home he seemed to
have no desire to do anything. Jerry was worried, Logan could
tell. "I know he's still recuperating," Jerry said, "but he just
sits around and stares at things. It's like he's not at home, if
you know what I mean, Logan."

Logan came over where Richard sat gazing out the window. "Well, boy, you're not doing anything. How about len-
din' an old man some help?"

Richard turned and studied Logan, who was wearing his
usual faded overalls. "Why sure, Uncle Logan. What do you
need? Something worked on?"

"Nah, that old Chevy of mine is runnin' for a change." He
pulled his straw hat off and scratched his thinning auburn
hair. "What I'd like is for you to give me a hand takin' some
fixins over to them young folks that live down in the crook
of the river."

"What folks are you talking about?"

"Oh, it's a bunch of young folks that took up land over
there. I thought I told you about it. They call the place the
Vine. I don't know what that means. Anyway, they're having
quite a struggle of it. They don't know much about farmin',
and they didn't get enough put back for the winter, I think.
There must be about twenty of 'em, and I reckon they could
use some extra."

"You gonna take some food over?"

"That's it. I'm gettin' all the leftovers from Merle. There was a whole turkey left, almost, and bits and pieces of another one. Anyhow, he said to come and get it. It's them young'uns over there; I hate to think of 'em missin' out on a Christmas dinner, even if it is a day late."

"All right," Richard agreed. He got up, put on his heavy fatigue jacket, and went out to the car.

Logan had hooked a two-wheel trailer to the back of the ancient vehicle. "I reckon we got enough stuff to fill that one up."

Richard got into the car, avoiding the sharp springs that were breaking through the seat covers, and slammed the door. The old car cranked slowly, laboriously, then burst into a noisy roar, and Logan winked at him. "Hear that thing? I hope we make it back."

Richard said little on the way to Mountain View to pick up the food, but Logan carried on a rapid-fire conversation pointing out different family homesteads and telling their histories. Richard asked with interest, "You know everybody in this county, don't you, Uncle Logan?"

"Well, I been here, man and boy, for sixty-eight years."

"You never left? Never wanted to go away?"

"Oh, I moved off for awhile, farmed a place for a couple years back in the twenties. But it was a poor farm. After your great-grandpa died I came back here. What would I go away to? The big city? Why would I do that, boy?"

"You may have something there." Richard looked out at the beauty of the countryside, the snow glistening, the firs topped with the crystal whiteness, and nodded. "It's not a bad place to be."

Logan looked at his great-nephew, thinking, *That must've been a bad thing over in Korea. A fella could get mighty sick of that. Something's wrong with this boy. He's sad and that ain't natural for a young'un his age.*

Logan stopped the Chevrolet at the Delight Hotel, and

when they went inside, they found Merle had packed up all of the remains of the feast in boxes. "You gonna take this to them young people out by the river, you say?"

"Thought I might. It looks like there's a lot of it."

Thirty minutes later Logan was steering the car down a rutted dirt road. "Can't get through this place in the spring," he said. "Mire up to the hubs." He gave his attention to steering, and they came out on a road that paralleled a winding river. "Used to swim in this when I was a boy. Caught some of the finest bass and perch you ever did see, too." A few minutes later he said, "There she is. Them folks done pretty well fixin' the old place up." He pulled in next to a long frame house circled by barns out behind and various outbuildings, the roofs all covered with snow. A curl of smoke went up from the chimney, and as Logan stopped the car, he said, "Don't have to worry about 'em bein' home. They ain't got nowhere to go."

Richard got out and turned to the trailer as Logan climbed laboriously out of his side of the car. The door of the house opened, and a tall man with sleepy-looking blue-gray eyes and a shock of black hair and a black beard came out to greet them. "Hello, Mr. Stuart," he said. His accent was not southern but was hard for Richard to place.

"Want you to meet Tom Henderson—and this is my great-nephew Richard Stuart." As the two men shook hands, Logan said briskly, "Had a bunch of grub left from our party, Tom. Hate to waste it, so I brung it over."

"Mighty nice of you," Henderson nodded. He noted Richard's jacket and said, "The Corps, I see."

"First Division."

Henderson studied him carefully and nodded. "You've seen some action then," he said. He turned to say, "Laurel, you think we could use some turkey and fixings?"

A young woman carrying a child came into the doorway and answered, "Yes, Tom, we sure can." She smiled at them. She wore a long calico dress, faded past all its original color, and a pair of men's boots. Though she was small, her figure was trim, and her cheeks glowed with health. Richard looked at the child, who was staring at him owlishly. "What's his name?" he said.

"John. I'm Laurel Jackson."

She said no more but turned away and moved back inside.

After the groceries were unloaded, Henderson looked at the stacks of boxes in the kitchen and shook his head. "It looks like enough to feed a regiment. But we'll make away with it quick enough. How about some hot sassafras tea?"

Logan said with an impish grin, "This here's a California boy. He ain't never tasted sassafras tea."

"It'll be a treat for you, Richard." The woman called Laurel soon came out of the kitchen with a pot that sent steam upward. Henderson removed some cups from pegs that hung on the wall, and as Laurel poured with a steady hand, he distributed them. Handing one to Richard, he said, "Hope you like this. It's a cultivated taste, I think."

Richard sipped the tea and opened his eyes with surprise. "Never tasted anything like it," he said.

"There ain't anything like it," Logan spoke up. Henderson smiled. "Here, you fellas have a seat."

Logan said, "Why, sure. Like to sit and visit a while. Tell me what you're plannin' for crops next year."

Richard found a cane-bottomed chair that needed some repair, but it held his weight. He moved it over toward the large wood-burning stove and soaked up the heat, listening as Logan and Tom spoke about farming. He watched people moving in and out of the room, apparently going about their business without regard to the visitors. Besides the two young men who had helped bring in the boxes, he saw several younger women and four or five children. The oldest person he saw was a grandmotherly type who came out of the kitchen from time to time and spoke to the younger women in a quiet voice.

Richard sipped his sassafras tea, and once Laurel came over and refilled his cup. "Do you like it?" she asked. Her voice was deep for a woman, especially such a small woman, and she smiled at him shyly.

"Real good," Richard said.

"You go out and dig the roots to make the sassafras," she said. "You've never done that?"

"No, I'm a city boy. Don't know beans about farming."

She hesitated for a moment, then asked, lowering her voice, "You in the army?"

"The marines."

"Oh!" She thought that over, and then something passed in her eyes, and Richard could not tell what it meant. He looked down at her hand and saw no ring there, and for the rest of the visit, he watched to see if any of the young men came near her.

Logan got up and reached for his coat, which he had tossed on the floor beside the door. "Got to get goin'."

"Thanks for the Christmas bounty," Henderson said. He shook hands with Logan, then with Richard, saying to the latter, "Don't be a stranger."

"Good to meet you, Mr. Henderson."

The three men went outside, and Henderson stood in front of the house until the Chevrolet chugged out of sight. Logan was mystified by the group. "Can't figure out what they're doin' here. They're sure not farmers, and I'm havin' a hard time figurin' out who's the wife to who."

"That woman, Laurel. I don't think she has a husband."

"What makes you think that?"

"No ring on her finger."

"Oh, I didn't notice." Logan swerved to dodge a pitted hole in the ground and said, "Pretty thing, isn't she?"

After a long silence, Richard said, "I didn't notice." He did not see the smile that touched Logan's lips, nor could he read the thoughts of the older man. *Well, he ain't too shell-shocked to notice a pretty gal, and that's good.*

Back home, Logan shut the engine off then turned to face his nephew. "I been thinkin', Richard. How'd you like to stay on for a spell?"

Richard turned to look at him, his eyes widening with surprise. "With you, here?"

"Why, sure. You ain't got a job to go to, do you?"

"Well, no, I don't."

"It appears to me like you could use a bit of peace and quiet." Logan's eyes sized up the young man shrewdly, and he said, "I could use some help around the place a little bit. You and me could go huntin' over in the hills. You're a sharpshooter—might get us a buck. I'd appreciate the company."

Richard said, "You know, I think I might like that, for a while, anyhow."

Logan reached over and slapped the young man's shoulder. He saw Richard wince, for the wound had not fully healed. "Oh, I'm sorry, boy. I forgot."

"It's okay, Uncle Logan."

He lifted his hand and arm and flexed the fingers, saying, "Almost well now. Are you sure I won't be in the way?" he asked.

"Why, shoot, boy. You see how much room we got in the house, and me and Annie just ramble around that old place. Pick any room you want upstairs. Don't even have to come down and talk when you don't want to. I figure me and you could have a good time together."

Richard said no more, but later that day he found his parents while they sat at the table drinking coffee. He sat down across from them and said, "I think I'd like to stay on here for a little while. Uncle Logan's asked me to, and I think I might like it."

"Might be a good thing," Jerry said quickly. He had not talked with Logan about this, but the idea seemed good. He knew that Richard was tight as a spring wire, and he knew that there was nothing like the quiet of this rural farm to calm a person's nerves.

Bonnie agreed, saying, "You know I'd rather have you at home. But it might be good for you to stay here for a couple of weeks. We'll go on back, and when you get ready to come home, you can fly in."

Richard nodded. "I'll stay then. Maybe I can be of some help to Uncle Logan on the place here." He smiled at them, seeming to relax more, and when Jerry was alone with Bonnie he said, "I think it's a good thing. He can unwind a little bit, and when he gets over the war, he can come home."

Stephanie had moved into an apartment with three other young women the previous spring. She felt her presence at her grandparents' home was creating too much extra work for her grandmother. The day after she returned with her grandparents from the Christmas get-together in Arkansas, Jake arrived at the apartment unexpectedly.

"Jake! What are you doing here?" Stephanie gasped, answering the door in her bathrobe and slippers.

"I came to talk to you."

"Now? It can't wait until tomorrow? I'll see you at work."

"No. Some things can't wait. Can I come in?" He slouched against the door frame, but there was an intensity in his eyes that confused her.

"Is it something about work?"

"Why don't you go get dressed," he quipped. "And put something over your head to cover up that messy hair."

Glaring at him for a moment, Stephanie said, "Well, come on in. There's coffee made in the kitchen. You'll just have to wait until I change."

When she came out a few minutes later, she found him in the tiny living room reading the paper, his feet propped on the coffee table.

He put down the paper and smiled at her, but there was tension in his face. He rose and walked over to her; something in his attitude made Stephanie stiffen. She put her hands on his chest as he reached for her and said nervously, "Now, wait a minute, Jake! What's this all about?"

Taylor took her arms and held them. For a moment his

eyes ran over her face, and then he said, "Black hair and green eyes. Stephanie, I've tried, you don't know how hard I've tried to keep from saying this, but you're the most attractive, beautiful, gorgeous, smart, intelligent, charming, sexy woman that I ever met."

She saw that joking wouldn't turn this aside. "Please let me go, Jake," she said.

He released her and said, "I might as well say what I want to say, and I might as well say it now."

Stephanie sensed danger, as if they were standing on a precipice—she knew if they went over it, there could be no going back. But it was too late—he was already saying the irrevocable words.

"I love you, and I want to marry you."

He spoke so matter-of-factly and his speech was so at variance with the intensity of his gaze that she could not respond.

"I'm not a very romantic guy, I guess, but I want to be. Right now I want to take you in my arms and kiss you. Would that be all right?"

Stephanie still felt too stunned to answer, but he took her silence as consent. He put his arms around her and kissed her. He held her for a moment, then lifted his head and said softly, "I'll say it again. I love you, and I want to marry you."

Never in her young life had Stephanie Stuart been so confused and so rattled. "Jake," she stammered, "I–I don't know what to say." She moved away from him, clasped her hands and pressed them to her lips, and her legs felt unsteady, but she determined to remain standing. "All of a sudden you walk in and spring this on me?"

Jake seemed subdued. Her response wasn't what he'd hoped for. "I know it," he muttered. "I'm just a mug, an ex-pug with no manners whatever."

"That's not true." Stephanie went over and stood in front of him. "Your manners are rough, but there's a goodness and a gentleness in you that I admire."

"You do? Well, that's good news."

"But, Jake, marriage to me is a very holy thing." She saw his eyes blink at the word "holy" and said, "The Lord is very important in my life, and that's not true of you. How could we get along as husband and wife if we are so different on that one point?"

"I could change," Jake said quietly.

"I've always been afraid of that sort of arrangement," Stephanie said, biting her lip. "I've known women who went with men who weren't Christians. They said, 'When we're married, he'll be different.' But I don't know of any who changed. It was the wives who changed. It's too important, Jake. And we're different—incompatible—other ways, too. I saw how you took to my family. You want a regular wife who'll stay home and have babies and cook for you. That's not me. I don't know if I *ever* want to have children, and staying home—well, to me marriage seems like sort of a trap for a woman."

He looked surprised at that, so she went on. "I've told you I always wanted to be like my granddad. He's gone everywhere, he knows all sorts of people, he's had an exciting life. He loves getting the story, and so do I. That's what I want to do."

Jake stood stock-still, his eyes fixed on her. "So that's it?" he said.

"I'm sorry, Jake, but you'd be sorry, too. It would never work."

She expected him to argue, but he did not. Moving across the room, he picked up his hat from the table where he had thrown it. He went to the door and turned back and said quietly, "All that's probably true, but it leaves one thing out."

"What's that, Jake?"

"I love you, and I got the strange feeling that I'm not going to get over it. Good-bye, Steph."

He shut the door. Without warning, Stephanie felt tears filling her eyes. She tried to fight them back and could not. She groped her way to the couch, pulled her feet up under her, and began to weep without knowing why, yet aware that something had happened to her that was not going to pass away easily.

Part 2

GOOD TIMES

7

A Trip to Town

January brought more snow, and Richard stayed out-of-doors constantly. He took many of the chores off Logan's shoulders, learning to milk the cows and take care of the beef critters, throwing their feed down to them from the loft. He became calmer, Logan and Anne noticed, and the hollows in his cheeks filled out as he began to gain weight on Anne's cooking.

It was at the end of January, on a sunny Thursday afternoon, when Richard took one of his walks to the hills. He carried a gun, but since meat at the house was plentiful, he didn't plan to shoot anything. The crust of snow broke beneath his boots, and the air was like wine. The sky was blue with fluffy clouds, and a feeling of goodwill ran through him. He followed the road, then crossed farmland, his eyes always darting here and there. Logan had taught him to recognize many of the birds, and he saw a gray fox that trotted smartly along, took one look at him, then reversed and disappeared into the brush.

He came to a fast little creek that fed into the river, and not wanting to get his feet wet, he decided to leap it. But his left leg, still weak, gave way so that he was off balance, and his right foot slipped and then was caught between two protruding rocks. He sprawled in the water, which instantly hit him in a cold wave. Instinctively holding the rifle out of the water, his face twisted, he pulled his foot loose and then tried

101

to stand up. Pain shot down his ankle, and he had to crawl
out of the creek.

"Well, this is a pretty mess!" he said in disgust. He looked
around for a stick and saw none. "Sure would hate to crawl
back home." He tried to get his bearings and was grateful he
had learned to know the land pretty well. The closest place
was the Vine, only a half a mile or so away. "I can make it that
far," he grunted. He unloaded the rifle, got to his feet, and
grasping the top of the barrel, used it as a cane. It was slow
going, and he had to stop several times to rest. He came to
an overgrown two-track road and said aloud, "This probably
goes to the Vine." He hobbled along, and his ankle gave out.
It had been numb, but now pain was shooting through it, and
he could not stand to touch it. *May be broken*, he thought, more
annoyed than alarmed. He stood there uncertainly and then
heard a sound. Looking up the road he saw a man coming on
horseback and knew a great relief. He kept his eyes on the
rider and soon recognized Tom Henderson. He waved, and
Henderson kicked the horse into a gallop.

Pulling up, Henderson took in the wet clothes and the
muddy end of the rifle butt. "Have some trouble, Stuart?"

"Twisted my ankle in the creek back there. Can't stand to
put it on the ground."

"Here. Get on board." Henderson slid off the horse, which
had no saddle. He led the horse closer to Richard and said,
"Whoa, boy!" then turned to Richard. "Let me give you a
lift."

Richard laid the rifle down and put his hands over the tall
bay's back. "Can't give much push," he said, then he felt his
left leg grasped, and as he was lifted into the air, he managed
to throw his injured leg over the horse. "Okay," he said, and
Henderson handed him the rifle and sprang up easily behind
him saying, "Better get you out of this weather. You might
catch pneumonia."

The horse headed for home at a walk. Richard said, "Glad
you came along, Tom."

Henderson's face broke into a grin. "Maybe I'm an angel sent to look after you."

Richard thought about that, then said, "Well, I need some lookin' after."

"Don't we all!"

The fire was warm, and the crackling of the white oak and the hickory logs had a soporific effect on Richard. For some time he had been watching the women work, and the men were all outside doing their chores. He thought over the past four days and was mildly surprised at the history of it. He had arrived at the house with Henderson and had been half carried inside. The older woman, who everybody simply called Granny, and the young woman, Laurel, had carefully removed his boot.

Granny Stevens shook her head. "You got a bad sprain there, sonny. Can you move that foot this way?" She made him move his foot every way and nodded. "Nothin's broke, but you ain't gonna be runnin' foot races for a week or two."

"Can you send for Uncle Logan to come after me?"

"Sure I can," Tom said. "But what's the hurry? It's already getting late. Let these women doctor that foot of yours, and I'll go over and tell Logan what happened."

"I wouldn't want to be intruding."

"You wouldn't do that," Laurel said unexpectedly. "I'll make up a bed for you in the back bedroom." She rose and left, and Henderson said, "There's your invitation, okay?"

"Well, all right. I guess I can stay the night."

The night had turned into two nights, then three. Logan had come over the day after the accident. He found Richard cheerful and comfortable, though his ankle was swollen to an enormous size. "Gonna take that thing a while to go down," Logan said. He looked around and said, "You can come home, but it looks like you got more nurses here and no stairs to climb."

Henderson, who had been sitting beside the pair, grinned and said, "The women are going crazy cooped up in the house. A sick man to practice on, that's just what they need."

Richard's ankle had grown steadily better, and now he came to his feet, grabbed the cane that Logan had whittled for him, and moved across the floor. Laurel came out of the kitchen and said sharply, "You shouldn't be on that foot!"

"Got to do something, Laurel," he said. "I'm going crazy."

"Well, you be careful, you hear?" She had a worried look and shook her head at him as if he were a naughty child. "Come on in the kitchen, then. You can help me peel potatoes."

Carefully Richard moved into the kitchen, and for some time he sat next to her, working on the potatoes. She had revealed little of herself, only that she came from Tennessee. She never once spoke of a husband, Johnny's father, which seemed rather strange. He asked, "How long have you been here?"

"Oh, I've been here for two years. I came just after Johnny was born."

Richard hesitated, then said, "Laurel, where's your husband?"

Laurel turned her head so that he could not see her face. She was very still, and Richard said quickly, "I'm sorry. I didn't mean to pry."

"It's all right." Her voice was tight, and she did not turn to face him.

Richard felt terrible. "If there's anything I hate, Laurel, it's a nosy parker that has to know everything." He put his hand on her shoulder, the first time he had touched her, and said quietly, "Never mind. Don't be upset. I'm just a hard-nosed marine who doesn't know any better."

Laurel Jackson turned to face him. He saw tears in her eyes, and he saw with astonishment that his kindness had touched her. "Johnny's father is dead," she said finally, and her lips trembled. "They took me in here when nobody else would. These are good people, Richard."

"I believe they are," Richard answered. He peeled potatoes, glancing at the young woman from time to time. She was not beautiful, but there was a cleanness and prettiness that drew him. He said, "I like it here."

"You gonna stay a while?"

"I might just do that."

Jerry and Bonnie were taking their first vacation without their children. Since her brother Jesse's death, Bonnie had felt alone, especially with her children grown and flown, so she was particularly enjoying Jerry's company. They had flown to Chicago and had stayed with Amos and Rose, and they'd also spent time with Lenora and with Christie and Mario Castellano—Jerry had been very close to them all when he'd lived in Chicago as a young man.

An added purpose for the trip was the purchase of a new car, which they were driving cross-country back to L.A., seeing some sights en route and visiting some of the other relatives—Jerry's large family making up for Bonnie's lack of family. After spending a couple of days with Logan and seeing Richard, they headed west, stopping in Oklahoma City to stay overnight with Pete and Leslie.

As they sat at supper, Jerry said, "You should come out to Los Angeles for a long visit. Spend time with Mona. You need to get out of Oklahoma for a while and take things a little easier."

Pete said, "It sounds inviting, but I can't come now. There's still a lot to do around here even though Stephen has taken on most of the responsibilities of running the business, since I've become an old man."

Leslie rose to the bait and slapped him on the wrist. "You're not old!" she said. "You're a young sixty-six."

Grinning broadly, Pete winked at Jerry, saying, "She always did have a yen for younger men." Then he grew more serious. "One thing is tempting. It looks like Mona is staying in California for a while."

Bonnie asked, "What do you hear from her? We see her very rarely, even though we're in the same city."

"She's very busy," Leslie answered. "She had a supporting part in one Monarch movie, and with Lylah's help she got small parts in a couple of Republic pictures. Then she talked Lylah and Adam into doing a feature film about the Korean War. The last I heard it was just called *The Soldier.*"

"I don't know how she did it," said Pete, "but she talked them into letting her star in the picture, which is pretty risky if you ask me. Costs a lot of money to make one of those things. But Adam said he thinks Mona can act better than most of the big stars. All she needed was a chance." Pete shook his head and added, "I'm not sure that's the right life for Mona. She hasn't been happy in show business. And she'll be thirty this year. That seems to bother her, too."

"Well, working with Lylah is better," Jerry observed. "She keeps on going, doesn't she?"

"Yes, she does," Pete said absently. He was silent for a moment, then said, "I can't keep up with Stephen. Besides running our business, he keeps starting new companies and selling old ones off like you or I would buy a loaf of bread. He must be pretty shrewd, though. He's worth a fortune."

"But it's all on paper, isn't it?" Leslie shook her head doubtfully. "Remember what happened back in '29. Lots of millionaires on paper couldn't pay their rent the day after the stock market crashed." She turned and asked, "What about your kids?"

Bonnie reached up and tucked a wisp of her black hair in, saying, "We'll see Stephanie even less now that she's a foreign correspondent."

"Funny she didn't say anything about it at the reunion," commented Pete.

"It's what she always said she wanted, and Dad knew somebody at International News Service who would give her a start on his recommendation, in spite of her being a woman and being so young," replied Jerry.

"So, she's in London learning to write what she calls news-briefs—condensing stories into one-sentence fillers. Sounds exciting, doesn't it?" Bonnie laughed. "I'm not sure it's quite what she expected!"

"What about her and the fella Jake she brought to the reunion?" asked Leslie.

"Well," Jerry answered, "something happened, but neither Stephanie nor Dad are saying what, if Dad even knows. He just says she'll do well—after all, she's got all of his talent."

"Amos never was broke out with modesty, was he?" Pete smiled. "He used to boss the lot of us around just because he was the oldest. He's a pretty smart fella though. Anybody that wins a Pulitzer has to have some sense. What about Robert?"

"Going great guns. Off every night playing somewhere with his band. I don't know how he keeps going. He sings all night and plays the piano. Every kind of little place where they can get fifty people together. Then they pile into cars with half a dozen other singers, and they head on out." He shook his head. "It's not a good life, but he's all caught up in it."

"And what about Richard?" Leslie asked. "I take it he's still down on the farm with Logan?"

"Well, he's still in Arkansas, but he's not living with Uncle Logan."

Peter lifted his head. "Where's he living?"

"You remember Uncle Logan told us about that group over on the Cartwright place? Richard's been staying with them for the past few months. I don't know. It worries me a little bit. It seems like such an aimless way to live." Jerry drummed his fingers on the table nervously, then shook his head. "He went into a shell, I think. It was pretty rough on him in Korea, but Uncle Logan thinks he's coming out of it now."

"Does his wound bother him any?" Leslie asked.

"Some, I think, but you know scars on the inside take even longer to heal. In any case, he's planting cucumbers or something now. You can't spend your life growing cucumbers."

Pete laughed and said, "Nephew, you and I planted our cucumbers, only worse. Don't worry about it," he smiled encouragingly. "He's got a good foundation. He needs time to uncoil, I suspect. He'll be himself again."

Richard moved down the long rows weeding the garden and thinking of nothing in particular. It was a habit he had gotten into, and it served him well. The memories of the war already came back less vividly. The smiling young soldier that he had killed still floated through his dreams sometimes, and he thought of men in his squad, and he thought about Jack Smith almost every day. But the keen edge of hurt had begun fading away. The radio kept him up on the news from that other world. He heard names of hills he'd fought on, still trading hands. The truce talks were in their third year. They stopped and started so many times Richard couldn't keep up. In April, prisoners of war had been exchanged, which was the only concrete progress so far. No one had any expectations about how much longer the fighting might go on.

He chopped at the grass, paused, pulled a file from the back pocket of his jeans, and put a razor edge on the hoe with four quick passes of the file, a new skill he had picked up. He moved on down the row and stopped to look up at the sky. A red-tailed hawk was circling overhead, and for a moment Richard thought, *If he's after the chickens, I'll have to discourage him*. But he saw the hawk was far away from the house. It fell like a plummet and did not appear again.

Having finished in the garden, he moved on back toward the house. He washed up outside at the faucet and went around to the back door, where he found Granny examining Harry Tate's catch after a night out on the river.

Granny was looking at the enormous snapping turtle that Tate had dumped out on the ground, and she spoke quickly,

as she always did, running her words together. "Don't let that
scoundrel get away!" she said to Richard. "We'll have him
for supper tomorrow night. Now, what you have to do is put
a stick out there and make him bite it! Here, let me get the
ax." She stepped to the side of the house, picked up a double-
bitted ax, and by that time Richard had enticed the turtle to
stick its head out and bite into the stick. Instantly the old
woman swung the ax. It flashed in the sun, and then the
turtle's head was separated, and the crimson blood stained
the dark ground. "Take that head away! It ain't fit for nothin'!"
Granny said. She looked up at Richard and asked, "Boy, you
know how to cook turtles?"

"Don't think I do, Granny."

"Well, you come along, and I'll give you your first lesson.
Pick up that varmint now. Harry, you go get those fish
cleaned," she ordered.

Richard picked up the huge turtle, and they walked out to
a black pot where a fire was already kindled. She had Richard
put the turtle on the grass, then bring several buckets of
water, and when the pot was filled and at long last boiling,
she said, "Now, dump him in there. You come back when he's
been boiled good and cut all the meat loose from the shell.
Gut it and cut it into chunks, then you fill that bucket and
put some salt in it and soak the meat all night. Tomorrow I'll
show you how to cook it. Tastes mighty good."

"I bet it does, Granny. I'll see to it."

Later that afternoon, after Richard had prepared the turtle
meat as instructed, Laurel stopped him as he headed for the
barn.

"I'm going to take Johnny down to the creek and fish. Why
don't you come? You look so hot and sweaty."

The invitation sounded good, and he said, "Well, I think
I will. Maybe go wading."

"I always do that," Laurel said. "Let me get Johnny, and
we'll go."

Fifteen minutes later, they were standing barefooted in

the water watching Johnny splash happily in the fresh, running brook. It was a clear stream, spring fed, and it felt very cold to Richard's feet. "Cold enough for trout," he said. "I'll bet there's some in here; doesn't take a big stream for trout."

"You can ask Tom. He knows all the fishing spots around here." Laurel was wearing a long skirt, as usual, but she hiked it up so that her legs were bare to the knees. They appeared startlingly white compared with her arms and face and neck, which had been tanned into a golden tint by the hot summer sun. Afterward they fished for a while but caught only a few small sun perch. They sat idly in the shade of a spreading hickory tree and were quiet for a long time. Laurel asked, "What are you going to do, Richard?"

"Haven't thought about it."

His answer somehow pleased her, and she pulled her legs under her, tailor fashion, and leaned over and stared into the water. "Look at the minnies," she said. "They're like little silver darts. Pretty."

Richard almost said, "Well, so are you pretty," but he held back. "I don't know as I ever want to do anything. I don't right now, except work in the garden and fix the truck."

Laurel looked at him and smiled. "You know, I feel more secure here than I ever felt in my life. My daddy was a tenant farmer, and we moved from one shack to the other as far back as I can remember. I have three brothers and sisters, but they're all scattered now."

"What about your parents?" Richard asked. Laurel did not answer, and he knew she would not. She had a way of breaking off conversations when she did not want to respond, and he said nothing more.

When they got back to the house, Henderson asked, "Catch any fish?"

"Just little ones. Didn't even keep 'em."

"Just fishing in the wrong place. I'll take you out someday, and you'll bring in pole benders." He hesitated then said,

"Richard, would you mind taking a load of vegetables into town tomorrow?"

"Sure, why not? What'll I do with them?"

"We sell 'em by the roadside. Just park somewhere close to the general store, and people will stop and buy 'em. We need a little cash money."

"Don't know if I'd be any good at selling anything."

"Laurel can go with you, can't you, Laurel? She can do the peddling. All you do is drive the truck and sit around and wait."

"That sounds good to me," Richard said.

"I'll pack us a lunch so we won't have to eat at the cafe," Laurel said eagerly.

It was ten o'clock before Richard got the old pickup running. Tom helped load it with squash, tomatoes, young potatoes, and cucumbers. Richard got in, and Laurel climbed in beside him. He started the engine, and they chugged off down the rutted road, still wet from an overnight rain. He drove slowly, pampering the old Dodge. When they reached the main highway, he said, "Where do we set up shop?"

"Oh, anywhere along here."

Pulling over to the side of the road, he followed Laurel's instructions. They set up a table with folding legs, and she set out some of the vegetables on it in an attractive arrangement, and he put up the sign that read, Fresh Vegetables—Cheep! He smiled but said nothing.

Midday passed swiftly. Richard had brought a book that Tom had given him, a book of poems by Gerard Manley Hopkins. He struggled with it for a while. Quite a few cars stopped, and he got up and helped Laurel wait on the customers.

During a season when no cars seemed to be on the road, she came over and sat down beside him in one of two folding chairs they'd brought. "Is it a good book?" she asked.

"How should I know," Richard mused. "It's over my head."

"Read me something, Richard."

"Well, here's one that I can understand a little bit. It's called "Heaven-Haven." He read slowly and clearly:

> I have desired to go
> where Springs not fail,
> to fields where flies no sharp and sided hail
> and a few lilies blow.
> And I have asked to be
> where no storms come,
> where the green swell is in the havens dumb,
> and out of the swing of the sea.

"That's so pretty," Laurel exclaimed.

"It is, isn't it? I never wrote a poem in my life. Don't think I could."

"Tom does, but he doesn't let anybody read them very much. He wrote one about me."

"I'd like to read that one."

She grew suddenly remote and said, "Maybe I'll let you read it some day." She looked down at her hands and shook her head. "That man just knows what's on the inside of people. That poem said more about me and what I've been and what I am now than anybody has a right to know."

"I guess poets are that way. What do you think this poem's about?"

"Let me see." She moved her chair closer and studied the book, turning it toward her. She was wearing a short-sleeved light blue dress with a dark green belt. It was not the long dress that she usually wore, for the skirt came only to her knees. It was more form fitting than her other garments, and Richard felt aware of her in a disturbing way. Her arm was warm and firm against his forearm. "A nun takes the veil," she read.

"That's the subtitle," Richard offered. "What do you make of the poem?"

"It sounds to me like it's a woman who's tired of the hard things she has to face, and she wants to go where things are easier. Isn't that what it means, 'where Springs not fail'? There's no sharp hail, and there are few flowers there." She looked up at him, and he was again struck by the beauty of her large violet-blue eyes. They were her best feature, though she often kept them lowered.

"I guess it does, but it doesn't have to be a woman." He started the poem again and shook his head. "That describes me pretty well, I guess. I don't want to become a nun or a monk, but I guess that's what the Vine is to me. There are a few lilies, and there's no sharp hail to cut me to bits. No storms, just a place where it's calm and peaceful. I guess that's what I'm looking for."

"That's what we're all looking for, isn't it?" She suddenly became conscious of her arm on his and took it away, flushing slightly. "Anyway, it's a good poem."

Richard felt embarrassed by the contact and said, "Let's go into town and get something cold to drink to wash those sandwiches down."

"We'll have to pack up all the vegetables."

"That's all right. After we eat, we can set up on down at the crossroads. We'll get people going both ways." They packed up and drove to the small country store. There were two gas pumps out in front, both of them rusty, and the weathered gray frame building was decorated with RC Cola signs, as well as advertisements for Redman Chewing Tobacco and other delights.

They entered the store and were struck by sounds of a song called "Moving On" by Hank Snow. The radio was loud, and gathered around it at the counter were four young men drinking soda and talking loudly over the music. Richard paid them little attention, for they seemed to be arguing about the results of a horse race that some of them had been involved in. He moved to the cold-drink box, opened it, and picked a Nehi cream soda for himself, then looked around for Laurel.

She was moving along a glass case that had an assortment of knives, inexpensive jewelry, and a few wristwatches and clocks. "What will you have to drink, Laurel?" he spoke up, lifting his voice over the music and the talk of the men.

Three of the men were wearing overalls, faded and well-worn. The other wore a pair of brown trousers and a dirty T-shirt. He was the biggest one. "Well, now. What have we got here?" the big man said loudly, leaning back on the counter, a red strawberry drink in his hand. "It looks like some of them so-called farmers from over by the river. Is that right?" he lifted his voice. "You folks from that farm over there?"

Laurel moved over to the cold-drink box. "I'd like an RC Cola," she said to Richard.

"Hey! I'm talkin' to you!" the big man said. He winked at the man next to him, a tall wiry fellow with eyes too close together and a shock of yellow hair. "I hear tell the menfolks do pretty well. Have the women any time they want 'em—any of 'em."

"Is that right, Alvin?" The tall wiry fellow grinned. He spat on the floor and said, "Wouldn't mind payin' a visit."

Richard walked up to the counter and cast a look at the four loafers before he turned to the clerk, a rotund man with gray hair. "How much for the drinks?"

"Five cents each."

Richard fished the change out of his pocket, put a dime down, and turned, saying, "Come on, Laurel."

They reached the porch, but as they stepped to the ground, the big man called Alvin came bursting out. "Wait a minute! I ain't through talkin' to you two!"

The other three came out behind Alvin, and Richard turned, saying under his breath, "Get in the truck, Laurel." Alvin planted himself directly in front of him, and the others spread out to make a semicircle. "I don't want any trouble," Richard said.

"Why, there ain't gonna be any trouble." Alvin laughed hoarsely and winked at his audience. It was obvious he was accustomed to performing, and he had scars on his face from old battles. He slapped his hands together, making a meaty sound, and took a step toward Richard, saying, "We're just going to have a little talk." He was six one or two and weighed at least 220. He had a bulge around his middle but he had the heavy muscles of a wrestler or a weight lifter. "Now about that little lady there." He winked at Richard. "If you're gonna pass her around like I hear you do out at that place, I won't mind waitin' my turn."

Richard knew then that there was no easy way out. His senses were heightened. He saw Alvin's grimy fingernails and the traces of tobacco juice that stained the corners of his mouth, even the wrinkles in his shirt. He noticed the tiny mole on the cheek of the tall wiry one and the similarity of the two others, obviously brothers. "I'm going to get in the truck with the lady and drive away," he said quietly. He knew, however, that this would never satisfy Alvin.

The bulky farmer reached out and grabbed Richard by the front of his shirt, bunching it up in his left fist. He raised his massive right fist and said, "Now, why don't you just go take a walk, city boy, and I'll have a little talk with Laurel, here." He grinned evilly and held the fist poised. "No sense your gettin' all busted up, a pretty boy like you, is there now?"

Richard's marine corps training stood him in good stead— the arduous hours spent at boot camp in martial arts training. "Don't call it self-defense," Sergeant Masterson had said. "You're not going to defend yourself. You're going to attack the enemy! Always get in the first lick," Masterson had snarled, "Always!"

Richard was wearing heavy work boots. He braced his left foot and with all his strength kicked out with his right. The full force of the blow took Alvin on the kneecap. He let out a sharp yell, loosed his grip on Richard's shirt, and fell into the dirt holding his knee. "You broke my leg!" he yelled. "Get him, Ed!"

The other three men spread out so that he could not face

them all. Without waiting for them to get close, Richard leaped forward. He held his right hand, thumb alongside his fingers, and although he did not have the hard edge that he once had along his little finger and the ridge of his palm, when he caught the tall wiry man across the nose, he heard the nose break and the scream of pain from the man called Ed.

But he had turned his back on the other two, and a blow struck him on the left side in the vicinity of his old wound. Pain shot through him, and the two men bore him to the ground. He was aware that Alvin and Ed would be on him soon, and reaching up on the man who straddled him, he grabbed him by the shirt front and jerked him forward, bringing the man's face against his skull. A kick grazed his head, but he rolled around to his feet.

All four men surrounded him, Alvin limping but his fists held high, Ed's face a mess from the broken nose spurting blood.

Laurel threw herself at one of the brothers, who brushed her off, ignoring her cries of protest. She ran to the truck to find something for a weapon.

The fight was wicked. Time and again Richard lashed out with a telling stroke, knocking one or other of the men down, but they were wearing him down. He was aware that a car had stopped, and then he heard a voice say, "What's going on here? Hold up!" He turned quickly and wiped the blood from his eyebrow where he had received a blow, and he saw a large, portly man getting out of the car. Richard was wary, thinking, *This might be another enemy,* but then he heard Alvin say, "Sheriff, this man needs to spend some time in the pokey. He jumped me."

"Is that right?" The bulky man turned and said, "I'm Sheriff Paulks. What you got to say for yourself?"

Richard had heard tales about small-town sheriffs. "Sure," he gasped. "I jumped all four of 'em."

"We don't need any smart talkin' Yankees down here." He looked at Alvin and said, "He really got in the first lick?"

"Shore he did!"

Sheriff Paulks said, "You're under arrest, fella!"

"No!" Laurel came forward, flushed and with a tire iron in her hand. "These men made trouble. Not Richard."

"They're from that place over by the river where they all got common wives," Alvin said, reaching down to massage his bruised knee. "You know what kind of folks they are, Sheriff."

"I'm gonna lock you up, boy. You'll get a fair trial. If you're found innocent, I'll turn you loose."

Richard said quickly, "Laurel, can you drive that truck?"

"I–I think so."

"The key's in it. You go on home now and tell Tom what happened."

"But what about you?"

"I'll be all right."

Laurel looked at him for a moment, then got into the truck. As she started it, Paulks grabbed Richard's arm. "You come along now. No more trouble."

"No more trouble, Sheriff," Richard said. He went over and got into the car.

It worked out about how he thought. He was brought up before the j.p., who ran a gas station in the center of town, and was asked how he pleaded. He said, "What if I plead guilty?"

"Then you pay a fine, and we turn you loose," the j.p. said. He was a short, thin man with a set of ill-fitting store-bought teeth.

"What if I plead not guilty?"

"Then we'd hold you in jail for a trial. If you're found guilty, you'll probably do three months on the county road gang. How do you plead?"

"I guess I plead guilty."

"Your fine's fifty dollars."

"I don't have it, but I'll get it from my uncle."

Richard did not have to spend the night in the small, filthy cell with its rancid blankets. He was standing at the window when he saw Logan's car pull up, and Tom was with him. Richard watched with interest as they entered city hall—the j.p.'s gas station—and within a few minutes the sheriff came and opened the cell. "Come on," he said. "Fine's been paid."

Richard followed him to the outer office. Logan got right in Paulks's face, and he gave the sheriff a thorough dressing down. Logan looked small alongside the big man, but Paulks looked afraid.

"You're a sorry excuse for a sheriff, Jeff Paulks! Election's coming up. I don't usually take part in politics, but I reckon I know everybody in this whole county. By the time I get to my friends, and they get to their friends, I reckon you're gonna have to make an honest living. Maybe pumpin' gas out at the Exxon station!"

"Now, wait a minute, Mr. Stuart! I just done my duty!"

Logan stared at him and seemed about to say something else, then shook his head. "You're a sorry excuse for a man, and even a worse excuse for an elected official!" He wheeled and said, "Come on, Richard. Let's get out of here!"

When they were outside, Richard grimaced. "Must be a lot of fun for you, bailin' your relatives out of jail."

"Everybody knows Jeff Paulks ain't worth spit! Come on, get in. I'll take you and Tom home."

As they drove back, Tom said, "I thought Laurel was going to get my shotgun and go down there and clean house. She was mad clear through! You have a few bruises there. Did you get your licks in?" Tom asked, a humorous gleam in his eye.

"My old judo sergeant used to say, 'Always get the first lick in,' so I managed to do that."

"Good," said Logan. "Alvin Hood's been needin' a come-down. I wish you'd a broke that knee of his instead of just bruisin' it up. Mebbe another time." Logan hadn't cooled off just yet.

"I hope not," Richard said. He sat between the two men, feeling good that they had come to his rescue. He said as much, and his uncle said, "Why, boy, we couldn't let the devil have one of our own. Don't you know that?"

By the time they got home it was dusk, and Laurel came out of the house to meet them. She reached up and touched the bruise on Richard's face. "Come inside," she said quietly. "I'll take care of you."

Tom and Logan watched the pair go in, and it was Henderson who said, "That's a good nephew you have there, Logan."

"Well, I reckon. You watch out for him, Tom. He ain't got over that war business yet. He's kind of vulnerable, you might say."

Henderson cocked his head and gave the older man a strange look. "I guess we all are, aren't we?"

8

COUNTRY MATTERS

I will always love you, and I'll always treasure what you did for your country."

Helen Maxwell put her arms around the soldier, whose left sleeve was pinned up.

"You can't love half a man," Roger Deerfield said bitterly. "I left most of myself over in the mud of Korea."

"No, you're here, and you've done your duty, and I love you for it." Reaching up, she pulled his head down and kissed him. His one arm went around her, and they held the embrace for a long moment.

"Cut! That's a take!" Stan Lem had been standing outside the range of the cameras. He came over and slapped the soldier on the back and hugged Mona. "That's the best scene in the movie—the last one," he said.

"Well, help me get myself out of this gear. My arm's breaking with these straps." William Castaine, who had played the lead in the movie, shrugged out of the marine tunic, and Mona helped him remove the straps that tied his lower arm to his upper arm. William flexed the member carefully and said, "You did great, Helen."

"Thank you, Roger."

"Come along. Get your clothes changed, and we'll go out and celebrate."

"Thanks, but another time maybe. I've got plans already." Mona smiled at him, then turned and made her way off the set to her dressing room. She had not dreamed how physically exhausting playing the lead in a movie could be. Stan Lem was a nice man, but he was a perfectionist, and for some scenes he had demanded ten takes or more. Now, however, *The Soldier* was "in the can," as they put it, and when Mona got back to her dressing room, she slumped down for a time. She thought about the two years that had passed—about all of the people that had worked on the film, about Adam and Lylah being in constant touch with it. She smiled, thinking about how she'd presented the idea as the first movie out about the war. There had been endless problems of every sort. It had been a gamble for Adam and Lylah, but they had stayed with it, and she hoped that it would pay off not just for her sake but for theirs.

She rose, showered, and put on a loose-fitting dress that came to just above her knees, made of an aqua-colored linen. It had three-quarter-length sleeves and a high neck with a dark green fabric bow tied around it. She went to find Adam and Lylah, who were waiting for her. "You want to go out or just have steak at my place?" Lylah asked.

"That sounds good to me, the steak."

"You're tired out," Adam said. "Come along. I have to leave early, but there are a few things we need to talk about."

They left the studio and went at once to Lylah's house. She had called ahead to the Japanese servant, and the steaks were ready within minutes after they arrived. They sat down at the table, with its spotless white tablecloth, and ate their filets mignons and fresh garden salads, and as they ate, Adam expressed his enthusiasm about the prospects of the film. "It's going to be great. I don't know if it'll set any records at the box office, but it's the kind of film that wins awards."

Mona had been lifting a bit of salad to her lips. She lowered it slowly and smiled saying, "I'd rather it make a lot of money than win awards."

"That's important," Lylah said, "but this is the kind of film

122

that will be better for your career in the long run. Other studios will be wanting you now. You wait and see."

The meal went pleasantly, and after they had eaten a light dessert and talked for some time, Mona said, "Would you think me awful if I took a little time off?"

"Not at all," Lylah said. She came over and kissed the young woman on the cheek, saying, "You need some time off, Mona."

"Why don't you go to the place we've got in the Rockies? The studio owns it," Adam offered.

"Thank you, Adam, but I think I'd like to go to Arkansas." She smiled at them and said, "There's something about that place that I like. I remember how beautiful the long drive was when we went there to visit when Stephen and I were kids. We called it going on vacation, not realizing the folks didn't have money in those days to go anywhere else! It's so far in the backwoods that nobody's likely to recognize me there. Not that they would in the Rocky Mountains," she laughed. "But I'd like to just stay in the old house and visit a little bit with Uncle Logan and Aunt Anne and spend some time, maybe, with Richard."

"That's a good idea," Adam said. "I'll get the plane ticket for you. When do you want to leave?"

"In a day or so, just so I have time to get a few things in order." She rose, and Adam came over and hugged her, saying warmly, "You did a fine job, Mona. I think you're at the beginning of a great career."

The bus that brought her north from Fort Smith to Mountain View had been a difficult ride, for Mona was tired. Getting off the Greyhound, which stopped at the Delight Hotel, she saw the only taxi in town. She walked over and saw a sign stuck inside the windshield instructing her that the driver could be reached around the corner at the funeral parlor. "Guess I'll call Uncle Logan instead," she said to herself. She entered the hotel and asked for a phone. Arlene Baxter said,

"Why, it's Miss Mona Stuart, isn't it? How are you, dear? How's that daddy of yours? He was always my favorite of the Stuart boys. We were in school together. Used to go out some." Arlene chatted away about all the news she'd heard about any of the Stuarts or anyone any of the Stuarts might possibly have ever known.

Mona tried to relax. She reminded herself that this was the small-town way, and especially so in the South. If you want to get anything done, you have to pay for it with conversation, so Mona offered Arlene a few bits of Hollywood gossip in return and told her about the picture she'd just finished. Then Arlene said, "Why, dear, you look all in. Why don't I just call Logan and Anne for you so they can come down and get you?"

Mona was expected, so Logan arrived within a few minutes, and soon they were at the house. Anne came out to greet her. They hugged and kissed, and Mona said, "I've come to freeload on you a while, Aunt Anne."

"Why, don't talk so foolish. Me and Logan are always glad to see our folks come. Now, I know you're tired, so how about the room in front up there. It looks out on the road and the fields. The one with the pretty pink wallpaper."

"That's just the room I would have picked." Mona smiled. *The wallpaper is hideous*, she thought, but the bed was comfortable, and Logan carried her suitcase up, then excused himself to get back to some chores. As she unpacked, Mona asked Anne, "How's Richard? Do you see him often?"

"Oh, he seems real well, though he got in some kind of brawl a while back. He stays over at the Vine, but we see him all the time. Logan goes over, or Richard comes here."

"What about that place? I've heard a lot of stories about it."

"I think they're just young people who want to get away from the world. Think some of 'em have a pretty bad background, but they don't cause no trouble," she added. Anne was a small, rather frail, woman, showing her age now, which was sixty-three. She was plain and had never been pretty, but Logan loved her and had married her and had raised her children, Helen, Ray, and Violet, as if they were his own. And they'd had a son together, Clinton.

"I think I'll lie down for a while, then I'll come and help you fix supper."

"Won't do no such thing! You take a bath and lie down, then put on some old clothes and you come down and eat with me and Logan."

"All right, Aunt Anne."

Following Anne's direction, Mona took a bath, then lay down and went instantly to sleep. When she awoke, she was startled to see that it was growing dark outside. She put on a pair of old faded jeans and a blue shirt with long sleeves, and after fixing her hair, she went downstairs. Logan was there and he came over to give her a kiss. "I always like to kiss beautiful movie stars," he said. "Now sit down and tell us all about that movie."

The table was piled high with country cooking including baked ham, fried chicken, mashed potatoes, and home-canned vegetables from the summer just past. Mona paid for her meal by entertaining the older couple with tales of how the movie was made. She was interrupted with exclamations such as "I swan!" and "You don't mean it!"

"Don't know if Richard will want to see a movie about the war in Korea. He's tryin' to forget it," said Anne.

"That's probably true, but the country needs to know what our men over there went through. They've signed a truce, but who knows if that will last, and there needs to be a record of what happened," Mona said.

"Guess that's so," Logan said. "I remember I never appreciated Owen's medal until I saw that movie with Gary Cooper, you know, *Sergeant York*. Owen don't ever talk about his time overseas, but when I saw that film I thought, that fella, York, he's just like Owen. Good ol' country boy who did his job. And I guess Richard done the same thing."

After dinner, they sat in front of the television and watched *George Burns and Gracie Allen;* then Mona yawned and said, "I had a long nap, but I'm still sleepy."

"You go on up to bed, honey," Anne said, patting her shoulder. "Sleep late in the morning. After you get up, I'll fix you a good breakfast."

Mona went to bed and left the window open a crack. It was October, and the smell of the hills was a raw, wild odor that came to her filled with evergreens and the fruitful earth, the time of harvest. She lay down in the feather bed and laughed when she disappeared. She pulled up a quilt that her grandmother Marian Stuart had made, and she lay for a while listening to the sounds that came from the outside—the cries of night birds and a far-off coyote singing his lonesome song, and she drifted off to dreamless sleep.

"Why don't you drive over and see Richard?" Anne said. "Or you can ride; we got a nice saddle hoss called Minnie."

"I'd like to. Be good to get out in the open."

"Well, I'll have Logan saddle 'er up for you."

"I can do that," Mona said. She had loved horses as a girl, and after breakfast she went out and found Logan examining his beehives.

"I'm going to ride over to see Richard," she said. "How do I get there?"

"Well, you can't hardly get lost." He grinned. After giving her instructions, he said, "Tell Richard to come over and shove his feet under the table."

"All right. I'll tell him." Moving out to the pasture, she called the roan mare, who came and took the apple that Mona had brought to entice her. Opening the gate, Mona led her into the barn and put the bridle on her. Then she put on the blanket, fastened the saddle, and adjusted the stirrups. She led the horse out of the barn, swung into the saddle, and touched her with her heel. "Let's go, Minnie!" she said cheerfully.

She left the farm and passed through orchards laden with apples, the smell rich on the air. She stopped under a tree, pulled an apple off and ate it, enjoying the firm, white flesh and the delicious taste. Logan's directions were fairly simple, and soon she saw the buildings in the curve of the river, as if held in the crook of an elbow. As she rode up, she saw an elderly woman sitting outside. "Howdy, missy," the old woman said, in a strong voice surprisingly deep. "Climb off that hoss and set a spell."

"Thanks. I believe I will. Is this the Vine?"

"Yep." The elderly woman watched Mona dismount and then said, "You can turn that pony into that corral over there. Might be a little hay for 'er, too."

Following the instructions, Mona returned after shutting the gate. "I'm looking for Richard Stuart. He's a relative of mine. My name's Mona Stuart."

"Well, he ain't here right now, but he orta be back soon. Why don't you set and wait."

Mona came over, and the old woman rose. "I'm Granny Stevens," she said. She put out a work-hardened hand, which Mona shook. "You're from the city, I take it?"

"That's right."

"Looks like your kinfolk comin' now."

Mona turned to see Richard, who had appeared from around the corner of the building accompanied by a tall man. Richard was wearing his fatigue jacket, and the other man was wearing a denim jacket worn white with many washings.

"Why, Mona!" Richard called and waved when he saw her. He hurried over and hugged her and kissed her cheek. "I'm glad to see you. Are you staying with Uncle Logan and Aunt Anne? How long can you stay?" He smiled at her and rattled on, not giving her time to even answer.

His companion came up and Richard turned and said, "Tom, this is the famous actress Mona Stuart."

Richard's companion smiled and said, "I'm Tom Henderson, Miss Stuart."

"What in the world are you doing here, Mona?" Richard asked.

"I needed to get a little rest, and this is about the most restful place I know of."

"I think so." Richard stopped and looked at Tom. "I'm glad you came, but I've got to work on that truck. I have to get it fixed this morning so we can take one of the kids to a doctor appointment in Fort Smith. I'm sorry I can't take time to show you around now. Can you come back over tomorrow?"

"Well, yes, I can do that."

Henderson said, "Richard's our only mechanic, Miss Stuart. But I'd be happy to show you around. I see you rode over. I can saddle up in a couple of minutes. Be glad to have you stay for lunch with us, too, if you'd like."

Mona hesitated—after all, she'd never met this man before, but Richard nodded approval. And Mona noticed that the tall man was quite good-looking—always a persuasive argument with her. "Well, I would like to see the place, and I'll be here long enough for you and me to get caught up, Richard. Logan told me to invite you to supper."

"It's settled then. Let me saddle up, and I'll give you the grand tour," said Tom.

"That would be fine." After Henderson headed toward the barn, Mona said, "I'm glad to see you looking so fit and strong, Richard. I was concerned when I saw you at Christmas. I'm sorry we didn't get to talk then."

"I'm pretty fully recuperated, Mona. Inside, I think, as well as physically. Funny thing, how work heals," he said. "Look, we'll talk later. I have to get that truck going."

Mona went back to the corral and led her horse out. She mounted when Henderson came back on a rangy bay, and the two of them rode out. It was a pleasant experience.

As they talked together, mostly about the work that went

on around the Vine, Mona was puzzled. Henderson was lean, and the wind and the sun had weathered his face, but he did not seem to be a farmer. He dropped a couple of names, including Tolstoy and Dickens, not ostentatiously, but enough so that her interest was piqued.

"Are you a farmer, Tom?"

"I guess we're all farmers here," he said. His eyes were sweeping the skies, but he turned to face her. He had steely blue-gray eyes, and his dark beard looked soft. It was clipped short, and it gave him a rakish look. "I guess you're wondering, like everybody else, what kind of a place this is?"

"Well, I must admit I'm curious. Richard's family seems a little curious, too."

Tom laughed. He had a pleasant laugh, and his eyes crinkled. "Everybody thinks we're living 'communally' here, but if you stay around long enough you'll see that it's not like that."

"Well, what sort of place is the Vine? What's it for?"

"That's a little hard to answer," Henderson said. He leaned over and patted the bay on the shoulder and thought about the question for a moment before he answered. He pulled up, and her horse stopped beside his. "Over there's where we're going to put in a new orchard," he said. "Apples and pears. Takes a long time to grow an orchard, but people have to think ahead." He turned to her then and shifted his weight in the saddle. "What kind of a place is this? I guess you might call it a hospital, in a way. Most of us here have been bruised by the system. We agree with what Wordsworth said." He quoted the poem slowly,

> "This world is too much with us; late and soon,
> Getting and spending, we lay waste our powers:
> Little we see in Nature that is ours.

"I guess that's our story. We've been wasted out there, so we've come here to try and find ourselves."

"But people find themselves sometimes in the city, in the busy world."

"Some maybe, but I couldn't handle it. None of us here could. Jefferson said, 'God made the country, but man made the town.'" He suddenly laughed and said, "Here I am spouting all this to a city girl. This is not for everyone," he said, growing more serious.

"I see what you mean, Tom. I think Richard needs something like this," Mona said thoughtfully. "He was badly cut up in the war, inside, I mean."

"Yes, he was, but he's getting better all the time. He won't stay here forever. Most people don't."

"What about you?"

"Me? Ah, I'm just the old man back in the hills." He smiled at her. "Now, tell me something about this movie you've been making. I've heard something of it from Logan. What's it about?"

They rode along, and although Mona had left the city to rest after the rigors of the movie, as they moved along under the reds and golds and yellows of the leaves, with the fall scents and sounds in the air, she found it relieved her to talk about it. She talked, as a matter of fact, until they wound around and came back to the house. Laughing self-consciously, she said, "Talk about a gabby woman. I haven't talked this much in years—without getting paid for it."

"Sounds like a good movie," Tom said. "The kind we need more of."

"You see many movies?"

He hesitated, then swung down. When she dismounted to stand beside him, he said, "Used to."

Something in his tone caught her attention. "You don't like the movies?"

"Now that wouldn't be tactful of me to answer, would it, Mona? Come on. Let's go see what's for lunch."

The lunch was delicious, and she found the people to be simple and kind; most of all, she was pleased with Richard.

She did notice that his eyes went often to a young woman named Laurel, who had a little boy that seemed to be hers. Mona determined to ask Richard about her later on.

Afterward, she helped clear away, then she talked for a while with Richard. She had to tell all about the movie again, and he said, "I don't know much about things like that, but Tom does. You ought to see the books he's got in his room. He tries to get me to read 'em, and I don't know what they're about. Art, music, theater."

Mona turned with interest to the tall man who was sitting loosely in a cane-backed chair. His eyes were lowered, but he lifted them and smiled at her. "Don't listen to what he says. I don't understand half of those books myself."

"I don't believe that." Mona smiled; she looked very pretty even dressed in casual clothing. When it came time to leave, she said good-bye to several of the people she'd met. She put out her hand to Tom and said, "I enjoyed talking with you, especially about the movie. I hope we'll get to talk some more."

"Sure," Tom nodded. "Come over any time. We never close."

She gave an account at supper of her visit, and Logan raised one eyebrow saying, "Hardly figure those folks out, especially Tom. He's got country sense."

"What does that mean, Uncle Logan?"

"Oh, it just means that he's one of those men that always knows the right thing to do and the right thing to say. Why, he could be anything, a politician, college professor, a preacher if he had a mind to."

The next week Mona found herself going every day to the Vine. There was little to do around the home place, and she enjoyed the ride. She liked Richard, of course, but found him most often engaged in some activity that took his attention, usually involving Laurel.

The big project for a few days was canning apples and applesauce and making apple butter. "Granny makes the best apple pie you ever tasted," said Tom. Mona peeled apples and tended the canner like everybody else.

By Thursday they had finished, and she and Tom were taking a walk through the woods. She had been amazed to find that he seemed to know everything about movies, even the history of them back to the silent days. He had strong ideas, and as they walked through the woods, the fallen leaves crackling under their feet, she took offense at something he said about modern-day movies. She stopped and said, "Tom, you're just obstinate and old-fashioned! You remind me of Uncle Logan. The last good movie he saw was Ken Maynard in *Here Comes Trouble.*"

"I'm not obstinate," Tom turned to grin at her. "I'm firm. That's the difference between us. You're obstinate and I'm firm." He laughed at her expression and said, "I'm sorry, Mona. I didn't mean that, and I don't set up to be any expert about the movies."

Mona was not a tall woman, though supple and very well shaped, as befitted a former Miss Oklahoma. She had given herself the best care, and as Henderson looked down at her, admiration showed in his eyes, but he said nothing.

Mona was annoyed about being called obstinate, and she was puzzled. Almost every male she had ever met since she was fourteen had tried to kiss her, but not once had Henderson even spoken a word that would be construed as a pass. A perverse notion came to her. *He's not as high and mighty as he thinks. I can make him kiss me!* And Mona certainly knew how. She looked up at him and let her lips go soft, and whispered, "I'm sorry, Tom. I didn't mean to say those things." She knew how to lower her eyes to make them more enticing, and she leaned forward just a fraction of an inch, an invitation that any man would have recognized instantly.

Tom looked at her, and something like humor came to his eyes. He ignored the provocative look and said, "Well, that's good. We'd better be getting back now."

Stunned by his seeming rejection, Mona said almost

nothing. She was short-spoken with Richard, and that night, back at the home place, she lay awake thinking about Henderson. "Maybe there's something wrong with him," she muttered. "Maybe he just doesn't like women. I'll ask Richard tomorrow."

She did so the next day, after riding over early, and Richard responded, "He goes to the dances some. Women seem to take to him. He likes them, too. He's spent a lot of time with a redhead named Colleen, but nothing serious, I guess." He grinned at her and said, "What's the matter, Mona?"

She turned away without answering. The resolve hardened in her, and when Henderson appeared and said he was going out to look for a cow that was about to calve, she asked, "Can I go along?"

"Sure, come along, Mona."

They left the house, and he spoke lightly as they strolled along. Though it was cold, he wore no jacket, only a flannel shirt, with the sleeves rolled up. "Always did like the cold," he said. "Don't like the hot nearly as much." When they entered the woods, he called for the cow in a soothing voice but finally gave up. "She's had that calf somewhere. She'll just have to come in on her own."

He turned and Mona brushed against him, making it seem accidental. "Sorry," she said, and she put her hand on his arm to steady herself. She waited then, and he turned to face her. She lifted her head and whispered, "You're a very attractive man, Tom. I didn't expect to find anyone like you out here in the Ozarks."

Henderson stared at her but made no move. He studied her for a moment—the pursed lips slightly open, the eyes that watched him with provocation—and then he shook his head. "You don't really want me to kiss you, Mona. It's just a challenge to your talents to find a man who won't come panting after you. That's Hollywood, and that's one of the things I don't like about it, and it comes out in the pictures. Anyone who stays in that place long enough gets hardened, and it's happening to you."

Curiously, Mona slapped him resoundingly across the cheek. "You're a stupid man, Tom Henderson! You don't know nearly as much as you think you do!"

She whirled and ran blindly away. She heard his footsteps behind her, and then his hand grabbed her arm. "Turn me loose!" she said, turning around furiously. "Or I'll slap you again!"

"You're going the wrong way," Henderson said. "The house is that way." He nodded in the direction opposite the one she had taken.

Mona's face flamed, and she jerked her arm away and walked silently back. She felt stupid and ashamed, and she refused to look at Henderson, who walked silently beside her. He said nothing either, and when the two got to the yard, she went at once to her horse. Henderson said not a word to her but turned and walked into the house. He passed by Richard, who came out as Mona swung into the saddle. "You're not leaving, are you?"

"Yes!"

Richard saw that she was disturbed. "What's wrong, Mona?" he asked quietly.

"Tom Henderson is an arrogant jerk! That's what's wrong!"

Her words were harsh, and her lips were drawn together into a tight line. Richard studied her carefully and said as gently as he could, "He's the smartest fellow I ever knew, Mona. And the best man, almost, outside of family. You're just mad because he won't dance to your tune."

"And you know all about it, don't you, Richard!" She kicked her heels against her horse's sides and rode away at a gallop. She did not turn, but she had the feeling that she had made a perfect fool of herself. She thought of Henderson's steady gaze and muttered, "He's not the saint he pretends to be!" Still, she could not get him out of her mind, and when she got back to the home place, she unsaddled the mare, walked her to cool her down, then put her in the corral. That night at supper she told Logan and Anne, "I've been here long enough. I have to get back to Los Angeles." She sensed their eyes on her and felt that these two people could read her through and through. She excused herself early and went to bed dissatisfied.

The next day she kissed both Logan and Anne good-bye and endured the bus trip to Fort Smith. When her plane was in the air, she looked down on the rolling Ozarks that lay beneath her and thought spitefully, *I hope I never see this place again—and especially I hope I never see Tom Henderson again!*

9

Doing the Right Thing

Hollywood had lost some of its glitter for Mona Stuart. She returned from the Ozarks and threw herself into a small part in a picture that she did not enjoy. The role was, the studio convinced her, worthy of her talents and would advance her career. It paid well, and since she had nothing else to do, she had taken it. She portrayed a woman of extremely low moral character, almost a prostitute. The stars of the picture she did not find to her taste, and every day when she left the studio, she felt gritty and dissatisfied with everything.

After the New Year, 1954, a call from RKO Studios came, and she went eagerly to talk to the producers there. They wanted her, she quickly discovered, for another minor role, this time portraying the companion of Machine Gun Kelly, a famous criminal of the Roaring Twenties. Once again she was assured that the role would help her, and again, the money was good. Still, she put them off for a few days.

Adam had been having a tea party with Suzanne when Maris poked her head in the room saying, "Adam, Mona's here."

"Oh, no!" Suzanne said. She shook her blonde hair, and the innocent blue eyes looked just for a moment rebellious.

"We'll continue this another time, sweetheart." Adam pulled her up and kissed her, nuzzling her neck saying, "Mmm! You smell good!"

"You don't smell very good, Daddy. I think you need a bath."

Adam laughed outright and released her. "Probably right," he said. He left the child's room and moved into the living area to greet Mona. "Well, this is a surprise." He grinned. "But you missed supper."

"Oh, Adam," Mona said. "I hate to bother you like this, but you're so busy at the studio." Her lips turned up in a smile as she continued, "So I thought I'd just come and bother you at home."

Maris smiled at Mona. "Just in time for dessert. Adam always eats so much I make him wait for dessert. Come along to the table."

Mona protested but gave in, and soon the three of them were sitting at a small table in the kitchen eating lemon meringue pie and drinking coffee. Mona commented as she watched the couple, "How perfect you two are! You look like something off the cover of a romance novel."

Adam and Maris both laughed heartily. He said, "Mona, not five minutes ago my about-to-be-seven daughter told me I need a bath because I don't smell so good. Don't take Hollywood too seriously. Real life is nothing like a romance novel. Is it, Maris?" He smiled at his wife. "Maris and I know the worst about each other, and as much time as you spend here I can hardly believe you don't see at least some of it." Just then the two children came in begging for bites from the pie. Mona enjoyed the teasing between Adam and his son, and she saw that the children adored him.

Saying, "It's time for baths," Maris rose. Ignoring Sam's protests, she hauled him off bodily while Suzanne came over and took her father's kiss. "You promised to come in and read me about the little train that could."

"You know it already by heart. And besides, you can read that yourself."

"I know," Suzanne said placidly, nodding her blonde head. "But it's better when you read it, Daddy."

As Maris and the children went upstairs, Adam said, "I'm

already dreading the teenage years—what'll I do when some boy wants to date my little girl?"

Mona smiled. She sipped her coffee, then pushed a morsel of pie around with her fork.

Noting her preoccupation, Adam leaned forward, putting his elbows on the table. "What's up, Mona?" he asked, his eyes fastened on her face.

Lifting her gaze, Mona said, "I'm worried about my career."

"You're doing fine. You've done good work, and you're going to do more."

"I got an offer from RKO today." She lifted a hand in expressing her futility. "They want me to play a gangster's moll. Some no-good woman who hooked up with a hood named Machine Gun Kelly back in the twenties."

"I heard they were doing some casting for that. Gangsters are big again these days. It seems like the worst ones have become heroes—Capone, Dillinger."

She looked up and shook her head. "Why is it that people want to see things like that?"

He sipped his coffee then said, "Something about evil attracts people. Don't know what it is. We've run out of heroes, I guess." He picked up the paper lying on the table and said, "It looks like we've lost another one."

"A hero? Who's that?"

"Joe DiMaggio. Look. He's marrying Marilyn Monroe."

Mona studied the picture and read a few lines of the story. She shook her head, saying, "That'll never last. That woman has no stability. Beautiful, but they say she has no self-esteem at all. All that beauty, and she still hasn't found herself."

"Some might say that sounds a lot like you, Mona," Adam commented. "I don't know," he went on when she made no reply, "why the stars don't seem to make it. This business is hard on souls, isn't it?"

"I guess it is. I want to do a good picture, Adam, something as good as *The Soldier*."

"So do I," he said wryly. "We've been looking all over the place for good scripts, but they're about as rare as the Hope Diamond. What I'd like to do," he added, "is *Bride of Quietness*."

"That book won the National Book Award, didn't it?" Mona frowned. "I haven't read it."

"You should. It's the finest novel I've ever read. Certainly, at least, of the modern ones."

"Why haven't they made a movie out of it?"

"Basically because the author, William Starr, won't let anybody have the rights to it. Everybody's made a try, but so far no cigar."

"Do you know him?"

"No, he's a recluse. He taught in a little college in Kentucky, wrote the book, and as soon as it hit big and won about every prize in sight, he just disappeared. Nobody can understand it; most people would be riding the crest of the wave. But why don't you read the book. I've got a copy you can take home with you."

Mona left an hour later and went back to her apartment. She undressed, showered, put on her gown, got into bed, and then began reading *Bride of Quietness*. She had intended only to skim through it, but the first chapter, almost the first words, riveted her. It was a simple book about a country woman who had to handle great emotional problems. After reading three chapters and noting that it was after two o'clock, she put the book down and shut off the light. She lay for a time thinking about the story. *How can a man write a book like that? He knows so much about what a woman's like.* Her last thought was, *I'd like to meet William Starr. . . .*

Amos called Jake into his office and said, "Get out of Chicago for a while. Cover President Eisenhower's address to the UN General Assembly. Go to New York. We need something fresh."

Jake was surprised. He'd done a lot of traveling on assignment before, but since he'd been promoted to assistant news editor, he'd assumed those days were over.

"By the way," Amos continued, his face expressionless, "Stephanie will be in New York, too, working on a report on Dag Hammarskjöld. She's only working as somebody's assistant, but she's never been to New York before. Guess she figured if she was going to see the great cities of the rest of the world, she might as well see our own." He tore off a piece of paper from a pad on his desk and handed it to Jake, saying, "This is where she's staying if you care to look her up."

In the months since Stephanie went overseas, Jake had poured himself into his work, putting in long hours and, after his promotion, concentrating on learning his new responsibilities as Amos's assistant. He liked being an editor, but he didn't much care for the administrative aspects of the job, so he concentrated on learning to do those particularly well. Mostly, he just didn't let himself think about her. He wouldn't go out with anyone else—when his pals commented about that, he told them he didn't have time because of the job. He wouldn't admit that he just didn't have the heart for seeing anyone. As he returned to his desk, he thought, *And here's Amos setting me up*. He didn't know how much Amos knew about things between him and Stephanie. Amos was certainly reporter enough to know something had happened to provoke Stephanie's sudden desire to get an overseas job immediately. *Should I go see her, as Amos is suggesting?* he wondered. Then he grinned at himself. *Of course I'll go see her.* Then a sobering thought arose. *If she'll even want to see me.*

Stephanie was out shopping New York's fashion district the first time Jake called her hotel. He left a number, almost glad she wasn't there—that way she didn't have to return his call if she didn't want to see him. He got back to his hotel about ten, after discussion over drinks and dinner with some other reporters about what Ike was likely to say, among other

things. The concierge gave him Stephanie's message: Of
course I want to see you; call whenever you get in.

She was staying at the Hamilton House, and when they
met in the lobby the next evening, Jake embraced her briefly
and kissed her cheek, then studied her with approval. "I see
you've been bargain hunting at the thrift shops again," he
said solemnly. Stephanie's dress was a simple but elegant
shirtdress made of a light rose silk. It had long sleeves, a narrow cloth belt around the waist, and came to just above her
knees. The top of the dress was covered by a short off-white
sweater that sparkled with beads, braid, and ribbon embroi-
dery. She looked beautiful in it, though he would not tell her
so. He was wearing a charcoal gray flannel suit with narrow
shoulders and lapels, and the trousers were also of a narrow
cut and had cuffs. His shirt was a light gray silk, and he wore
a gray-and-black striped tie that peeked out of the buttoned
jacket and a new black fedora purchased for the occasion.
Stephanie smiled at him and said, "You look nice, too. I like
that suit. My dad would say you look good enough to be
buried in it some day."

"Thanks a lot," Taylor grinned. "You say the nicest
things."

"Just like you."

They went to dinner at the most outlandish restaurant
Stephanie had ever seen. Jake insisted on taking her to the
Forum of the Twelve Caesars. When they were seated and
looked around, Stephanie's eyes opened wide. "This isn't a
restaurant, it's ancient Rome!"

Laughing under his breath, Taylor nodded. "Two fellas
called Baum and Brody bought portraits of twelve Roman
emperors, and they made up their minds that New York was
a whole lot like imperial Rome. So they set about replicating
the Appian Way—that's what we passed in the vestibule—
and did you see the waiters? They're all wearing togas!"

Stephanie looked at the wine bottles in ice buckets shaped
like Roman helmets and said, "I think it's a bit much."

The waiter came, and Stephanie wanted to giggle, for he had hairy, pudgy legs. She studied the menu and was amused by it. There was "Fiddler Crab a la Nero: The noblest Caesar salad of them all" and "Sirloin in red wine, marrow, and onions, a Gaelic recipe Julius collected while there on business." Finally she tossed the menu down and said, "You order, Jake."

"Bring us each a sirloin, medium well, salad with Italian dressing, and a baked potato."

The waiter looked at him as if he were a strange being from outer space, and his lips grew tight. "Very well, sir, if you insist."

"I think you hurt his feelings, Jake," Stephanie said as the waiter walked away.

"Well, he hurt mine with that idiotic menu."

The food was good though the atmosphere was bizarre. They chatted through dinner about Stephanie's family, Jake's new position, Stephanie's work, and politics.

"Do you believe Communism can be as pervasive as Senator McCarthy says? He hasn't produced any convincing evidence," Stephanie said.

"He is a spellbinder, though. The senate seems to think he might be on to something. Did you see where they voted $214,000 for his investigation of Communism in the government?"

"No, I missed that tidbit."

After the restaurant, they went to see *The Crucible*, Arthur Miller's new play about the Salem witch trials, which gave them further food for thought about hysteria and fear and Senator McCarthy. When they got to Stephanie's hotel, Jake saw her to her door. She turned and said, "It was a lovely evening. It seemed nice to see you and to get caught up on what you've been doing."

Taylor seemed preoccupied and somewhat downcast. Stephanie inquired, "What's the matter, Jake?"

"I've missed you," he said.

"I've missed you, too."

"You never really said, but I got the idea that you left because of me."

"I thought it would be too uncomfortable for both of us if I stayed around."

"Maybe you're right. Can I ask you something, though? As a reporter I just want to make sure I understand."

"Of course. As a reporter." Stephanie was puzzled. She hadn't known what to expect of this evening.

He looked her directly in the eye. "You gave me two reasons why you wouldn't marry me. Neither of them was because you didn't love me. Is that correct?"

Her face felt stiff. "Yes, I'd have to say that's correct," she whispered.

"So, again, just to be sure I get the story straight, you wouldn't marry me, but you were in love with me. Are you still? Or have you gotten over it?"

"No comment," she whispered hoarsely. She turned quickly to go in, but he stopped her, turned her face to him. He looked into her eyes, his face very close. He ran his finger lightly over her lower lip. Stephanie was in tears then, and so was Jake. He blotted her tears gently with the back of his hand. Neither could speak. He kissed her lightly, opened the door for her, then gave a wave and a semblance of a smile, and turned toward the elevator.

She regained her composure enough to call out in a stage whisper, "See you tomorrow?"

He nodded, then was gone.

On the third day of Stephanie's stay in New York, she got a phone call from her father. "Did you know Bobby's there in New York doing a performance? He's at the Imperial Theater. It'd be nice if you could go by and see him."

Stephanie called Jake, saying, "Bobby is performing here in New York. I'd like to go see him. Will you go with me?"

"Sure." He paused and said with a stern tone, "But I don't

want you mauling me after we get home like you did last night." There was silence on Stephanie's end, and he imagined the flush rising to her cheeks and laughed aloud. "It's all right. You're safe enough. I'd like to hear your brother perform again."

The Imperial was headlined by a group called Bill Haley and the Comets. Haley's name was outside on the marquee and, in much smaller letters, three other names. One of them was Bobby Stuart.

They entered the theater and looked around. Taylor said, "I feel like a grandpa in here. Why, these are all kids, Stephanie."

Stephanie was also struck by the youthful crowd. There were some as young as twelve or thirteen, she estimated. The girls wore short skirts and saddle shoes or penny loafers. The boys were lean and undernourished-looking, for the most part.

"I see what you mean. I have no idea what to expect."

The two found their seats. First up was a trio who gyrated a great bit and sang nonsensical lyrics at the top of their voices.

"I don't think these kids will replace Frank Sinatra or Perry Como," Taylor murmured.

The next act was a young woman who had a good voice, indeed, and sang songs such as Stephanie had never heard before.

"That's New Orleans jazz," Taylor said. "Got a lot of the blues in it, too, from Memphis. She's good."

The emcee came forward and quieted the crowd and said, "And now, here is Bobby Stuart!"

Stephanie had heard Bobby sing and play many times, but not recently. He was twenty, but she thought he still looked seventeen. He had auburn hair and large, direct eyes, and there was an assurance about him as he came out and went at once to the baby grand piano. Without sitting down or even greeting the audience, he ran his fingers across the keyboard and began to pound out a wild beat and to sing a song that Stephanie had never heard before. The crowd began to cheer, evidently familiar with it, and Stephanie leaned over and said, "I guess this is what they call 'rockabilly.'"

Jake was studying the young man, watching his assurance and poise and listening to the music. He turned to Stephanie and said quietly, "Well, he's got it, kid. Sex appeal, charisma, whatever you want to call it. Some people practice a lifetime and can't even get mild applause. Others, like Crosby and Sinatra, all they have to do is step out on a stage, and they've got the audience crying for them. Your brother's going places in this business."

The crowd demanded that Bobby come back again and again, and finally the emcee came forward and said, "Well, folks, I can see how you feel about Bobby Stuart. He'll be having his own concert the first thing you know. Now, it's time for Bill Haley and the Comets!"

Stephanie did not really pay much heed to the group that played. They were clean-cut young men who had a great beat, but she was thinking about Bobby and wondering where he was headed with his career.

Stephanie wanted to go backstage after the performance, so Jake took her by the arm and firmly brushed by those assigned to protect the performers, holding up his press card and saying, "Hearst Papers." This proved to be an open sesame.

They found Bobby sharing a small dressing room. He had put on his street clothes, and he opened the door immediately when they knocked. "Steph! I'm so glad you made it. Mom called and said you might be here. How are you?" He hugged her and kissed her on the cheek, then turned to look at the man beside her. "Is that Jake with you? He looks like an FBI agent."

"No, they look much better than I do," Jake said. "Most of them are lawyers, college graduates. I'm just your sister's bodyguard this trip."

Bobby laughed. He was still energized from his reception by the fans. He said at once, "Come on! I'm starved to death. Let's go get something to eat."

They went out to a little restaurant where Bobby ate enormous portions of spaghetti, while the other two toyed with their food. There was an electricity about him that he could not seem to turn off. When he'd finished eating, he talked rapidly about his music and about different places he had been.

"I'm gonna have my own concert. It won't be as big as this one, but it'll be a start. I wish you could be there, Sis, for my solo."

"I'm going back to London in a couple more days, but maybe Mom and Dad and Richard can come. Where will it be?"

"Memphis," he said. "It's where a lot of this music starts. The blues had their birth there, not far from New Orleans. But tonight we leave for Detroit." He grew thoughtful then and stared at Stephanie. "How are you doing?"

"I'm doing fine," she said and started to tell him about her UN assignment.

Jake interrupted, "I made a good reporter out of her. She didn't know a thing when I got her, but I taught her everything she knows."

Bobby grinned, liking the reporter very much. This was obvious to Stephanie. She brought Bobby up to date on her work in London and her part in the trip to New York to interview Hammarskjöld. "I won't even get to meet him; I just do background research for the interviewer and write up his notes. I'm filing some other reports on the UN's activities, though."

When they parted, Bobby said, "Take care of yourself, Sis."

"And you take care of yourself, Bobby," Stephanie said, hugging and kissing him. "Write to me."

Jake and Stephanie spent the next afternoon seeing some of the sights in New York—the Empire State Building, the

Chrysler Building—and taking the ferry to see the Statue of Liberty. In the evening, they had supper at a sidewalk cafe, then rode through Central Park in a horse-drawn carriage.

At her door, he put his arms around her and held her close. She was returning to London the next day. "When will I see you again?" he asked.

"Don't ask, Jake. Maybe never."

He looked in her face and smiled. "Maybe I'm a romantic after all. I believe true love will conquer all."

"Sometimes it doesn't. You know that, Mr. Hardboiled Reporter. Remember what happened to Romeo and Juliet."

He saw she was near tears. He bent his head and kissed her, lingeringly, then longingly.

She felt something virile and strong and heady in his embrace and in his kiss, and she put her arms up around his neck. She clung to him, pulling even closer. All the world faded away, and she was aware only of this man, this moment, and the love she felt for him.

Some sense of propriety returned. She removed her arms from his neck and put her hands on his chest and pushed him back. His arms were still around her, and she breathed with difficulty as she looked up into his eyes.

Taylor shrugged. "You mad at me?"

"I guess not, but—" she halted, composing herself, and then said, "you must never do it again."

"I know. You don't trust yourself, do you, Steph?" He smiled broadly.

Stephanie's face grew red, for she knew he was well aware of her capitulation, and it made her angry. "Good night, Jake."

Taylor reacted to the anger in her tone and said, "You don't have to treat me like I'm Attila the Hun, and you don't have to be afraid of me."

"I'm not afraid of you," Stephanie said defiantly.

He turned and walked to the elevator, angry too. But by

the time the door opened he was over it, and as he got in he raised his hand and said, *"Chemain de Fer."*

She looked at him quizzically. "I don't understand French," she said. "What does that mean?"

"It means railroad," he said. "Road of iron."

Stephanie laughed. "That doesn't make any sense."

"I know, but it's all the French I know. Good night, Steph."

As it turned out, Stephanie's departure was so rushed as to prevent a long good-bye—there were many details that at the last moment became her responsibility. She was both relieved and unhappy as the DC–3's props began to warm up for take-off. She offered a prayer of thanks that she'd gotten a job that would keep her away from Jake, because she felt that if she'd remained anywhere near him she'd have married him, right or wrong, no matter what the obstacles between them. "I want to do what you say is right, Lord, even if it's hard." *And it is hard,* she thought, tears welling up in her eyes.

10

"FIND A CAUSE WORTH LIVING FOR!"

Richard entered the country store. Behind the counter Phineas Morgan was cutting a thick wedge of yellow hoop cheese with a large knife. He tore a length of brown paper from a roll, carefully wrapped the cheese, and sealed it with tape. His customer took a long swig from the chocolate Nehi he was holding, handed over a dollar bill and took his change, then ambled out, the cheese under his arm and his left thumb hooked under the support of his bib overalls.

Moving along through the stacks of clothes, shoes, pots and pans, tools, and food items, Richard picked up a can of Hershey's chocolate syrup and smiled, then moved back to the counter. He added four cans of pork and beans, two packages of weenies plus the buns to go with them, and half a dozen bottles of Nehi strawberry drink.

"That be all, Richard?" Phineas inquired. He was a slight man with a shock of salt-and-pepper hair and a drooping cavalry mustache usually stained with either tobacco, snuff, or nicotine.

"That's all. How much, Phineas?"

Adding up quickly on a small tablet, Phineas replied, "Four dollars and sixteen cents." He took the five-dollar bill that Richard handed him, and counted back the change.

Bluegrass music, Bill Monroe's version, was playing on the

radio. Richard picked up his paper sack and started out but stopped when he met Alvin Hood at the door, the burly man he'd had a fight with. "Hello, Alvin," he said. "How are you today?" Hood did not speak, but glared at Richard. "I hear you're a coon-dog man," Richard continued.

"A fella could hear anything," Hood snapped. "What's it to you?"

"Tom Henderson's got a female he claims is the best he ever saw. Had a litter of puppies, and he told me to scout around to see if there's anybody interested."

"How much you want for 'em?"

"Oh, no charge, Alvin," Richard shrugged. "I don't know dogs myself, but one of them, I tell ya, really took my eye. Biggest of the litter and smart as any animal I ever saw." He smiled and said, "Why don't you come out and take a look at him? Might be you could use another dog?"

"Might be." Alvin looked disturbed and stared down at the floor for a moment. It was a long moment. He was stunned by the offer, and, indeed, he had never been able to figure Richard out. Alvin had spread rumors about him throughout the community and was still rankled that in a fight he'd been bested by a smaller man. But Richard always greeted him with a smile and never appeared to notice his churlish behavior. Looking up, Hood bit his lip and said, "How come you gonna offer to give me a dog? We ain't been friends."

"Well, I'd like to be, Alvin. I know I'm just a city boy, but I'd like to learn. Even like to learn a little bit about coon hounds. They tell me that you wrote the book on that subject."

"Well—reckon I'll come out, maybe this afternoon, and look them pups over."

"Fine! Fine! I shot a buck day before yesterday. The fattest thing you ever saw. You might like a little of that, too. See you this afternoon."

Richard left, and Hood slouched over to the counter, put his fist on it, and shook his big head. "I can't make that fella out, Phineas. By rights he oughta be out to get me, but he don't seem to be headed that way."

"Nice fella."

Hood shifted uneasily. "I been shootin' my big mouth off about those folks out there at that place they call the Vine. Maybe I been a bit hasty. Guess I'll go scout 'em out today." He leaned across the counter and said, "Gimme one of them cream sodas, Phineas."

Richard and Laurel found that one of the chief pleasures of life—better than radio, better than television—was listening to Granny Stevens.

Late on Thursday afternoon, they were both seated out where she was stirring soap in the huge black iron kettle over a fire that Richard had built for her out of dried hickory.

"Tell us about your courtin' days, Granny. Did you have lots of boyfriends?" Richard asked. Laurel was sitting with her back against the wall, wearing blue jeans and a pale blue cotton blouse. Her light brown hair caught in the breeze, and she reached up and smoothed it down. Richard didn't notice the apprehensive glance she cast his way.

"Boyfriends? Why, I never heard of such as goes on these days," Granny said. "I had a few young men callin' on me, but we always sat with my daddy and my mama on the front porch."

"That must have been exciting." Richard smiled.

"Better'n what goes on this day and age," Granny Stevens grunted. "When I agreed to marry Mr. Stevens, he had never even seed me alone."

"Did you kiss 'im much, Granny?" Richard looked at Laurel, for they both knew her response to this. Laurel kept her eyes on Granny so she wouldn't have to let Richard look into her eyes.

"Kiss him? Why, he never held my hand until after we was married!"

Laurel sighed. "That must've been a nice time to live."

Granny looked over, her sharp gray eyes studying the young woman. "It was a heap better'n now, but the good Lord's the same yesterday, today, and forever," she said and smiled. She had a good smile. Her face was wrinkled, but there was a pleasantness and goodness in it that made people trust her intuitively. "You better go help get lunch started. I'll be finished with this soap directly. Wait, what's that I hear?" She looked toward the road. "That looks like your Logan Stuart coming."

It was, indeed, Logan Stuart. He pulled up in the battered Chevrolet and got out slowly, as if his joints hurt. Moving over to where the three were sitting, he greeted them. "Howdy! That's a fine batch of soap you're makin' there, Granny."

"I'll fix you up a little when I get it dibbed," Granny smiled. "Better than any of that store-bought stuff."

"I'll say amen to that." Logan took off his hat and wiped his brow. It was May and it had been a hot, blistering day, but the breeze was beginning to stir in the tops of the trees. "Glad to see it cool off." He looked over and said, "I come to give you an invitation, Richard. Your uncle Owen pulled in today, and he's gonna preach Sunday. Brother Crabtree said the church needs a good skinnin'."

"I'll sure be there, Uncle Logan."

"Bring anybody that wants to come with you. Better come early. You know how it is when Owen preaches. Church house is always full. And why don't you come to supper tomorrow night so you can visit with him?"

"I got some fresh buttermilk," Granny said to Logan. "How 'bout I get a glass for you?"

Logan nodded. "How about I just do your stirrin' while you fetch it for me."

She handed Logan the paddle, and as the old woman walked toward the house, Richard recounted his conversation with Hood at the store earlier that morning and said, "I've been making it a point to be nice to him. I treat him as if there never was any fight, and I think at last it's paying off."

"Well, Hood's a pretty rough fella, but no rougher than some of the rest of us when we was his age, I guess."

Richard laughed at Logan. "I seem to remember you telling me you wish I'd broken his knee instead of just bruising it. I'm glad to see you getting mellow in your old age."

Logan laughed, too. "I meant what I said about Paulks, though. Me and a couple of other old fellers are workin' to get him out."

Granny came out with a brimming glass of buttermilk, took the paddle, and said, "Get this down in your gizzard, Mr. Stuart. It'll do you good."

Logan drank the buttermilk, which left a white mustache on his upper lip. Wiping his mouth with his hand, he handed the glass back to Granny and grinned. "It did me good." Nodding to Richard, he said, "I'll see you at supper."

Reverend Harlan Crabtree looked out over his congregation with satisfaction. The hard pine benches were packed, and all the chairs from the Sunday school rooms had been brought in, and they were filled, too. A few people stood at the back.

After greeting the congregation, Reverend Crabtree said, "I know that you come to hear not me but our guest, Reverend Owen Stuart. This is homecoming for Owen, for he came to this church when he was just a boy, with his parents and his brothers and sisters. He's gone around the country preaching the glorious gospel of Jesus Christ. After the singing, he will come without any introduction, and, Brother Owen, I pray that you will speak the Word of God as it's laid on your heart. Now, let's all stand, and Brother McCoy will lead us in that great old hymn, 'All Hail the Power of Jesus' Name.'"

Laurel was wedged in tight, with Johnny on her right and Richard and Tom on her left. She was very conscious of sitting so close to Richard, and she could not look at him. He pulled a brown paperback songbook from the rack of the pew in front of them, turned to page 29, and began to sing heartily. Laurel had never heard this song before, but the small frame church seemed to tremble with the volume raised by the congregation.

Owen raised his eyes from the page, for he knew the song by heart. As he sang, he studied the church, memories flooding back of times when he had sat with his father and mother, both gone now, and nostalgia seemed to fill him up.

The singing went on a long time, then the offering was gathered. The choir sang "Jesus Is Coming to Earth Again." They were untrained for the most part; nevertheless, they put their hearts into it, and the light on some of the faces stirred Richard. He glanced around and saw the toil-worn farm families and small-town storekeepers and thought how limited their world was. Many of them had never gone outside the Ozark Mountains. Their parents and grandparents had grown up here, and the great things that happened in the world outside did not seem to matter so much to them. They were concerned with families, with making a living, and, beneath all of this, with the world that is to come.

As this thought grew in Richard, he realized that this was missing from his life. He had been busy growing up, going to school, going to war, and in all of that time, he had not taken time to think about Jesus coming back to earth again. Of the fact of that return Richard was fully convinced. He could not ever forget the faith of the Stuart family. Despite their falls and mistakes and tragedies, always there was that vein of faith that Jesus Christ is the Son of God and that he is coming back to earth again.

As he listened to the choir, Richard's throat swelled and grew full, and something came into his spirit. He had heard the song before, but never had it struck home as now. *Jesus is coming back*, he thought; *the same Jesus who went away, and what will he find in me when he comes?*

Richard had heard the gospel since he was a child and had

responded, but it had not been the same for him as for his parents and grandparents and for many of his uncles and aunts—even for his sister. He had seen in them a full-fledged dedication and determination to serve the Lord, and, sitting in the little weather-beaten church, he suddenly realized that his life had not been turned toward God.

The singing concluded, and Owen rose, put his Bible on the cedar pulpit, and tapped with his steel hook gently. "I'm glad to be back in this church," he said, his voice clear and modulated. He was still strong even at seventy-one. An unpretentious man, he wore an inexpensive gray suit, purchased at Sears & Roebuck, and there was a genuine love and strength in his face that held his listeners captive. He began to read the Scripture.

> And a certain ruler asked him, saying, Good Master, what shall I do to inherit eternal life? And Jesus said unto him, Why callest thou me good? none is good, save one, that is, God. Thou knowest the commandments, Do not commit adultery, Do not kill, Do not steal, Do not bear false witness, Honour thy father and thy mother. And he said, All these have I kept from my youth up. Now when Jesus heard these things, he said unto him, Yet lackest thou one thing: sell all that thou hast, and distribute unto the poor, and thou shalt have treasure in heaven: and come, follow me. And when he heard this, he was very sorrowful: for he was very rich.
>
> Luke 18:18–23

Closing the Bible, Owen laid his hands on it for a moment in silent reverence and prayed a quick prayer. Then he began to talk. "This young man who came to Jesus did one right thing. He did come to Jesus. He could have gone anywhere, for the Scripture says that he was rich, but he came to Jesus. That is the right thing for every man, every woman, and every young person to do, to come to Jesus."

Owen spoke quietly about the young man who had all that

the world could offer: riches, position, place. "He did one right thing in coming to Jesus, this young man—but he did one tragic, terribly wrong thing. Matthew 19:22 says that 'he went away' from Jesus. He would have been welcomed in any church in the land, for he was respectable and wealthy and a good, moral man. But he was a lost young man. He was lost because he did not let Jesus Christ do with him as he pleased, and that is the essence of being unsaved. He was lost because he had nothing to live for. You may say he had his business, he had his fortune, but where did that go when he drew his last breath and stepped out into eternity to meet a just Judge?

"I've always hoped that this young man did come back to Jesus sometime, that he did not go out to meet God unsaved and to face hell and judgment. But he had nothing to live for. What do you have to live for? Your business? That will be gone. You say you live for your family? No one is stronger than I about the obligations of the family, but your family will not go with you to meet God, and you cannot serve your family unless you serve Jesus Christ."

Richard felt crushed in a way that he had never known, for he realized that he had nothing, indeed, to live for. His hands tightened as he locked them together, and he was not aware that he was trembling. Laurel was looking at him, stealing glances sideways, noting his pale face and his lips drawn into a hard line, and she could not understand.

Owen said, "Find a cause that is bigger than you are, that is bigger than business, that is bigger than the home, bigger than the nation, bigger than anything, and throw yourself into it with all your heart. I know of but one cause like that. It is the Lord Jesus Christ and the kingdom of God."

Richard felt weak and drained, yet there was something in him that said plainly, "This is for you, my son." It came to him in his spirit as clearly as if a trumpet had sounded. Owen motioned for the congregation to stand, and he said, "I want you to come and give your lives to Jesus Christ." Richard, brushing blindly against Laurel and Johnny and stepping on toes, achieved the aisle and went forward, and Owen was there putting his arm around him, shaking his hand, and praying with him. Richard never forgot the pressure of that arm around his shoulder and the hand holding his and in Owen's eyes that light of joy and delight at seeing him there.

Those who came forward stood at the front, and Owen and the pastor prayed with each of them while the congregation sang. Then Crabtree said, "We are so happy that every one of these has come. One that Brother Owen is especially interested in is his great-nephew Richard Stuart. Richard has told me that he was converted when he was a child, but he did not surrender everything to Jesus. This morning he comes to say that he feels that God is putting his hand on him, and he will follow wherever God leads him." He smiled and looked at Owen and winked. "I wouldn't be surprised if you have a disciple here to take up your work, Brother Owen."

"Amen!" Owen's voice boomed, and loud cries of "Hallelujah" and "Amen" went around the room.

After the closing prayer, the congregation began to file by to shake hands with and hug those at the front and to encourage them.

Laurel did not go to shake hands with Richard. She slipped outside and stood beside Tom. "What does it all mean?" she asked.

"Well, for one thing, we'll be losing one of our members at the Vine."

"He'll be leaving?"

"I think so." Seeing the alarm in her face, he added gently, "That would be sad for you, wouldn't it, if Richard left?"

"We're very good friends. Johnny loves him so much."

Henderson almost said, "Johnny's not the only one, is he?" but he held his peace. He put his hand on Laurel's shoulder. "Any man that gives his life to God can't go wrong, or any woman either. It's something you ought to think about, Laurel."

Late that afternoon when the sun was falling rapidly toward the jagged hills in the west, Laurel saw Richard leave the house and walk down toward the creek he seemed to love so much. She turned to another of the young women, saying, "Mary, will you watch Johnny?"

"Sure. Come on, Johnny. Let's make some cookies."

Taking off her apron, Laurel hurried out of the house, then across the yard and down the path that led to the woods. She had been troubled ever since the service that morning. She found Richard staring into the stream. "Richard," she called softly. "I–I want to talk to you."

Richard turned and smiled at her. "Sure. Come on. Let's sit on the log." He moved down the stream to where a large hickory tree had fallen, and the two sat down. "You're upset? What's wrong?"

Laurel had come to the Vine filled with fears and apprehensions about the future. For her it had been a haven, a place of safety. "Are you going to leave, Richard?"

She was wearing a simple cotton dress and a pair of low-heeled white shoes, well-worn and scuffed. Her hair always seemed beautiful to him, rich and thick, slightly curled as it blew in the May breeze, and her eyes—he could never describe their color. Sometimes they seemed violet, but now they looked dark blue, and he saw fear in them. Her vulnerability and sweetness and goodness had drawn his attention from the first time he saw her. "I think I will leave, but you mustn't worry about it, Laurel," he said, wanting to make that look of fear disappear.

She turned her head away from him. Her voice was muffled when she said, "I'll miss you, and so will Johnny."

"You mustn't feel bad. I may not leave for a long time." He began to tell her how he had grown up in a Christian home and had always lived a fairly moral life, even in the marines.

Then he tried to explain how God had come to him that morning. "I don't know how to put it to you, Laurel, but God is real. Jesus is real, and I'm going to follow him. I've got a good example in Uncle Owen. Sometimes it's hard being a minister, but I want to do it."

She turned to face him, and he saw tears in her eyes. "When you first came here you asked me about Johnny's father. I felt too ashamed to tell you. And as we've grown closer, I was afraid I'd shock you and that I'd lose you. But I feel like I have to tell you the truth. His father was in the service, like you. I'd never had a boyfriend, and he'd never had a girlfriend. He was shy, and so was I. We were very young, and we knew that he would be leaving, and he was all I had, Richard. All I'd ever had, and," a flush came to her face, and she bit her full under lip, "we—we did wrong." She dropped her head then, and her hair curtained her face. She did not speak for a long time, but her shoulders began to shake. Then she lifted her eyes, and there was tragedy in them. "He went away to an army camp in Louisiana, and he was going to send for me and we were going to be married, but he died, in a training accident. He never even knew that he was a father." She put her hands over her face. "My parents threw me out when they found out."

Richard did feel shocked. He'd never considered that Johnny might be illegitimate. But he also cared deeply for this young woman and wanted to comfort her. He put his arm around her and drew her close. Her hair smelled sweet. He let her cry for a while simply because he didn't know what to say. "I know it's hard, but God will take care of you and Johnny just like he's going to take care of me."

Some inflection in his voice told her it was as she'd feared. He hadn't said, "God will take care of *us*." Laurel looked up, her eyes dewy and her lips trembling, but she stopped crying.

Richard leaned over, kissed her forehead, pulled a handkerchief out, and wiped the tears from her face. "We're in

God's hands. All we have to do is be obedient, and we'll be all right."

She knew it had changed between them. Suddenly he was treating her like a sister, not like a woman he was in love with.

They sat silent until the sun dropped behind the low-lying hills, then they rose and made their way back. In the growing darkness, Laurel felt cold and alone but no longer fearful. And the two passed out of the woods and walked toward the house.

11

No Man Is a Match
for a Woman!

What are you saying, Max?"

"I'm saying that you may want to just step aside."

"Leave the picture?"

"We've only shot a few scenes with you. It wouldn't be hard to shoot around them til we get another actress."

"You're firing me?" Mona felt like her heart had stopped.

"Nothing like that," Danenberg said, spreading his hands wide. "It's up to you. I'm willing to go on, but you're going to have to do better than you have."

This can't be real, she thought. *I feel like I'm saying lines.*

Max said, "Well, what do you say?"

Mona was miserably aware that she had failed to convey the performance he wanted. "I just can't seem to get into this picture," she said.

"Look, Mona. You're a good actress, but sometimes in this business, roles just don't fit. This may be one of those times."

"Can you give me a day or two to think about it, Max?"

"Sure. You go home, or go for a walk. Whatever you decide, sweetheart, I'll stay with you. But you've got to come through for me."

"Thanks, Max. I'll give you my answer soon."

Since it was a costume picture, it took some time for Mona to remove her makeup and change. She had just finished putting on her street clothes when a knock came at her door. "Come in," she said.

A head bobbed inside, and Ted Franklin said, "Miss Stuart, there's a fellow at the front gate asking to see you."

"Who is it?"

"Says his name is Tom Henderson. You want to see him?"

"Tell him to wait. I'll be right there." Mona was wearing a peach-colored dress with a full skirt, heavy pleats, and large side pockets. She put on a maroon bolero jacket, fastened a soft, wide belt, then after a few passes at her hair, grabbed her bag and left the dressing room.

As she passed through the busy activities of the sets, she wondered what Tom could be doing in Los Angeles. Every day she thought of him, and every night. *Maybe that's why the picture isn't going well. I'm too distracted.* It had puzzled and frustrated and angered her that she could not get the tall man out of her mind. She was accustomed to the admiration of men, but Henderson had certainly not overwhelmed her in this respect. She thought, *Perhaps it's just my strange form of pride that keeps bringing him to mind.* As she walked toward the gate, she saw him lounging outside wearing the familiar faded jeans and white T-shirt and a bill cap pushed back on his head. She was disgusted to find herself having to conceal her eagerness and embarrassed at the memory of how she had parted from him. She slowed her walk, took a deep breath, and exhaled, and as she stepped through the gates, she said as coolly as she could, "Hello, Tom."

"Hi, Mona. You're looking fine. Have you gotten over your hissy fit?" His grin was wide, and there was in his sleepy-looking, blue-gray eyes admiration, she felt sure.

She decided to ignore his question. "What are you doing in Los Angeles?"

"Oh, I have a chore to do. Thought I'd drop by, and we could go somewhere and talk a little bit."

"Well, I'm free for the rest of today."

"Are you hungry?"

It was only a little past four, and Mona had little appetite. But she really was glad to see him, and she wanted to talk, so she said, "Yes, you can tell me all about Richard, and about the others at the Vine. Where do you want to eat?"

"I've already found just the place. Come on."

Mona expected him to call a taxi, but he said, "It's only about fifteen blocks from here."

"Fifteen blocks?"

"It'll do you good. All this fresh air and sunshine. Think about how many people come to Los Angeles just for that. Come on," he urged.

Mona felt his hand on her arm, and he shortened his stride so she could keep up with him. As they walked along under the sunny skies, he said, "I suppose you heard about Richard's decision."

"What decision?"

"He's going to be a preacher."

"A preacher?" Mona missed a step, but he caught her.

He grinned at her and said, "I think it's a good idea. Nobody around like Owen Stuart, and one day he'll have to quit. Nice to know another Stuart will be in there preaching the gospel."

For the rest of the hike—as Mona felt it to be—she questioned Henderson about the details, especially asking about Laurel.

"I'll tell you about it after we eat. There's the place."

Mona looked up to see a building with a tile roof line, large windows, red-and-white horizontal tile, and two yellow arches running from the back to the front of the building. "Is this it?" she asked.

"Yes, this is McDonald's. They make the best hamburgers you ever tasted. I tried one on my way to the studio just to see what it's like. Come on in."

Amused by his choice of a restaurant but knowing he had little money, Mona accompanied him inside.

Five minutes later the pair were seated in a booth, and

Henderson said, "They make the best french fries you ever tasted."

Mona found that she was hungry after all and pitched into her meal. She listened enthusiastically as he described what was happening at the Vine, and she said wistfully, "I bet it's beautiful there now."

"Yes, it always is in those hills. I was down at the creek the other day and found myself wishing you were there with me."

Mona managed to keep her mouth from dropping open in surprise. "Did you really, Tom?"

"Why, of course; I thought you'd know that!"

And just how would I have known that? she thought, but said nothing. They talked for a long time, and it was growing late. "I've got to be alone for a while, Tom. I've got a decision to make."

"That's hard work sometimes."

She said, "I want to tell you about it. It's too busy here. Come on to my place?"

Forty-five minutes later they arrived at Mona's apartment. Tom looked around and said, "Nice place." He saw her bookshelf, walked over, and studied the titles. "Have you read all these?"

"Well, I've read all of some of them and none of some of them and part of some of them." Mona smiled.

"Did you ever read any of them twice?"

"Oh, yes! My favorites."

"Who was it that said, 'An illiterate man is one who reads a book only once'?" He saw a book lying on the table and went over to pick it up. He ruffled through it and said, "What about this one, *Bride of Quietness*. Is it a oncer?"

"Oh, it's a great book, Tom! Have you read it?"

"Yes."

"What did you think of it?"

"Oh, it has its faults."

"Don't be like that," Mona said. "What did you really

think of it?" Then without waiting, she said, "I thought it was one of the finest novels I've ever read. Adam wants to do a movie of it, but nobody can find the author."

"I don't like movies made from books. I don't know a single one that was better than the book itself."

"This one could at least be as good. Adam and Aunt Lylah want to do it." She hesitated and said, "I think they'd give me a chance at the starring role."

This caught Henderson's attention. He studied her carefully and said, "You wouldn't be a bad choice. You're a lot like Helen in the book."

Startled, Mona said, "You don't really think that?"

"Once my dad told about a fellow who brought a young woman home that he had just married, and she was really homely. His dad got him alone and said, 'Son, she's not very pretty.' And the son said, 'Well, beauty's only skin deep.'" Henderson's eyes crinkled and humor came to his eyes. "The old man said, 'Let's skin 'er!'"

Mona laughed uncomfortably. "You're crazy, Tom. What is that story supposed to mean?"

Henderson grew very serious. "I think deep down you're like the heroine of this book, so deep down that it's hard to recognize, but it's there. Good and sweet and honest, everything a woman ought to be."

"Do you really think that, Tom?"

He shrugged and said, "I wouldn't have said it if I didn't, but—I'd have to skin you to get at it."

Mona felt hurt by what he'd said in such a matter-of-fact manner, but he obviously didn't see that she might be.

"Now, what's the problem? What's the decision you can't make?" he asked.

She put the hurt feelings away, and she told him about the film, about how unhappy she was with it. When he inquired into the nature of it, he said, "No wonder you don't like it. That's not a good woman you're portraying. The film, to me, doesn't seem to have anything that would help people."

They talked for two more hours, and finally Tom stood up to leave and said, "We all have to make our own choices. Richard's made his, and I think he's made a good one. I'm no preacher, but maybe you ought to listen to Richard and your Uncle Owen. Well, it's late, and I better say good night."

"Where are you staying? Give me your phone number. Can you have lunch with my brother Stephen and me tomorrow? He's in town on business."

Henderson hesitated, and at first she thought he meant to refuse, but he said, "I'm at a little fleabag called the Majestic." He grinned broadly. "It's not very majestic, I might say. It's over on Twenty-eighth Street. I guess it's in the phone book. I'm in room 211."

"Meet me tomorrow at noon at the studio. I'll get Stephen to meet us and we'll go out somewhere. I'd like for you to know my family."

"Why would you like that?"

She came over and touched his chest, pushing it gently. "I don't know. I just would."

"All right," he said. He took her hand, studied it, then squeezed it and said, "See you tomorrow at noon."

The lunch with Stephen was not as much fun as going to McDonald's. They went to a fancy restaurant, at Stephen's insistence, and Mona knew that her brother was amused at Henderson's T-shirt, jeans, and half-boots. They sat down, and Stephen ordered for all of them without asking, saying, "I know this place. Trust me."

Mona said, "Tom, tell Stephen about Richard's decision." She watched Stephen's face as Tom briefly outlined Richard's decision to go into the ministry, and she saw that he was not impressed.

"I'm sorry to hear that. He seems like a bright young fella. He could do well at anything he tried."

"I think he'll do well at what he's trying," Henderson said. He picked up his glass of water, sipped at it, and said, "He's happier now than he was when he came. He was pretty fragmented from the war."

"Well, he's had time to get over that." Stephen looked very successful. He was wearing the latest fashion in men's suits, and it did *not* come off the rack at Sears & Roebuck. "Tell me about this place you run, the Vine," he demanded. He listened for a while then interrupted Tom in midsentence. He shook his head. "Sounds like you need a little business advice," he said. "You're just barely scraping by there. Look, there's no point in that. We could put that place on a business basis. Throw some money into it. Get some tractors out there. You need to have a business that pays."

Tom listened, his sleepy-looking eyes fastened on Stephen as if trying to read him. He glanced at Mona and saw that she was watching him carefully. Stephen said, "What about it? I can get the cash, and we can make a successful business out of that place."

"Thanks a lot, Stephen, but most of us were in business some way or other before we arrived there." He smiled wryly and said, "And most of us were mangled by it. That's what the folks are like who come there. We've been cut up by the world, so we're not really interested in getting back into that sort of thing."

Stephen was offended. His lips grew tight, and he shrugged. "Well, if that's the way you feel about it, that's all there is to be said." He changed the subject, asking, "What are you doing in L.A.?"

"Came to help another mangled victim, somebody else who got caught up in the machinery."

Stephen stared at him as if he had discovered some sort of fault. He glanced at Mona and said nothing. It was a strained meal after that, and when it was over, Stephen paid the bill, put down a large tip, and said, "I've got a meeting. Can I drop you anywhere?"

"I've got my errand to run." Tom stood and put his hand

out. "I know you want to help, and I appreciate it. It was kind of you."

Stephen was mollified by the words. "Well, anytime I can help, let me know. And you tell Richard that I'm pulling for him."

Mona rose and hugged Stephen, saying, "I'll call you later, maybe tomorrow."

When they left the restaurant, Mona said, "I still haven't made my decision whether to go on with the movie or not." She hesitated then said, "Could I go with you on your errand?"

Henderson shook his head slightly, saying, "It won't be much fun for you, Mona. But come along if you like."

The taxi took them to a part of Los Angeles that Mona did not know. The businesses were dingy, run-down. There were many bars, hock shops, and dilapidated hotels. She said nothing, but when the cab driver pulled up in front of a tenement with several broken windows, she began to question whether she should have come. After Tom paid the driver, they walked up to the front door. Half a dozen youngsters were playing there, most of them under six, and they seemed to have no one watching them. Their enormous brown eyes watched the strangers, reminding Mona of wild animals alerted at danger. Tom knocked on the door, and a large woman with hard brown eyes and hair growing gray said, "What is it?"

"I'm looking for Carmen Rio."

"She's upstairs. Second door to the right."

Mona followed Tom into the dark hallway. There was the smell of cabbage and grease and bodies not thoroughly washed and decay. The stairs gave under their weight, and when they came to the door, Tom knocked. A small man, wearing a dirty white undershirt, faded trousers, and no shoes, opened the door and peered at them, saying in a heavily accented voice, "What you want?"

"I'm looking for Carmen Rio."

"What you want with her?"

"A friend of mine asked me to look in on her. He thought I might be able to help her. Is she here?"

The man hesitated then said, "Sí. You come in."

The two entered and saw a room cluttered with cast-off furniture. An old couch with broken springs and a faded orange cover sat against one wall, with a battered coffee table in front of it. Along another wall, two double-decked bunk beds were fastened, and from two of the beds, which had flat pads for mattresses and ragged blankets, small children looked out, like owls from a tree. A doorway led into a kitchen. The man said, "My name is Manuel Gonzales. I will get Carmen for you." He disappeared into the kitchen, and the sound of voices could be heard.

A young woman emerged, no more than twenty-five, Mona judged. A small girl was hanging to her skirt, and a boy of about six, wearing only a pair of shorts, followed her, his eyes carefully watching the visitors. "I'm Carmen Rio," the woman said. She was not tall, but her figure was well formed, as revealed by the thin cotton dress she wore. The dress had been washed until it had little color left. Carmen's hair, tied at the nape of her neck, was black and fell almost to her waist and had a lustrous glow to it. Her dark eyes studied the strangers. She was a very pretty woman, Mona saw, and if she had proper clothes and her hair and nails were cared for, she would be beautiful.

"My name's Tom Henderson. We've got a mutual friend, Juan DeSilva."

"You know Juan?"

"Yes, we've been friends a long time. He asked me to come and see you."

"What for?" The instant response was blunt, and Tom looked around and saw that the man had appeared in the kitchen with a heavy woman beside him. There were two more young people there, and it was apparent that they all shared these two rooms.

Henderson said, "Is there any place we could go have a cup of coffee?"

"There's a cafe half a block from here."

"Sounds good. Can we go there?"

"I have to keep my children."

"Why, bring them along. What are their names?"

"This is Consuela, and this is Enrique."

"This is Mona Stuart, a friend of mine."

For a moment the woman seemed about ready to refuse; then she shrugged wearily and said, "All right."

Tom turned to the little girl and knelt down so he could look her directly in the eyes. "I bet you're hungry. What would you like to eat, Consuela?"

Consuela stared at him, then buried her face in her mother's skirt. Tom laughed and said, "Well, you're shy, but you'll like me later on. What about you, Enrique? Are you hungry?"

Enrique looked up at his mother and said nothing. Henderson got up and said, "Well, let's go." He walked along talking about DeSilva, their mutual friend. "He's had a pretty hard time lately, but I think he'll pull out of it." He waited for Carmen to answer, but, sullenly, she said nothing.

The cafe was a dingy hole-in-the-wall, and Tom cheerfully said, "Looks like we're the only customers. We ought to get good service."

The proprietor greeted them with a smile and took them to a table, handing them several flyspecked menus. Mona noticed Carmen did not even look at hers. There was suspicion in Carmen's eyes, as if she had been deceived many times, and she kept her eyes fixed on the pair in front of her.

Tom gained the confidence of the children before long. Soon he ordered for Carmen and her children, explaining that he and Mona had just come from lunch, and when the food came, it didn't take any encouragement to get them to eat. Then Tom ordered pie all around, and Mona could not eat hers, but he said, "Well, I bet Enrique and I can take care of that." He cut it in two and shoved it to the boy, who had loosened up considerably. "Sí, it's good," he said.

Carmen said, "What is it you want with me?"

"I live in Arkansas; that's a state about in the middle of the country. I live on a farm we call the Vine," Tom said, speaking quietly. He told her of the Vine and what it did and how people came there who had no place else to go. He made no pleas but said, "If you'd like to go there, Carmen, there's a place for you. It won't be fancy, but there's good food and a place to sleep and work to do."

Her eyes were unfathomable. "Why are you doing this?"

Henderson shrugged. "I was badly hurt at one time. I needed to get away. Then I found that there were others like me. So I bought a piece of land, and we all work, and I know it must sound strange, but it's like a big family. Juan said you and your children are in trouble. He isn't in a position to help you, so he thought I might be able to."

Carmen was silent. Her dark eyes were fixed on Henderson's face. When he said no more, she put her hands on her children and drew them closer to her. "You would not want me. We are not American."

"If you want to come, you'll be welcome," Henderson said. "About being American—well, I guess you can become citizens if you want to."

"I'm Cubano. I would not fit in. I do not read or write English." Fear became obvious in her eyes. "And my children. I am afraid for them."

"I can't make you any guarantees, Carmen," Tom said quietly, "but if you come, you'll find people who will love you and accept you just as you are. Just exactly as you are. And the children will have enough to eat and a place to play and beds to sleep in, and Enrique can go to school." He did not urge her, but she began to ask many questions. It was obvious that she had a terrible fear of not being able to provide for her children. She said, "My husband was killed in a holdup. If he had been captured, he would have been in prison." She glanced down at her children and said, "He was a good man once, but he fell into the wrong company."

"Do you have any relatives here?"

"No. My parents are in Cuba. They're old. Manuel lets us stay with him, but it is very bad."

"I think you should come to the Vine, and if you don't like it, I'll bring you back."

Carmen suddenly turned to Mona. She had not spoken to this expensively dressed woman, but her eyes narrowed, and she asked, "Do you live there, too? At this place?"

"No. I live here in Los Angeles. I've visited there, though, and I think you'd like it. It's a nice place, with very kind people."

Carmen took a deep breath. "There's nothing here for me or my children. I have nothing to lose, but I do not believe I will be accepted outside the barrio."

Tom nodded, saying, "You'll just have to come with me and find out. When can you leave?"

A bitter smile touched the wide, full lips of the young woman. "Right now," she said bitterly. "It will only take a few minutes to gather our clothes."

"We'll have to stop at my hotel long enough for me to pick up my things, then we'll go to the bus station and take the next bus to your new home."

Tom and Mona stood on the sidewalk in front of the tenement while Carmen got her and the children's things together.

Something troubled Mona, and she came out with it. "She's very pretty, isn't she?"

"Yes, she is."

"Tom—be careful."

He turned to her with surprise. "Be careful of Carmen? Why, don't be foolish, Mona. I just want to help her and her children."

"She's a pretty woman, and you're a man. No man's a match for a woman in things like this."

Henderson turned his full attention on her. "I don't understand why you'd say a thing like that."

"She'll be there all the time," Mona tried to explain, "and you'll be there, and I know you get lonely at times."

Surprise came to him then. "I didn't know you saw that."

"You do, don't you?"

"Yes, I do. Very lonely, but there're always friends, and it's better than what I've had before."

"It would be like you to marry her out of pity, but she wouldn't suit you."

"Why are you saying these things, Mona?"

"I don't want you to be hurt again, Tom. I don't know what hurt you so badly in the past, but I can see one thing. You're educated, and you love books and art and music. You keep it covered up with that rustic outfit of yours and the act you put on, but I know you better. Carmen could be a good wife for someone but not for you."

"Well, in that case, I'll keep my guard up."

He tried to laugh it off but saw that she was not smiling. "I will be careful. Loneliness makes people do odd things." He took her hand and held it, and surprise came to her eyes. "I get lonely for you." He lifted her hand to his lips, kissed it, and then looked at her and saw her shock. "It's nice that you're worried about me—but I'm worried about you. What about this picture?"

"I'm not going to do it."

He squeezed her hand and said, "I'm glad. I think that's a wise decision."

He summoned a cab for her. When she got in, he said, "Will you come back and visit?"

"If I can, Tom." She flushed slightly and said, "I didn't mean to interfere in your affairs. It's just that I wouldn't want anything bad to happen to you."

Henderson leaned in, kissed her on the cheek, and said, "That's nice, and I feel the same about you. Come to the Vine."

12

FALL OF A MAN

Richard felt uncomfortable around Laurel. He had a sense of obligation toward her—he knew that for the past year there had been something growing between them. And he couldn't find it in his heart to blame Johnny for the circumstances of his birth. But Richard had begun to think about the future. He was serious about becoming a preacher, and he didn't know what to do next. And what should he do about Laurel? A minister couldn't marry an unwed mother with an illegitimate son.

He put these concerns in a letter to Owen, and he'd gotten a response within a few days.

Dear Nephew,
 The questions you raise are important, and I wish I could come and talk to you face-to-face, but my schedule just won't allow that.
 I'll call you next Sunday afternoon at the home place at 3 o'clock. (I figure things will be quieter there than the place where you're staying.) In the meantime, read John 8:3–11. And pray for God's light.

Love,
Owen

Richard looked up the verses Owen suggested. They were about a woman brought to Jesus who had been caught in adultery. Was Owen suggesting that Richard disregard

173

Laurel's past? He had a couple of days to think about it before Sunday. And he took Owen's advice about praying, too.

The phone rang at exactly three o'clock. Logan and Anne had gone for a little stroll so Richard could have privacy.

"Hello."

"Howdy, Richard," said Owen's voice. "Glad you got my note. I'm sorry I couldn't come to see you just now, but I didn't want to wait a long time to talk about these things."

"Hello, Uncle Owen. I'm glad you called. I sure need your advice."

"Well, what did you think about what you read in John 3?"

"It sounds like you're saying I should forget about Laurel's past. Is that what you mean?"

"There's more to it. You dated some in high school, didn't you, Richard?"

"Yeah, some."

"Anyone serious?"

"Well, I went out with Annie Regan for about a year. It seemed pretty serious at the time. But I was only sixteen. It didn't mean anything. What are you driving at?"

"Now, I'm gonna get real personal with you, Richard. Be honest with yourself even if you don't want to tell me. Did you and this Annie Regan kiss much? Did you spend much time alone with her?"

Richard flushed even though no one was there to see. "Well—yeah, I guess."

"Did you ever feel like maybe the two of you got a little too intimate—like you went a little too far?"

Richard was silent.

"If that happened to you, maybe you can put yourself in Laurel's situation. Maybe things just went a little too far."

"But it's up to a girl to make a guy stop, isn't it? Annie sure stopped me. Laurel should have made her boyfriend stop."

"Did your daddy teach you that?"

Richard was silent again. Then he said, "No. He said a man has to control himself."

"See, Richard, girls are taught that it's up to them to say no because boys are just born more aggressive. But the truth is, it's up to both a girl and a boy to say no."

"So, it's as much her boyfriend's fault as it is Laurel's."

"Yes. And to my way of thinkin', in Laurel's case maybe even more his fault. Maybe that boyfriend was taking advantage of her loneliness. She thought she was his first girlfriend—maybe she was and maybe she wasn't. Or maybe he was lonely, too. Or maybe he didn't have a daddy who told him it was up to him to control himself."

"So it's not so simple, huh?"

"Maybe. Now think about John 8 again. Do you have your Bible there?"

"Yes."

"See where it says, in verse 7, 'He that is without sin among you, let him first cast a stone at her'? What do you think that means?"

"I think it means that even though I didn't sin in that way—but maybe not for lack of trying—I have sinned other ways, so I have no place pointing my finger at Laurel."

"I think you've got it, boy."

"But Uncle Owen, does that mean I should marry her?"

"You have to decide if you really want to marry her. You haven't been in too much of a hurry, it seems to me. Do you love her?"

"Well, yes, but what about being a preacher? If I marry Laurel I can't be in the ministry, can I?"

"Richard, there's all kinds of people and all kinds of preachin'. Seems like maybe you need to think about if there's people that wouldn't care if Laurel had a baby out of wedlock."

"Who wouldn't care?"

"You're a smart boy. You think about it. And what about Bible school. You think about that?"

"You didn't go to school."

"No, but times are changin'. When I started preachin' most people didn't have any more education than I did. There's a school in Chicago you might think about. I'll send you some stuff I've got that tells about it. And it'd be nice if you was there near your grandma and grandpa."

"You've given me a lot to think about, Uncle Owen."

"Good! It's good for a young man to think. Keep in touch. Tell me where your thinkin' leads you. And keep on prayin' like I told you. Good-bye, Richard. Tell Logan and Anne I'll talk to 'em soon."

"Good-bye, Uncle Owen."

Richard sat quietly after he hung up the telephone.

He had supper with Logan and Anne, and when he returned to the Vine that evening, he was a bit warmer to Laurel than he had been since she'd told him about her past. She looked at him in cold surprise and turned and walked away. *Looks like I've got some making up to do*, he thought. *But I've got to sort this all out first.*

Vaguely aware that the phone was ringing, Mona climbed out of the black pit of sleep into the twilight zone of semi-consciousness. "All right. All right," she muttered. She groped for the phone, picked it up, and fell back on the pillow. "Hello?" she said, her voice slurry with fatigue. It was her father's voice.

"Mona?"

"Yes, Dad. Is something wrong?"

"Bad news, honey."

"What's wrong? Is it Mom?"

"It's Stephen."

"Is he sick?"

"No, Daughter, he's not sick or hurt. He's been indicted for fraud."

Mona sat straight up in bed and cried, "Oh, no! It can't be true!"

"I think it's pretty straight, Mona. I just wanted you to know before you heard it from somebody else."

"I'll come right away, Daddy. Is Mom okay?"

"We're holdin' up. Do what you need to do, Mona."

Mona held the phone tight and whispered, "Okay. I'll see you soon."

He answered, "I love you, Daughter." The phone clicked and Mona put it back on its cradle, then she leaped out of bed trying to think what she had to do.

Pete and Leslie met her at the airport.

"Hello, Daughter," Pete said and put his arms around her and took her kiss on his cheek.

She hugged and kissed her mother, whose face was stiff with strain.

"Have you talked to him, Dad?"

"Yes."

Her father's reply was bleak, and that single word told Mona a great deal. "What does he say? How in the world could it have happened?"

"He says it's not his fault. He was in a deal with some other men, and he claims they maneuvered him into this."

"Dad, he couldn't have done it, could he?"

Peter took her arm and Leslie's and said, "Come on, let's get out of here." He did not speak until they had gotten Mona's luggage and were in the car, and then he began to tell her the details, as he understood the case against Stephen. There was little hope in his voice, and Mona felt fear touch her spine. "Dad, he couldn't go to jail, could he?"

"Yes, he could. As a matter of fact, from what the lawyer says, there's not much hope of anything less."

"It's hit us pretty hard, Mona," her mother said quietly. "It looks like we'll lose the business, but we're hoping we can keep the house."

Mona felt horrified. She hadn't considered that her parents might be at risk. She suddenly saw how old they were. They had worked hard all their lives building their business and providing for themselves and their children. And to lose it now—and because their son was in some crooked deal. She felt some of their grief and shock.

Mona went to see Stephen that afternoon, but the interview was terrible. He'd been drinking and kept casting blame on the other men involved. Mona tried to find out the details but with little success. She ended up nearly screaming at him for what he was doing to their parents. Before she left, he said, "Don't worry. I got a good lawyer. I'll beat it."

"It might not work that way, Stephen," Mona said icily.

"Sure it will, Sis." Stephen's confidence was a veneer. When Mona saw that he was afraid, she put her arms around him and held him tightly. She could not keep the tears back, and she whispered, "I'll be praying for you, Stephen."

Mona and her parents endured the long trial, which was so complicated that they understood very little of the details. Apparently Stephen had falsified financial statements to the Securities and Exchange Commission, failing to accurately report his own transactions—and profits—as required by law. He'd improperly used "inside" information. SEC investigators had uncovered these violations when they pursued a complaint by one of Stephen's former business associates.

By the first day of the trial, Stephen had recovered his self-assured manner. He entered wearing one of his expensive suits, smiling and looking rather cocky—even Mona thought so. But by the end of that day, he appeared pale and shaken. The government investigators presented document after document—boring in their details but clearly showing his deliberate duplicity. After three days of testimony by investigators and by two of his business associates, the jury deliberated over a weekend and brought in a guilty verdict. Sentencing was the same day—confiscation of all the assets held by his companies, in payment of the fines, and ten years in a federal penitentiary.

Mona felt turned to stone. She saw that Stephen's face was twisted with rage. Her parents went to him, and he received their consolation coldly, not moving, not putting his arms around them, enduring their embraces. Mona's heart was breaking. Her father was weeping, and her mother looked as if she might faint.

Mona went, just before Stephen was led away, and put her arms around him. He was stiff and unyielding. "Don't worry about me, Sis," he said. "I'll get out, and they won't catch me again. I'll be smarter next time."

"Oh, Stephen," Mona whispered, but then the guard was there, and her brother disappeared, his back erect and anger written in every line of his body.

Part 3

CHANGING TIMES

13

YE MUST BE BORN AGAIN

Reverend Harlan Crabtree came asking for Richard, and when the young man came out, the two shook hands. The minister said without preamble, "Richard, I want you to preach Sunday morning."

Dusk had begun to fall, and the swallows were making their swooping, wheeling turns in the gathering darkness. For a moment Richard thought he had misunderstood the man. "Preach? You mean this *coming* Sunday?"

Crabtree stood on the porch smiling. He'd left the motor running on his ancient Oldsmobile coupe. He said reassuringly, "I think it's time, Richard."

"But I don't even know how to put a sermon together! I haven't been to Bible school."

"I don't suppose Elijah went to Bible school," Crabtree said dryly. "I think this is important for you, Richard—and don't worry about the sermon. Nobody expects a Billy Graham message for a first-time sermon from a young man. One thing you'll want to do is give your testimony, how God has dealt with you throughout your life. Then anything else you'd care to add—why, we'll just look on it as a bonus."

Richard moved his feet uneasily and twisted his shoulders. "I–I'm not sure that it's time."

"I think it is. I been praying about it some time, and the impression came very strong this morning in my quiet time." He put his hand on the young man's shoulder, squeezed it, and said, "All right. Can I count on you?"

183

"Well, if you think so, Brother Crabtree. I'll do it, but don't expect too much."

When Tom stopped by the Stuart farm, he found Logan and Mona engaged in a game of checkers. After they invited him in and offered him a glass of tea, which he accepted, he sat down and watched them for a while. It amused him to see that Logan took checkers seriously.

"I got a reputation to maintain," Logan growled and slammed a checker down in a triple jump.

"You're too good for me," Mona commented. "I give up." She had returned to Arkansas to recuperate from the emotional aftermath of Stephen's trial and to see Tom. The home place was an infirmary at present, for Anne had recently succumbed to pneumonia, and Logan was grieving her death.

Logan stood to his feet, stretched his back, nodded. "You entertain Tom. I gotta go out and feed the cows."

After the old man left, Tom said, "I came to invite you to church Sunday."

Mona was surprised, and she hesitated. "I don't go to church much."

"I think you'll like it this Sunday. The minister will be a relative of yours."

Looking up with surprise, she asked, "Uncle Owen's coming?"

"No, another relative. Richard's going to preach. He told me this morning."

Mona smiled and laced her fingers together, then stretched. "I *would* like to hear that."

"Service starts at eleven. I'll pick you up at ten thirty." He rose, then hesitated. "Feel like going for a walk?"

They took the path towards Logan's pond. "Any decisions yet?" he asked.

"Oh, I don't know, Tom," Mona shrugged. She was wearing a pair of worn jodhpurs and a white silk blouse, with a navy blue silk scarf tied around her neck. She ran her hand through her hair. "Life's passing me by. I'm getting to be an old woman. Pretty soon I won't be able to play anything but character roles."

They stopped at a wood fence and leaned on it as they talked. "You're not old," he said. He reached over and touched her cheek. She looked up at him, blinking with surprise. "You've got the complexion of an eighteen-year-old."

He drew his hand back as if a thought had come to him, and she demanded instantly, "What is it, Tom?"

"Nothing."

Mona studied his face carefully. "I don't know what it is with you," she murmured. "At times you just go into a room and slam a door and hang a sign out, No trespassing! Keep out!"

Surprised, Henderson lifted his eyes. "I didn't mean to show that to you."

"Sometimes it helps to talk about things."

An ivory-billed woodpecker lit on a tall pine forty feet away and began drilling a hole, looking for the grubs within. Henderson watched it for a while, seeming not to have heard her. Then he turned to her abruptly. "I guess I do hide from people. I told you once I was battered by life, and part of it was my wife."

"You have a–a wife?" Mona found this hard to say. She had thought it strange that a man as attractive as Tom would not be married, but since he had never spoken of a family, she had assumed he was not.

He looked at her, and his lips grew tight. "I did have," he said, his voice brittle as glass. "I had a good friend, too." He said no more, but something in the stillness of his face and the stiffness of his back spoke to Mona.

"You mean they betrayed you?"

"Yes. They ran off together."

"Did they marry?"

"No. They meant to—but they were both killed in an automobile accident two months after they left."

Silence filled the summer air. A flock of red-winged black-birds argued noisily as they fluttered down into a field. Mona did not speak for some time, but then she moved closer and leaned against his arm. "I'm sorry," she whispered. "I know it hurts."

"It was some time ago," he said stiffly.

"But the echoes are still inside you."

Henderson turned to face her. Her lips were slightly parted, and there was compassion in her fine eyes. "You're an understanding woman, Mona," he said. He leaned forward and gave her what he intended to be a simple kiss, but the softness of her lips under his drew him. He reached out and drew her to him. He savored the wild taste of her lips for a moment, then he drew back. "I guess," he said quietly, "that was my confession."

Again Mona said, "I'm sorry, Tom."

"We'd better get back," he said—and it was to Mona as if the door had slammed shut. "I have to get home. Dinner will be ready."

On Sunday, they walked in to a full church. "Carmen's got a seat for us," Tom whispered. They moved down the aisle, and Mona was conscious of the stares she got from people. To them she was a strange, exotic species from Los Angeles, a movie actress. She saw suspicion in some of the faces, but she merely smiled and took her seat beside Tom. He sat next to Carmen, who was wearing a bright multicolored dress made out of a thin gauze material that clung to her shapely body. It was too showy for church, but Tom knew she'd spent a lot of time picking it out.

"A new dress. It looks nice," he said. "And the kids got new clothes, too."

"I guess we're celebrating." She turned and smiled at him. She had full lips and very white teeth, and her liquid brown eyes were large and lustrous. Her eyes slipped over to Mona, who greeted her. "Hello, Carmen."

Carmen merely nodded, and then the service started.

Richard was sitting in one of the two chairs on the platform. His eyes went over the congregation, and he braced his feet against the floor, sweat popping out on his forehead. He knew many of those packed into the little church, but still this was new territory for him. He thought, *I didn't get this scared in Korea when the shooting started!*

After the preliminaries, Brother Crabtree rose to say, "I know we're all praying for our young brother Richard Stuart. He's given his life over to God, and I've asked him to come this morning and share his testimony and tell us anything that's on his heart. Brother Stuart?"

Richard got up and moved stiffly to the pulpit. He fumbled with his Bible for a time until he found his text. He breathed a quick prayer, and he got a wink of encouragement and a nod from Logan. This settled him somewhat, and he began by saying, "I hope you didn't come to hear a polished sermon because you won't get it."

A fly appeared, buzzing around his head, and he brushed it away, then steadied himself and said, "I want to tell you what my life has been, for a few moments anyway. . . ." He briefly told the story of his youth and referred to his service in Korea, of which he said, "Every day men died over there, and I often think of them going out to meet God. I wish," he said slowly, "that I had been more faithful in my witness for Jesus, because, as the Scripture says, we are watchmen and are sent to warn those who do not know the Lord.

"God has called me to preach, and he's got a big job to do to use me, but I know God can use some mighty crooked sticks." Laughter went around and, encouraged, he said, "Now, that's the testimony. The sermon is one you've heard probably a hundred times, those of you who know the Lord and have served in this church for many years. Every evangelist that comes preaches it. The pastor preaches this message constantly. I take my text this morning from the third chapter of John. What verse do you think I will center on?"

Laurel was startled when four-year-old Johnny piped up, "I know, Richard—John 3:16."

Laughter went around again, and Richard laughed with them. "That's right, Johnny—John 3:16. I believe you could all say it with me. 'For God so loved the world, that he gave his only begotten Son, that whosoever believeth in him should not perish, but have everlasting life.'"

The sermon was very brief, lasting no longer than ten minutes, but as Richard spoke, something happened to Laurel. She had come eager to hear Richard preach, but she did not expect what happened. As he spoke of the love of Jesus, for the first time in her life, it came alive in her heart—the knowledge that Jesus Christ was not just someone in a book—he was different. Richard quoted another Scripture. "Ye must be born again." He had talked to her about this before, but it had puzzled her. Even now she did not understand it, but as he preached she lowered her head, unable to meet his eyes. Her heart began to constrict, and a terrible guilt came upon her. She was frightened and wanted to get up and leave but knew that she could not.

Richard said, "I want us all to stand, and we're going to sing a song that you know without your books. 'Just As I Am.' You know how it goes—

"Just as I am, without one plea,
But that Thy blood was shed for me,
And that Thou bidd'st me come to Thee,
O Lamb of God, I come! I come!

"As Billy Graham says, I'm going to ask you to get up out of your seats if you do not know Jesus. All Jesus requires is that you confess that you are a sinner. That's all, and look to him. Ask him to save you in the name of Jesus."

The choir began to sing and the congregation joined in. Mona felt very moved. She was shocked to see Laurel go forward, tears streaming down her face. Reverend Crabtree

met her, and he sat down with her on the front seat. He was
reading from his Bible to her, and Richard continued the
invitation through six choruses. Others went to the front,
and Mona thought, *There's something to all this!* A longing
rose in her, and she was aware that Tom, next to her, had
his head bowed and his lips were moving. The impulse
came to ask him to help, but she fought it down, and when
the service was over and they left together in his truck, she
said, "That was sweet, wasn't it? Laurel going forward to
pray."

Tom responded, "It does something to me to see someone
come to the Lord. Does it affect you that way?"

Mona could not answer. She could not meet his gaze as he
turned to look at her. Quickly she looked out the window and
shook her head, pressing her lips together.

"What's wrong, Mona?"

"I don't know, Tom. I feel so–so strange."

He said quietly, "I think the Lord is working on you."

"You sound like my father and mother."

"They're very wise people. You come from a great family."

"I guess I'm just the black sheep."

"We're all black sheep, as far as God's concerned."

He said no more, and she turned to him and said, "Tom, I
don't know what to do. I've got my career to think of. I've
worked hard to get to where I am. I can't just give it up!"

She expected him to argue, but he was quiet for a long
time. Then he said, "Mona, how many really happy people
do you know in the motion picture business?"

"Why, there's Aunt Lylah and Adam—" But then Mona
ran out of names. Most of the people in her profession were
unhappy, struggling to get to the top in a dog-eat-dog world,
caught up in a lifestyle that no one could really admire. She
did not answer further, and when he let her out, she said,
"Thanks for taking me to church, Tom."

"We'll do it again. That's a fine young preacher you've got
in your family." He drove away, and she watched the truck

until it disappeared down the road. When she went in the house it seemed too quiet, and as she took off her dress and put on her faded jodhpurs and a T-shirt, she was thinking of the expression on Laurel's face after the service. There had been a triumph there, and Mona Stuart, the movie star, envied her!

14

"WILL YOU FORGIVE ME?"

Laurel stooped over and picked up what looked to be a weed. "Oh, this is wonderful," she said. "I've looked everywhere for this!"

"What is it?"

"It's pepperwort," she replied, then stooped over to pick the plants, roots and all.

Bending over, Richard plucked some of the plants, asking, "What do you do with them?"

"Eat 'em! The roots are so good, real crisp and tasty." When she was satisfied, she glanced over at a clump of another sort of plant, saying, "Look, there's some checkerberry." She moved over and began to pull some nodding, waxlike flowers off a small plant, explaining, "You can boil these leaves and it makes a fine tea—better than store-bought."

"How do you know so much about plants?" Richard asked, dropping some of the stems into a small sack. As she bent to pull more of the plants, he thought how attractive a picture she made, for there was a grace in her movements that he found pleasing. She moved like a dancer, never jerky or awkwardly.

"Oh, my grandma taught me. She was an herb woman. People came from all over the hills to get her cures."

When Laurel had her basket full of various herbs and flowers, they started back toward the house. She was silent, and her brow was creased with thought.

Richard offered, "I've been doing a lot of thinking—about us."

"Oh, I didn't know there was an 'us.'" He could feel her anger.

"Of course there's an 'us.' You know there is."

She stopped in the path and turned to look him in the face. "Richard, you've made it clear that there is me and Johnny, and there's you. I'm sorry I wasn't married to his father when he was born. But I don't regret keeping that beautiful boy. After Joe was killed, his baby was all I had. Maybe it would have been best to give Johnny up—better for me, anyway. Maybe better for him. But I couldn't do it. I never wanted to give up my baby. I don't know how a mother could do that." She grew calmer. "I guess I have to look for a man who's big enough to forgive the past and love both me and my son. I think there's such a man. Tom says there is." She paused and he saw tears in her eyes. "I just haven't met him yet."

Richard had tears in his own eyes when he said, "I'm sorry I didn't take the news as you hoped I would, Laurel. I was shocked, and I felt confused, and I didn't reassure you like I should have. I'm ashamed of myself. I hope you can forgive me."

She was silent, so he continued. "I suddenly felt alive again, like I'd been dead, or half dead, at least, since I came back from Korea. What happened in church that morning changed everything. And it was the result of all that time of healing—healing my soul, my heart. And you were so much a part of that healing time. You listened when I talked, you cared even when I couldn't talk, even when I couldn't care. Can you forgive me, Laurel?"

Still she said nothing. He couldn't read her face.

"I talked to Uncle Owen about it. He gave me a lot to think about. And I've been reading and studying the Bible. This is what I think."

She still was quiet.

"Laurel, everybody does wrong—sins. And to God one sin is just as bad as any other. So you and I are the same—I had no right to think you having a baby out of wedlock was any

worse than anything I've done." He thought her face soft-
ened just a bit. "And as to you being a fit wife for a minister,
well—you're a healer, Laurel, a healer of people's souls.
You're kind—" he made bold to push her hair back from her
face, and she didn't pull away "—and sweet and caring." He
kissed her gently. "Will you forgive me, Laurel? I'm so sorry
I hurt you and made you feel disappointed and alone."

"I don't know, Richard. You're confusing me. I want to be
alone to think about it."

He smiled. "I love you," he said. "Will you marry me?"

"Yes."

Carmen looked over where Consuela and Enrique were
splashing in the creek. After lunch Tom had said, "Let's take
the kids out to the creek. It's too pretty a day to waste." Mona
had gone back to Hollywood in the middle of the week after
Richard preached, and Carmen felt relieved that she was
gone.

Consuela was five, and Enrique was seven. "They're growing up," Carmen said wistfully.

"Consuela's so kindhearted. And Enrique, he can't decide
whether he wants to be a star for the Yankees or fly airplanes.
And he's very protective of his little sister." Tom was reclining, watching the children fondly. He spoke for a long time
of Richard and of the service the previous Sunday. "I was glad
to see Laurel make her peace with God," he said.

Carmen murmured something. She felt uneasy, for she had
been raised a Catholic and did not understand the things that
went on. She said, "I do not understand this–this being born
again. I was baptized when I was a baby."

"You know that's not enough, Carmen. There's more to
serving God than baptism."

"Then why do you baptize and put people under the
water?" She had seen a baptism and had been highly impressed, although she pretended not to be.

"Oh, a baptism is just an announcement to the world that

a person belongs to Jesus Christ. That he or she is going to
serve God."

Carmen thought this over, and for some time she listened
as he spoke of the Lord. It was a side of him that she could
not touch. She called out, "You! Enrique and Consuela, it's
time to go."

After the usual complaints, they put their shoes on and
Enrique said, "Can we go down and see the new calf?"

"I suppose so, but then go straight to the house."

"They sure like animals, don't they?" Tom said. They had
brought a quilt out and were sitting on it. He turned to her
and said, "Are you happy, Carmen?"

Carmen watched the children disappear down the path.
She knew they would stay with the calf until she went after
them. She turned to him and studied his face carefully. "I am
content," she said. Then she added, "If it were not for you,
Tom, I do not know where the children and I would be." His
hair had fallen over his brow, and she reached out and pushed
it back from his face in a shy gesture. She let her hand linger
for a moment.

Tom felt startled. She put her arms around him and put
her head down on his chest. "I have never been able to thank
you," she whispered.

Tom was disturbed. He put his hands on her shoulders,
and she clung to him in a way that was not what he had expected. "Carmen," he said, "you don't have to thank me."

She lifted her face. She reached up, pulled his head down,
and her lips were soft and warm on his. She held him, and his
arms went around her, but gently, not with the passion she'd
looked for. He responded not to her sensuality but to her
love.

Tom pulled her close and spoke very quietly, "You're a
beautiful woman, Carmen, a good woman. But you know that
this isn't right for us. Have I done or said anything to mislead
you about that?"

"No–no." Tears started in her eyes.

"None of us knows if we'll find the love we look for. I think and I hope that you will. I know it's difficult, but in the meantime try to focus on those great kids and on the love of the people around you here, even though it isn't everything you want. It's something, something good—it makes your life better, just as your love for them—and for me—makes life better." He lifted her chin and looked directly into her eyes. "Try not to let wanting what you don't have ruin what you do have." He hugged her and released her, then he stood up and offered his hand and helped her up.

Carmen was puzzled. She knew there was some streak in this man that she had never touched, and she also knew that there was something in him that was not in her.

She studied his face. She had been prepared to surrender herself to him, but she saw that such a thing would not happen. "All right, Tom," she said. Then she bent over and began picking up the quilt, adding, "We'd better go to the children."

15

A Fork in the Road

The prison was not as grim as Mona had feared. Perhaps she had seen too many old James Cagney and George Raft movies and expected something like Alcatraz or San Quentin—huge, cold blocks of stone, gray, cheerless, with all light shut out by stone, concrete, and steel.

When she got out of her car and stared across the parking lot, all she saw was a series of low, buff-colored buildings with high windows and low-pitched roofs. The November weather was cold, and she drew her coat around her and shivered. She noticed that flower beds surrounded the buildings, and she could imagine in the spring that the gay colors would lighten the mood. Walking across the asphalt toward the entrance of what appeared to be the main building, she had to stiffen her resolution. The thought of going in there frightened her. She shook her shoulders in a nervous motion, straightened her back, and walked toward the entrance. When she stepped inside, she was struck by the resemblance of the prison to a business office, for it was painted white, with desks lined along the walls, and men and women were busy at their office work. The only difference, she noted, was the blue uniforms that the personnel wore.

"May I help you, miss?"

Mona turned quickly to face a young woman who had come up behind her.

"Yes," she said. "I'm here to visit my brother, Stephen Stuart."

196

"Step right over here, and I'll get you started." The young woman smiled. She had a moon face, glowing skin, and was as pleasant as any clerk in a department store.

As Mona soon discovered, getting in to visit a prisoner was not quite as simple as if this were a hotel. She had to sign numerous forms and provide all the identification she had in her purse, but finally the preliminaries were over. "If you'll go right over there," the young woman nodded, "I'll have one of the guards take you to see your brother. You may have to wait for a time in the visitors' area."

"That'll be all right," Mona said quickly. "Thank you very much."

Rising from the plastic chair, she moved over and gave the guard the papers that the young woman had provided. "Right this way, ma'am." He led her through a doorway and down several halls. On their journey they passed guards and inmates, who did not wear stripes as Mona had halfway expected.

She was led into a large room with banks of green plastic chairs against the wall and around the three tables that were in the center of the room. "If you'll wait here, miss, I'll get your brother."

"Will we have to talk through glass?"

The guard laughed. "Why, no, ma'am. That's not the way it works here. This ain't a maximum security institution. No hard liners, really. You can talk with your brother right in here. Even have coffee if you'd like."

A feeling of relief washed over her, and she paced nervously waiting for the guard to return. She sat down and began to thumb through the dog-eared magazines that were scattered on top of an oak coffee table: *Popular Mechanics*, *Field and Stream*, *Cosmopolitan*, and several tracts from religious organizations.

She started when the door opened and came to her feet instantly. Stephen came in, and the guard withdrew and shut the door. At once, Mona went to him and put her arms around him, noting that he wore no uniform, rather a pair of jeans and a blue cotton T-shirt. "Stephen!" she said. He stood very still, and there was coldness in his expression. He did not respond to her embrace. She'd hoped that he'd be happy to see her. Stepping back, she said, "I'm glad to see you. You're looking well."

"Well, a vacation in a health resort does a lot for a man's appearance." Stephen's tawny hair was cut short, and his complexion was pale. Seeing her helplessness and embarrassment, he said, "Might as well sit down. Would you like some coffee?"

It was something to occupy her hands and her eyes. "Yes," she said eagerly.

Stephen walked over to the globular glass containers, picked one up by the plastic handle, and stared at it. "It looks like tar," he murmured. "Probably been here since yesterday." Nevertheless, he poured the black liquid into two Styrofoam cups, then asked, "You still take sugar and cream?"

"Yes, both please."

Stephen added the condiments and sat down across from her at one of the tables. He watched as she sipped the rank coffee, and a cynical grin touched his lips. "It's good, isn't it?"

"A little strong for me," Mona said, trying to smile. She put the cup down and twirled it with her hands, then lifted her eyes to him. "I'm sorry I haven't been here before, Stephen," she said.

"It doesn't matter."

His reply was clipped, and Mona nervously asked, "Mom and Dad have been here pretty often?"

"Pretty often. Dad comes more than she does. I don't think she's forgiven me."

"I don't think it's that, Stephen. She can't stand to see you here. It breaks her heart." Mona tried to find a subject of conversation. It sounded stupid to say, "How have you been?"

She said simply, "I don't know how to talk to you, Stephen. I've never been in an institution before."

"Well, this isn't a bad one," Stephen shrugged. "Not like some of the real tough ones down in Louisiana. I ought to be grateful."

Mona saw the misery in his eyes and said, "I'm so sorry. Is there anything you need? Can I give you money?"

She reached for her purse but was cut off sharply.

"You're not allowed to give me anything. Not even a book," he said. "You'll have to send it to me—but I really don't need anything, Mona."

"I don't understand sentencing," she said, putting the purse back. "You read about people getting sentenced to fifty years and then getting out in five years."

"It's a big joke but not very funny. I read in the papers," he said, keeping his eyes on his hands in front of him, "about a man in Memphis who killed a woman. They caught him standing over her with a smoking gun, and he could be out in a year if he gets any sentence at all."

"That's not fair."

"Now you've got it, Mona. Life's not fair! I hate to break it to you, but you'd find out sooner or later." As if he heard the harshness of his own voice, Stephen got up and stood over her. "There's no point in trying to make small talk in a place like this. What am I going to talk about? What we had for breakfast? Cold oatmeal and bacon that wasn't too fresh. What am I going to do this afternoon? The same thing I did yesterday afternoon. Go out in the yard and try to get a little exercise, read a book, work at a meaningless job." He clapped his hands together in an angry gesture. "Go on home, Mona! Get away from here! Don't think about me! There's nothing you can do!"

Mona snapped under all the stress of this awful place and seeing the brother she loved so unlike himself. She stood up and leaned toward him across the table "Sit down, Stephen! I came here to visit, and *I am going to visit!*"

The tension was broken. Stephen seemed to relax. He sat down again and managed his first real smile. "Well, go ahead and visit. James Dean died last month. How about that? All that money and fame—and now what good does it do him?"

Mona sat down and they talked about Dean. The young actor had been idolized by millions—and his untimely death had affected Stephen. Mona was surprised to discover that her brother had thoughts about life and death that she'd never known.

He changed the subject. "Tell me what's going on with the family." They talked steadily for an hour. They drained the coffeepot, a guard came in and made fresh coffee, and finally it was time for her to go.

"Don't give up hope, Stephen. You're young, and all the family's praying that you'll get out as soon as possible. You can start all over again."

His anger resurfaced. "Oh, sure. All of us criminals start all over again. Maybe I can start an import business—bringing in heroin from Hong Kong," he said bitterly. "Narcotics is a business with a big future."

"Don't give up," she pleaded. "I'll write the folks and tell them I've seen you. Isn't there anything I can give you or send to you?"

"Some books maybe." He forced a smile and said, "Thanks for coming, Mona. It was a break in the day. It really helped."

Mona came to him, put her arms around him, and kissed him on the cheek. She turned and knocked on the door. As it opened, she turned back to look. "Good-bye, Stephen. I'll be back soon."

"Good-bye, Sis."

She left the prison, got in her car, and struggled to keep the tears back. "He's lost everything," she said. "There's a deadness in him that I never saw in a human being." She thought back over the conversation and searched to find something she could do to make things easier.

Amos Stuart had occupied the same office at the newspaper for as long as anyone could remember. He had gone to work for Hearst as a young man and had risen steadily to become one of the best editorialists in the country. He had written half a dozen books and had been a frequent guest on radio and television programs, for his wit and quick mind made him an interesting interview. He had been a friend and confidant of presidents, beginning with Theodore Roosevelt, and his access to the White House was a priceless asset in his profession.

A hazy sun streamed in the window lighting up the gloomy corners of Amos's office, which had never been neat and in later years had grown disreputable. The walls were lined with books, the shelves double and sometimes triple stocked, with white edges of manuscripts and newspapers sticking out of every crevice. Even the tops of the bookshelves were cluttered, mostly with awards that he had won in his profession. Silence reigned in the room, and its single occupant sat in a rocking chair that had been made by his father out of stout white oak. The cushion was a patchwork covering filled with cotton and had been roughly sewn together by Amos himself. He said once, "I won the Pulitzer sitting in this chair thinking. I'm not about to get rid of it for one of those newfangled reclining outfits."

The sunlight fell full on the old man's face, picking out the seams and outlining the sunken cheeks. He had been a heavy man until two years ago, and then he had lost weight so rapidly that it alarmed his wife, Rose, and the rest of his family. He hated doctors and went only when practically threatened with a divorce action. He was dozing with his arm across his chest and his head nodding when a sudden stab of pain in his chest drew him up into an upright position. He groaned slightly, shut his eyes, and massaged his chest, noting at the same time that the fingers of his left hand were numb, as was that same forearm. He stared at the arm as if offended and muttered, "Here, this won't do!" in a voice of irritation.

A knock at the door pulled his attention away, and he took a deep breath carefully, for there was something in his chest that was very delicate, and he felt that if he moved too suddenly it would all break like fragile crystal.

"Come in! Don't beat the door down!"

Taylor, accustomed to his boss's irascibility, stepped in and moved around to take the chair opposite Amos's rocker. His sharp eyes at once picked out the pain in the old man's eyes, but he let nothing show in his own expression. He had been aware, as had everyone, that Stuart was not a well man. He also knew that Amos hated to be reminded of it, so he said cheerfully, "I got the dope on the opening of the Tappan Zee Bridge in New York. Do you want to read it?" He extended a sheaf of papers, but when Stuart shook his head, Jake shrugged and tossed them on the floor beside him. He began to speak of other aspects of his work, aware that Amos was paying little attention. He half rose to go but slumped back when Amos lifted his head and spoke to him. "What's going on between you and that granddaughter of mine?" he growled.

Jake grinned and shook his head. "Certainly not as much as I'd like for there to be going on," he answered. "Why? Has she been complaining all the way from London?"

"She's been talking to me." Amos leaned back and made a temple of his fingers and studied them for a moment. When he spoke again, his voice sounded frail and reedy, not at all like the husky bark that Taylor remembered when he had first come to work for the paper. "I've always been very close to Stephanie. She's a fine girl. I'd hate to see her ruin her life on some half-baked newspaperman."

"So would I." Taylor studied the older man carefully and then said, "You don't have to worry, Amos. I've already made my play, and she turned me down cold."

"Did she now? I wonder why that is, Jake."

"It's because I'm not a Christian."

"Then I'm not surprised she turned you down," Amos said. "She's been well brought up. What are you going to do about it?"

The question caught Taylor off guard, a difficult thing to do. "What do you mean, what am I going to do about it?"

Amos responded testily, "You got something against the English language, Jake? I mean exactly what I said. What are you going to do about it? I've known for a long time that you were in love with my granddaughter. Don't blame you a bit. Question is, how much do you love her?"

Shifting uncomfortably in his chair, Taylor thought about the question. "I'm not much on talking about things like this," he admitted, "but I've got the suspicion that I'll never love another one like her."

"If that's so, why don't you marry her?"

"I've already told you—"

"I know what you told me, and all you have to do is become a Christian."

Amos laughed at the blank expression on Jake's face. "If you're such a smart fella, I'm surprised you didn't figure that out for yourself." He leaned forward and said, "For years now I've been talking to you about what fools people are to ignore the most important thing in life. Has it all gone over your head? Didn't some of it find a lodging in that thick skull of yours?"

Amos's abrupt attitude amused Taylor. "You would have been a wonderful member of the Inquisition," he said. "Put a man on the rack and make him answer one way or another." Then he became more serious. "I know you think I'm an irreligious dog, Amos, but believe it or not I have paid attention to the things you said. As a matter of fact, I went out and bought a Bible." He smiled cynically, adding, "I keep it at home so none of my fellow workers will know what good ways I'm falling into."

The sun was a fraction lower now, and its beam struck Taylor's face, illuminating his craggy, scarred features. He was totally serious, and he was honest with Amos. He had been far away from God when he had first come to work for the *Examiner*, but Amos's fairness, steadiness, and apparent goodness, in spite of his gruff manner, had been the telling factor on Taylor. He had said little, but as Amos had spoken of his faith with him time and time again, it had sunk in. Then when he met other members of the Stuart family and found the same vein of rock-hard conviction about Jesus Christ, it had caused him to consider his own life. He had not been happy, though now he was moderately successful, the rising star of the paper, a sure bet to replace Amos when the old man retired. Taylor had spent many sleepless nights thumbing through the Bible and had gone to a few different churches, listening carefully to the sermons, trying to unite what he heard with his own hard-bitten creed of naturalism. He had learned growing up that the world was dog-eat-dog, but Jesus of Nazareth, as he appeared in the pages of the Bible, had shaken that resolution.

After a long silence, Taylor said, "It's hard for me to talk about things like this. Stephanie said I'm a sentimentalist, but I keep it covered over."

"Most men do that, Jake. But it takes a strong man to follow Jesus in these times. I think you're strong enough to do it, and to be truthful, I may not have many more of these talks with you, so I wanted to make it clear how I feel."

The words tilted Taylor's face up quickly, and for a moment he could not speak. He said awkwardly, "I lost my father when I was very young. You may not like this, but I've kind of put you in his place, in my own mind."

Amos opened his eyes wider, then he, too, smiled. "Well, I guess we're falling into sentimentality, but truth is, I've wanted to see a young man like you as a son. You'll be sitting in this office one day, and I want you to do it as a Christian.

Now, let's talk about how someone comes into the kingdom of God. . . ."

The phone rang, and Stephanie put down the toast she had been eating and reached across the table to pick up the receiver. "Hello."

Stephanie heard first the voice of the overseas operator, then her mother's voice. "Stephanie . . ."

Instantly she heard the note of fear in it. "What is it, Mom?" she said quickly.

"It's–it's Grandpa. He's had a heart attack," said Bonnie.

"Is he alive?"

"Yes, but he's in intensive care at Mercy Hospital. Your dad and I are leaving for the airport in a few minutes. Can you get to Chicago?"

"I'll get the next flight."

Twenty-four hours later, more weary than she'd ever been, Stephanie sat in a hospital hallway outside a door with a glass panel.

The elevator door opened, and Stephanie saw Jake get off. She rose and ran to him, and he caught her in his arms. "How is he?" Jake asked.

"Not good. He can only have one visitor every four hours. Grandma is with him now. Dad and Mom and Aunt Maury and Uncle Ted went to get something to eat." She trembled in his arms, and he led her over to the seat.

"What are they doing for him?" he asked. They sat down and he held her with one arm, his other hand pinioned by hers as she held to him desperately.

When she had finished the details, she looked up at him with tears filling her eyes. "We've been so close. He's such a wonderful man."

Jake's throat was full, and he found himself blinking back the tears. He cleared his throat, then whispered, "He'll pull through. He's a pretty tough old bird."

Jerry and the others returned and brought sandwiches with them for Rose and Stephanie.

When Rose's visiting time was up, she came out in the hall. "Mom," Jerry said, "Let me take you and Stephanie home for a while. She's beat and you need some rest, too. Maury will be here, and I'll come right back. We can call you if anything changes."

Jake said to Jerry, "I'll be glad to drive them, if you'd rather stay." So it was arranged. Jake took Rose and Stephanie to Rose's house, promising to pick them up again at six.

Stephanie dropped into an exhausted sleep immediately, and Rose lay quietly, crying at the thought that she might never again share this bed with her husband of so many years.

Back at the hospital that evening, Jake sat with Stephanie and her family for hours, and during that time his mind was absorbed with three concerns. He was worried about Amos, lying with tubes and electrodes fastened to him. He was concerned with Stephanie and with trying to comfort her when he knew he had no comfort to give. He had never felt so empty or so helpless. And his mind was on the conversation he'd had with Amos just two days before, about Jesus Christ. Jake had lain awake most of that night thinking about it and since news had come about Amos's heart attack, it had been an insistent beating in his brain, the pleas of Amos for him to turn his life over to God.

When another four hours had passed, Stephanie said, "You go see him this time," and when Rose nodded her agreement he went. He was shocked by the array of wires and tubes attached to the sick man, and when he looked down at Amos he thought with a start that he was dead, but Amos opened his eyes and whispered, "Hello, Jake."

Jake leaned over and put his hand on the thin shoulder. "You're all right, boss," he said. "You'll come out of this."

Amos lay quietly and then said, "Have you thought about what we talked about?" His eyes opened wider. "It would make me feel a lot better, Jake, if you would find God before I have to leave."

Jake suddenly knew that there was no other way. His own heart had inclined him to this, and with Amos looking up at him with a plea in his faded eyes, he made a decision. He was a man who knew how to make decisions and how to make them quickly and cleanly and sharply.

"Amos, I'll give my life to God right now. I'll follow Jesus Christ no matter what it costs." He bowed his head and began to pray, and when he had finished and opened his eyes, he saw Amos studying him and the old man said, "You're a man who knows how to be tough and to stand with what you decide." He was quiet for a moment, then he smiled and whispered, "Go tell Stephanie."

Stephanie looked up to see Jake coming through the door. She stood up and said, "How was he?"

"I can't tell. He doesn't look any better." Then he took her hands and said, "I can tell you one thing, though, I've made up my mind to obey God!"

Instantly Stephanie knew that this was a different Jake Taylor. Something about him had changed, and as he pulled her over to the bench and began to speak, her heart began to fill. When he finished, she saw the tears in his eyes and threw her arms around his neck. An attendant passed by and looked at them askance, then smiled and disappeared through the door.

16

THE FIRST LOSS

C layton Robbins was a tall man with warm brown eyes and a thick shock of brown hair badly in need of trimming. He had graduated from medical school at the top of his class, and insofar as technology, technique, and skill with the tools of his trade, there was no one better in the city of Chicago. He was, however, less certain and able when it came to giving bad news to the families of his patients. Always when it was necessary to give the sort of news that he had to give to Rose Stuart and her children, Dr. Robbins wished he was pumping gas or selling aluminum siding.

As soon as he stepped into the waiting area, his eyes fell on the family. He went at once to Rose, with whom he had talked several times. She was in her mid-seventies, he judged, and probably a very striking woman when she was young. She was still trim, and her hair was a beautiful silver. As cheerfully as he could, Robbins said, "Well, he's still holding his own."

Rose Stuart was not a woman easily fooled. She had studied the doctor's face as he had crossed the room, noting the effort he had to put forth to smile and the fact that he could not meet her eyes. "We want to know the truth, Dr. Robbins. Is he going to survive this?"

Nervously Robbins cleared his throat. He studied the woman's face, also the face of the tall, fine-looking man with the graying hair and green eyes. He remembered that this was Jerry, the son. The red-haired woman at Jerry's right was a daughter, but he could not think of her name for a moment. She was watching him carefully. He didn't recognize the other two women there with them, one in a wheelchair.

"These cases are always difficult." He wished that he was more of an actor. Still, it did not matter in the end. They had to know the truth. With his hands outspread he said, "It's not good news, Mrs. Stuart. The attack damaged the heart very severely. If you have other family, I would suggest that you send for them."

Jerry stood stock-still for a moment, feeling as if all the air had been sucked out of the room, and then he said, "Are you sure about that, Doctor?"

"I don't put things like this unless I'm very sure," Robbins said kindly. "I'm so sorry. I wish there was more we could do, but he's only hanging on by a thread now."

Rose's eyes closed, and her lips drew tight. She swayed slightly, and Jerry steadied her. His sister, Maury, came around and put her arm around her mother, saying nothing, but holding her and weeping. Rose opened her eyes and said evenly, "Thank you for your honesty, Doctor. We'll send for the rest of the family at once. Can I see him now?"

"Yes, you may see him any time you please, Mrs. Stuart." He hesitated, then put out his hand. When she put hers in it, he enclosed it with his other one and said earnestly, "I'm so very sorry. I wish there were more that I could do."

"You've been all that a doctor could be, and we thank you so much," Rose said. She turned to Jerry, who wrapped his arms around her, and they cried quietly. After a few moments, Jerry turned to Maury and said, "I'm going to get to a phone and call everyone. You go with Mom."

"Jerry, why don't you let me do that," said Lenora, dabbing at her eyes with a handkerchief. "Stay with your mom and dad as much as you can."

"I'll help you," said Christie. "Mario's waiting for me to call, then I'll call Lylah and Owen, and you can call Pete and Gavin and Logan—it'll be hard on him so soon after losing

Anne." Both women felt less overwhelmed by the impending loss when there was something they could do. Jerry kissed his aunts and thanked them.

Amos's heart was so fragile that the nurses and doctors kept a round-the-clock watch on the machinery and instruments that monitored him. One of the nurses rustling about in her starched uniform was a pretty young woman in her mid-twenties. She leaned over once and patted his cheek. "You're going to be fine, Mr. Stuart."

Amos, weak as he was, smiled at her and said, "I don't have many virtues, missy, but stubbornness is one of them. You can bet your big starched cap that I won't go to meet my Lord until I have seen all my brothers and sisters and my grandchildren."

The family began to arrive in Chicago at once. Mario, Christie's husband, reserved rooms at a nearby hotel, including one for his sister-in-law to rest in when she could. As they arrived, each sibling and each grandchild had a private visit, a chance to share final thoughts and words, a chance to say good-bye. It seemed to comfort them, and all of them marveled at the clarity of Amos's mind in spite of his physical weakness.

Rose began her vigil. She went into Amos's room and sat down. She took his frail hand in hers, and the two smiled at each other.

"I hate to leave you, Rose, but I think it's best," Amos whispered. He found the strength to squeeze her hand and added, "You were always tougher than I was. You can make it for a little while without me—but I couldn't make it without you, sweetheart."

Rose leaned over, kissed him on the cheek, and smoothed his hair back. "I won't be long," she said. "You never had to wait long for me, did you? It won't be any different this time."

"We've had a good time, haven't we, Rose," Amos said.

They spoke of their love for each other that had been the strongest thing, aside from their love for the Lord. They smiled again at old jokes and things that happened when they courted, at funny things the children had said when they were tykes. "I love to see you smile," he said.

Jerry and Maury each came in from time to time, not staying long for fear of weakening him more quickly. But sometime before first light, Amos indicated that he wanted them to stay. There were chairs brought in and they sat at one side of the bed, while Rose sat on the other, holding his hand.

The end came just as the sun rose and threw its beams across the bed. Amos turned, looked at the sun for a moment, then turned back to Rose, this woman he loved with all of his heart. "Sunrise," he said, his voice clear, and then he looked up and said, "Kiss me, Rosie."

Rose leaned over and kissed his lips, and when she lifted her head, she saw that his eyes were closed. His chest moved so slightly that she barely sensed it. She did not know when he actually went away, it was so easy. She leaned over again, kissed him, and whispered, "Good-bye, Husband—I'll see you very soon."

Lenora, Christie, and Mario made most of the arrangements, trying to keep things simple. But the public funeral in Chicago for Amos was big and busy and crowded. The huge church was full, for Amos had made many friends—and enemies—in his long life in that city. The seats were filled with judges, lawyers, politicians, and most of all with journalists. Editors, reporters, and anyone who cared about the profession of journalism were there.

Rose came in with the family after the building was filled. As she sat down, she turned to Jerry and whispered, "This would have amused your father. I know what he would have done."

Putting his arm around her, Jerry whispered, "What's that, Mother?"

"He would have made a speech telling them to give the best they have to their professions and to their families and encouraging them to do more, to be more honorable."

"I think you're right. He would have done a good job, too."

The funeral was long. There were many tributes, but finally it was all over. The family felt drained and dazed. Bonnie came and kissed her mother-in-law and said, "I know you're glad that's over, but it had to be. People wanted to show how they felt about Dad."

"Yes, and now we can take him home."

The family funeral was held in the small church only a couple of miles from Amos's birthplace. Although Amos had been away from the Ozarks since he was a young man, still the home place had been maintained, and Amos and Rose had come back many times. The church was filled with Stuarts and with a few farm families who were close to them. Reverend Crabtree knew there had been a fine and fancy funeral in Chicago, but Rose had told him plainly, "Amos would have wanted you to conduct the service as you see fit. He always had confidence in you, Brother Crabtree."

He led in singing several of Amos's favorite hymns. Then he stood behind the pulpit and looked over the congregation and said, "It is my privilege to make a few remarks about our brother Amos Stuart. I feel that there are others here—Owen Stuart, and now Richard Stuart, both ministers of the gospel—who could do a much better job, and I asked them to do so. They both declined, and I will say it was the first time I ever knew of Owen refusing a chance to have his say."

The minister smiled at the murmur of agreement that went over the congregation. Crabtree went on to make his remarks, which were brief and to the point. "He did better than that fellow with the doctor degree, I think," Gavin whispered.

"I think that minister had more degrees than he had temperature," Pete answered, grinning.

Crabtree said, "The Stuarts are a resolute family, and as some of you may know, it is their custom to come back to the hills every Christmas. They made this vow many years ago when they were young, and very few Christmases have passed when this family celebration has not occurred." Crabtree turned and smiled at Owen and said, "I believe you want to say a word about this, Owen."

Owen stood and turned to face the congregation. He was worn and tired from his years of bare-handed evangelism and with grief at his brother's death, but there was a light in his eyes as he said, "We have not lost our brother. When you lose something, . . ." he said in a ringing voice that carried without effort through the building. "When you lose something," he repeated, "you don't know where it is." And then he smiled, and his eyes were filled with joy. "But we know where Amos is. He's not lost, he's just gone ahead as he always did with his family. We will have a reunion with him someday. And we'll have our reunion here a few days early this year. The Delight Hotel is already filled with the smells of cooking. Soon there'll be singing and happiness as we gather around and rejoice in our family. We invite all of you dear friends to come and join us after the burial this afternoon," he said. Then he paused and laid his hand on Rose's shoulder, adding gently, "We will miss him, but we will see him soon!"

17

PRISON BLUES

The cold January wind struck Peter Stuart in the face as he stepped outside his car and turned to face the prison. He had come here every month, and it never got easier. When he crossed to the entrance and entered, he was greeted by name by a tall guard who smiled and said, "How are you, Mr. Stuart?"

"Fine, Tony. How's that little one of yours?"

"Growin' like a weed. You go right on over. I reckon your son will be glad to have a visit from you."

As Peter traveled the familiar path through the labyrinth of the prison and came to the visitors' room, he thought of what the guard had said and found it bitter as the memories of his previous visits. He had come as often as he was allowed, neglecting other things in order to show his concern for Stephen.

As he entered the familiar waiting room, with the same dog-eared magazines, the same green plastic chairs, a sense of despondency came over him. *If there was only something to fight, something I could do,* he thought. *But what can you do besides send small gifts and try to encourage a little?*

The door opened, and Stephen walked in. His face was still, without a flicker of response in his eyes, and he made no attempt to smile. "Hello, Dad," he said. Moving over to the coffeepot, he poured a cup, then turned and asked, "Would you like one?"

"That might be pretty good. It's cold outside."

214

"I suppose it is." There was a faint mockery in Stephen's tone. Peter had noticed that this was becoming more and more his attitude. A bitterness had been born in his son in this place. It had hardened him and taken away his sensitivities. As Pete studied Stephen, who came over and sat down, pushing one of the Styrofoam cups toward him, a moment's silence fell between the two.

"Not much to talk about, is there, Dad?"

Forcing himself to manifest a cheerfulness that he did not feel, Peter spoke about Amos's funeral and how different family members were coping.

"How's Mom?"

"Pretty well. She misses you, of course. She said she'll come next month. She can hardly bear to see this place and you in it, and especially in the winter, she says."

For just a moment a faint light that could have been pleasure showed in Stephen's eyes, but then he blinked and turned those eyes downward again. "I'd tell you about what's going on in here, but it would bore you to tears," he said.

Pete leaned toward him. "Is it so bad, Son?"

"Bad enough, but look at it this way. I've only got eight more years to go."

"Not that long," Peter protested. "With time off for good behavior—"

"You don't know how hard it is. Nobody does." A shadow seemed to fall over Stephen's face, hooding his eyes. "Yesterday I left a soap wrapper on the window sill. Just forgot to throw it away. Then the guard came along and gave me a demerit. That adds three months to my sentence." His lips twisted into a bitter smile and he said, "I never thought I'd see the day that I'd be licked by a soap wrapper."

Peter wanted to reach over and touch his son in some way, but he had learned that Stephen was quick to resent any overt signs of sympathy.

The visit limped along, and when the time was up, Peter

rose and went over, still unable to reach out. "Anything you need—books, cash?"

"No. Nothing. You don't have to come back so often, Dad. I know it's hard on you."

"Nonsense. I'll be coming every time I get a chance." He hesitated, never knowing how to end these meetings. There was a temptation simply to turn and walk away, but he did his best to smile, saying, "Don't give up, Son. God knows what we're going through, and he'll see us through it."

When God was mentioned, Stephen's face immediately turned hard. He did not respond except to say, "Good-bye, Dad. Tell Mom hello."

As Peter left the prison, the gloom in his spirit thickened. He walked with his head down, got into the car, and then put his head on the steering wheel and wept. He and Leslie had been worried about Stephen's materialism, his leaving God out of his life, but now it was so much worse. Peter had prayed until he knew no more words to say. He had said them all a hundred times, but still, he believed God, and as he calmed down and was ready to turn the key, he breathed up one prayer. "God, bring my son to know you; then all will be well."

Jerry and Bonnie returned to Chicago to help Rose with Amos's business affairs. Stephanie went too, wanting to spend a few days with them before returning to work in London. Jake stayed away deliberately, not wanting to intrude on the family's grief. He had been assigned to take Amos's duties at the *Examiner*, at least temporarily. He took Stephanie out to dinner shortly before she was to leave. They went to a quiet Chinese restaurant under the el.

"I see Daley won the election for mayor," said Stephanie.

"Yes, at least maybe he'll provide more unity in the city's politics."

Their conversation continued in this desultory manner for a while. Then Jake raised a more personal matter.

"Do you realize it's been three years since you turned me down?"

"Yes, Jake, I know."

"I'm still in love with you."

"Yes, I know that, too."

He waited for her to continue, but when she didn't, he said, "Do you still love me?"

"I don't believe I ever said I loved you."

"Well, you didn't deny it, either." When she just stared at him, expressionless, he felt a little off balance. But he proceeded to take a small velvet-covered box out of his pocket and put it on the table. "I know this isn't the time, so soon after Amos's death, but with you leaving again—I wanted to do this in person rather than by mail or telephone. Stephanie—"

She reached across the small table and put her finger over his lips to interrupt him. "Jake, I gave you two reasons why I wouldn't marry you. One is gone now, but the other is not. I still want to be an overseas correspondent. Matter of fact, when I return to London, it will only be for a couple of weeks. Then I'm going to Tangier."

"I haven't forgotten that second reason," he said, taking her hand. "But I've had a lot of time to think about that one, too. To be perfectly honest, I would like a so-called normal life, with the little woman at home every night waiting for me. And I would like to have kids, I think. But I've had the bad luck to fall madly, head-over-heels, lock, stock, and barrel in love with another woman—you. And I can't seem to fall out of love with you. So, will I be unhappy married to you? Maybe. But I'm miserable without you now, so unhappy is a step up."

She laughed and blotted her tears away with the back of her hand, then said, "Jake, I just don't see how we can work it out."

"Stephanie, will you marry me? Then we'll work out the details of how we're going to manage it."

"Put the ring away. I'll have to think about it. It seems terribly unfair to you—you don't get much out of it that you want. I can't believe you'll be content to live that way for long."

"Well, in the Bible it says that a husband should love his wife like Christ loved the church—that means sacrificing himself for her. Will you allow me, Stephanie Stuart, to do that for you?"

"Oh, so now you're quoting Scripture to me?" She paused. "I'll think about it."

Three months later, in a tiny Christian chapel outside Tangier, Morocco, Stephanie Stuart and Jake Taylor were married. Jake held Stephanie's warm, strong hand in his and from time to time looked into her eyes, repeating the ancient words, "Love . . . honor . . . with this ring . . . as long as we both shall live." He knew this living, vibrant, lovely woman beside him was more than all the words.

When the missionary performing the ceremony said, "You may kiss the bride," Jake turned to face her, lifted the short veil, and kissed her firmly and with ardor. As they left the chapel, Stephanie squeezed his arm and said, "Did you mean all of what you just said, Jake?"

"I meant every word of it. It just wasn't strong enough."

Jerry and Bonnie stood together reading the letter, their arms around one another. "Wasn't it only yesterday," Jerry whispered, looking at the wedding picture enclosed, "that we brought her home in that pink receiving blanket? And only the day before that that you and I were that young and in love?"

"I was never as lovely as Stephanie."

"Don't talk nonsense. She got all of her good looks from you." His brow furrowed, and she knew he was thinking of his little girl leaving the nest for good, but neither of them said a word about it. Instead Bonnie pulled at Jerry's arm and said, "Come on. Let's go wire them our congratulations."

18

A SURPRISE FOR MONA

Lawrence Sutton had a great deal of patience, but it was practically exhausted by the woman who sat across from him. She pressured him to reveal the address, or at least a clue, to the whereabouts of William Starr. Sutton was a gentlemanly man of English stock and looked like an English actor, with his clipped British mustache and his dark hair turning silver at the temples. He stared at Mona Stuart, who simply would not take no for an answer. He said with exasperation, "I'm very sorry, but I cannot tell you what I do not know! I would like to know more than anyone where William Starr is!"

"Does he have a contract to do another book, Mr. Sutton?"

Sutton's face dropped. "I played the fool there, Miss Stuart. No one else would touch *Bride of Quietness* until I saw the possibilities and bought it. I should have signed him up for half a dozen books. It was the biggest mistake I ever made in my career."

"And you haven't heard from him since he disappeared?"

"Not a word, and I've had people looking for him. They've gone to his hometown, but he has no people there. He had no brothers or sisters, and his parents died some years ago. His friends say they haven't heard from him. His royalty checks are deposited at a bank in Kentucky, near where he taught, and the bank absolutely will not tell us

219

where the money goes from there. Personally, I don't think he's in the country. Perhaps he's gone to Mexico, or who knows where."

Mona felt the keen edge of disappointment. But she said, "I'm going to keep on trying. Will you give me the name of the college where he taught? I'll go there next."

"Certainly. The more power to you. Would you care to become one of my agents? I'd be glad to pay you a handsome sum if you could get him to sign a contract to do another book—any book!"

"I wouldn't care to do that, Mr. Sutton." She rose and put out her hand and when he took it said, "Thank you for your help."

"Well, I haven't been any help, Miss Stuart." He released her hand and said, "Why are you so determined?" Then enlightenment came. "I know. You want to do a movie of *Bride of Quietness*."

"That's right."

"Well, so does every major producer and studio in Hollywood. It's a fine book, but I don't think you'll have much success."

"Perhaps not, but I must try."

Sutton escorted her to the door. He put his hand on it and started to say something and then broke off, for Mona was staring at a framed photograph on the wall. It was one of seven or eight, and she stood carefully examining it.

"That's a very old photograph of William Starr," Sutton said. "We didn't think it good enough to put on the jacket. It was a blowup made from a snapshot. He's probably the most unphotographed best-selling writer in the country. Maybe in the world."

Mona was staring at the photograph as if transfixed—it was the eyes that arrested her—the half-lidded look. She got as close to the picture as she could. It's true it was a poor photo. *No, it isn't—couldn't be,* she thought. "But—but," she muttered. She looked at Sutton, then back at the picture. *It's all in my mind. Because of my feelings I think every man I see looks like him.* It looked enough like Tom Henderson to be a son or a brother, though. Her mind was going in circles, for the man she saw was Henderson! A younger version, without a beard and looking very fresh and unlined, but it was him.

Actress that she was, Mona composed herself. "Thank you very much for your time," she said, without any explanation. She left the office and stopped outside the building, the bright sunlight causing her to blink. She leaned against the wall a moment and took a deep breath. Then she hailed a taxi and gave the name of her hotel. All the way through the busy streets she heard none of the angry clamor of the traffic or the shouts. She heard nothing, for her mind was grappling with what she'd learned.

He's buried himself in those hills, she thought. *It's like he killed William Starr, and there's another man.* She knew some of it. His broken marriage had no doubt embittered him. She knew, also, from what she had heard that he had grown sickened by the publishing business, the biddings, and the underhanded methods of many agents who had pursued him relentlessly. Publishers had been no different, and she had heard enough from Lawrence Sutton to know that for a sensitive man like—William Starr—as she must call him now in her mind, that would have been unthinkable.

As soon as she got to her hotel room, she picked up the phone, and when the airline answered, she said, "I want a ticket on the next flight to Fort Smith, Arkansas."

Mona made no pretense this time that her visit was to see her uncle Logan. She arrived late in the afternoon and spent the night. Logan was glad to see her, welcoming any company, and he talked enough so that Mona could simply smile and agree, adding a comment from time to time.

The next morning, she saddled Logan's horse and rode to the Vine. Tom was coming out of the barn when she rode in. She dismounted and walked toward him quickly, and when he saw her, his face lightened. He put down the buckets he was carrying and came at once to meet her, wiping his hands on a bandana, which he stuck into his back pocket.

Taking her hand, he held it for a moment, then said, "Come inside. Most everyone is still at breakfast. They'll be anxious to see you."

"No. Not this time, Tom. I have to talk to you alone."

Her seriousness brought a surprised look to Henderson's face. "What is it?"

"Can we go for a walk?"

"Why, of course." He offered his arm, and she walked along beside him. He gave her a curious look sideways from time to time and made a few remarks about what he had been doing on the place. They followed the path that ran along the edge of the woods to a pasture where some of the livestock grazed. A broken down section of rock fence ran close to the woods, and Tom asked, "Is this private enough, Mona?"

They sat down on a part of the fence that was still shaded by the woods from the morning sun. Mona had been wondering how to speak of her discovery. She finally discarded every approach except one. She lifted her eyes to Tom's face and asked, "You're William Starr, aren't you?"

For just an instant, his sleepy-looking eyes didn't look sleepy. He shrugged his shoulders. "I used to be. Well, that was my pen name. Now I'm just Tom Henderson."

"Will you tell me about it?"

Hesitation showed in him, but he said, "All right. It's a long story and not a happy one."

Mona listened as he struggled to tell her how he had come to give up a successful life, with everything that most people dreamed of, for a small farm in the Ozarks. His eyes revealed how deeply he felt about what he had done. "I couldn't stand that kind of life, and there was no escape from it. Everywhere agents, publishers—all calling, all wanting me to write another book."

"But didn't you want to write another book?"

"Of course I did, but I didn't want it butchered. It was just a commercial thing to most of them, and I thought it was more than that, Mona."

"It is more than that." Mona began telling him again how deeply moved she had been by *Bride of Quietness*.

Henderson listened carefully, but then he interrupted her. "You've come, Mona, because you want to make the book into a movie, and you want to be in it."

"Yes. That's why I came." Mona's answer was simple, and she made no apology. "I think it could be a great movie, not just a good movie. Adam has talked about it many times, that it needs to be available for those people who will never read a book but would go to see a film. Would you consider it, Tom? You don't know Adam, but you know the family. Adam would never do anything to harm your book."

"Maybe not intentionally," Henderson said, slowly, "but Hollywood has a way of ruining everything it touches."

His words raked across Mona's nerves, for it had been said to her before, by him and by others. She said resignedly, "I guess that's your final answer then."

"Why, it's final for today." He looked at her and noted the loveliness of her hair as it framed her face. She looked very young in the dapple sunlight under the trees, and he said quietly, "I don't know what tomorrow will bring. Nobody does."

She had said all she could. Her surrender touched him. He expected a battle, but he recognized her honesty and integrity in refusing to give one. She smiled at him and said nothing more.

A woman's silence may mean many things. He wondered what it meant in her. He was enticed by the mystery. It touched his own solitary thinking, and he felt a slowly rising excitement. She had the power to stir him, to deepen his hungers and his sense of loneliness.

She got to her feet, and he rose quickly. He asked, "Are you staying on for a while?"

"Do you want me to?"

The heat of something rash and timeless and thoughtless brushed them both. He opened his arms and she came to him. She put her arms around his neck as he embraced her, and she offered her lips. There was sweetness and richness and enjoyment of an intimacy they'd both longed for. When they released each other, Tom took a deep breath and said, "We're having venison stew for lunch. Will you stay?"

"Oh, yes. I'll stay."

Mona's visit was strange—at least to her. She saw Tom every day. She spent time with her uncle Logan. She listened to Richard preach in the church for Brother Crabtree, and for two weeks nothing changed.

She had come here to coerce Tom to do something, but she had discovered a softness and a gentleness in herself that would not permit her to do that. So her days passed in quiet contentment.

One blot marred her visit. After supper at the Vine one night, she went to the kitchen to help Carmen do the dishes. Mona felt a resistance in Carmen and with feminine wisdom knew what was troubling her. This was confirmed when Carmen faced her suddenly, her eyes narrowed to slits. "Leave him alone!" she whispered fiercely. "You have everything. When you come here, he's restless. You could have any man you want. Why do you have to come here for him?"

Mona knew there was nothing she could say. This young woman admired and revered and, seemingly, loved Tom. It was natural enough—he had come for her and for her children when nobody else cared. He had given them safety, had become a haven, and Tom himself, Mona realized, had become the symbol of all that Carmen longed for.

"I'm sorry, Carmen," she said quietly. She turned and walked away, knowing nothing else to say.

Later, when Tom spoke of Carmen, he seemed unaware of what was happening. He walked Mona to her car, and she made a tentative attempt to speak to the situation she saw developing.

"The kids are growing up. She's happy," Tom said.

"Are you sure about that?"

Henderson said nothing.

Mona continued. "I think she's a very lonely woman. She craves what most women want."

"I know she does," he said.

"She's a young woman. She wants a husband and a home. You know, don't you, that it's you she wants?"

"So what would you have me do, Mona? Throw her out because I don't want to marry her?"

"Well, no, but—"

"Sometimes you just have to give people time to work through their own emotions. I think she can't help what she feels."

"That makes sense," Mona conceded. He opened the car door and she got in.

"Love is a rare thing in this world. Shouldn't I value hers for me and love her in return, even if it's not the same? I don't think Jesus was afraid to let people love him."

She smiled. "I'll have to think about that." Mona didn't agree with him altogether, but she saw that he'd given the matter a lot of thought. "Good night, Tom."

He leaned in and kissed her. "Good night, Mona. Ride over in the morning. We'll go on a picnic."

Part 4
QUIET TIMES

19

OUT OF THE SILENCE

M ona sat down across from Irving Segal, one of the better-known producers in Hollywood. She felt nervous. At once he demanded, "Well, it's a great script, isn't it? I think it'll be big-time, Mona."

She hesitated for only a moment, then shook her head. "I think it's not for me, Mr. Segal."

Segal prided himself on casting his pictures well. He considered long before making a choice, and his temper slipped a little, for he had expected an instant acceptance. "I wouldn't have offered you the role unless I was convinced you can do it!"

"It's just not for me. I know you wouldn't want anyone in your picture who couldn't give it her best, and I just couldn't do that."

Segal was unaccustomed to people turning him down, and he glared at her. "You're getting pretty choosy, Miss Stuart! I've heard you turned down a picture for Hopkins over at RKO, one that turned out to be pretty hot stuff."

"Yes, I did."

Segal puffed angrily at his cigar, then said, "Big stars can afford to do that, but you can't. I'll give you one more chance. We'll say no more about it. Will you do it?"

Mona knew this decision would affect her future. She would never be asked again by Segal to do anything, and word would get around, just like it had gotten around to him about the RKO deal. But the script seemed to her a tawdry thing without any significance at all. It was full of not-so-subtle sexual allusions and guns and noise, and nothing in it appealed to her. She got to her feet and smiled, saying graciously, "It was kind of you to think of me, Mr. Segal, but I just can't do it." She felt his anger strike against her, and when he grunted and sat down and began going through papers without giving her another look, she turned and walked out of the office. Her knees felt slightly weak. Instead of taking a cab back to her apartment, she began to walk.

She searched the faces she met and saw several pretty young women—there seemed to be a superabundance of them in Hollywood—and she thought, *Any one of these would give anything to have a chance like I just turned down. What's wrong with me?* She walked until she grew tired, then went back to her apartment. It was a period in her life when she could not reason clearly. Her thoughts went to Tom Henderson, and she knew that if he were here he would tell her something about the way she was acting. She thought about her life and, once more, was not pleased. She shook her shoulders angrily and muttered, "Mona, you've got to get over this!"

But she did not get over it. There was a hunger in her that she could not identify, a sadness that would rise in her every time she grew still, and, in desperation, she made a decision.

Mona had not been intimately acquainted with her aunt Lenora, but for years, at the family reunions, she had made it a point to spend time with this aunt. Though Lenora was confined to a wheelchair, she had worked tirelessly for the Salvation Army and had more life in her than almost anyone Mona knew. Something about the silver-haired woman drew her. How could a woman who had never had a so-called normal life be so filled with joy?

"You'll have to come to Chicago and spend some time with me," Lenora said every Christmas. At the last reunion there had been something more pressing than usual about her invitation. Her sharp, hazel eyes had held Mona's, and the younger woman had the idea that her whole personality was exposed to Lenora.

"I've got to talk to *somebody*." She located the number and called, and after warm encouragement from Lenora to come, she thought, *I must be losing my mind going to see a Salvation Army lassie—but I can't talk to anyone else, and I've got to have some help.*

Mona arrived at the Salvation Army headquarters in Chicago, and she was shown to Lenora's office. The colonel, as Lenora was called, was in a modern office with every kind of up-to-date equipment surrounding her. When Mona entered, Lenora gasped and said, "Look at you!"

As soon as the door closed, Lenora wheeled herself around and came over and lifted her arms. "Give me a good Hollywood kiss," she said. She took Mona's kiss on her cheek and said, "Now, are you hungry? Do you want lunch?"

"Not really. I ate on the plane."

"Then come along and let me give you a tour. That'll make you hungry!"

Mona laughed at her aunt's enthusiasm, and the tour of the organization was revealing. She discovered at once a strange marriage of spiritual content to expert business practice.

"We try to do two things here in the army—one is to present the Lord Jesus Christ as Savior to everyone who will hear. That's what General Booth, the founder, had in his heart," Lenora said. "The other thing we try to do is to help those who need it."

"You certainly do that, Aunt Lenora—or must I call you Colonel Stuart?"

Lenora laughed and shook her head. She was a youthful-looking woman in her sixties, and her ash-blonde hair was streaked with light gray, but her crippling injury had neither affected her zest for life nor her general health. She spoke in glowing terms of the work that the army did all over the world. Finally she said, "Now, we're going out to dinner and celebrate."

"What are we celebrating?" Mona said.

Lenora took Mona's hand, and she smiled. There was a sweetness and intensity about her that was missing in most people.

"To celebrate my niece coming to see me after all these years."

During the days, when Lenora was busy, Mona spent some time simply wandering around the city, and she visited her aunts Rose and Christie and some of her cousins, but every night she and Lenora talked together until such a late hour that Mona felt guilty, knowing that her aunt had to get up early in the morning.

On the third night at eleven o'clock, Mona looked over at her aunt, who was quietly studying her. "I shouldn't be keeping you up this late, Aunt Lenora."

"Of course you should. I've had the best time ever since you've been here. I don't usually have time to get lonely, but I like to have family around."

"I know you miss Uncle Amos."

"I do, indeed. He came every week, at least. We went out to eat together and talked about the days of our youth. Yes, I miss him a great deal, but I visit your Aunt Rose a lot, and Maury, and I hear great things about Richard." Lenora paused. "But you haven't told me your problem yet. I know you have one."

Mona knew that the moment had come. She shook her head in despair. "I don't know what's wrong with me, Aunt Lenora. I have everything I always thought I'd want, but I'm not happy. I'm miserable, and I don't think it's going to get any better."

Lenora smiled and wheeled her chair closer so that she could put her hand on Mona's knee. "I wondered how long it would take you to get to this," she said.

"You knew something was wrong with me, didn't you?"

"Why, child, one look into your eyes and my heart just bled! You're so lonely and hurt that people would have to be blind not to see it."

"They must be blind then," Mona said, shaking her head. "I haven't talked to anybody about it. What's wrong with me, Aunt Lenora?"

"You've heard of Saint Augustine?"

"Well, yes. A little."

"A great man of God. He said, 'There's a vacuum in every human being, an empty spot, a God-shaped hollow, and until God fills that no man or no woman will ever know peace, or happiness, or joy.' Isn't that wonderful, Mona?"

"I–I don't think so. I mean, what does it mean? It isn't good to have a hollow space inside, is it?"

"Why, it's the way we were made. The first humans were made like that, to have communion with the Lord God, and when they violated God's commandment and couldn't face him anymore, that's when all the misery of this world started." She spoke quietly and reached over and took her Bible, which was never far away. After reading several Scriptures she said, "You're unhappy because you're not complete. You need Jesus Christ."

"I've heard that all my life, and I know you found completeness, and my parents certainly have, but Stephen and I have missed it. He's bitter and angry and hates the world."

"I know he is. I write to him often, and I pray for him every day. God's not through with that young man yet." Lenora fell silent for a moment and then said, "But what about you? You've heard the gospel, but I want to share it with you again. What Jesus has done for me . . ."

Mona listened. She ordinarily did not like to be preached to, but there was something in her aunt that held her captive. Lenora read the old Scriptures over again: "All have sinned, and come short of the glory of God"; "Except ye repent, ye shall all likewise perish"; "Christ Jesus came into the world

to save sinners; of whom I am chief"; "Ye must be born
again."

"Do you believe all of these things I'm reading out of
God's Word, Mona?"

"Yes, I believe them, but I don't know how to—well, I
don't know how to make them real. Suppose I did give my
heart to God and got saved. Would I have to play a trumpet
in the Salvation Army?"

"Would you be willing to?" Lenora's reply came back like
a shot.

Mona lowered her head. "No," she whispered. "I wouldn't
be willing to do that."

"Then you're not ready. Jesus calls us to be his disciples,
his servants, and the first thing that we learn in the Bible is
that God's children are called to obey. I have no idea whether
he'd call you to toot on a trumpet, but until you're ready to
do it, you're not ready for Jesus."

"I don't know what to do. I wish God would just *make* me
do what he wants."

"He'll never do that—though most of us who are Christians think we would like it if he did. Did you ever hear of
John Donne?"

"The English poet?"

Lenora nodded. "He wrote a poem in which he said he
wanted God to just *make* him be good."

"Do you have a copy?"

"Yes—right here," Lenora said quickly, tapping her temple. "I memorized it a long time ago. My favorite part goes
like this:

> Yet dearly I love you, and would be loved fain,
> But am betrothed unto your enemy,
> Divorce me, untie, or break that knot again,
> Take me to you, imprison me, for I
> Except you enthrall me, never shall be free,
> Nor ever chaste, except you ravish me."

Mona listened carefully. "That's very strong stuff, Aunt Lenora—I can never be chaste until I'm ravished. And I can't be free until I'm imprisoned? How can that be?"

"I think all women and men are in some sort of a prison, my dear. For some it's alcohol, for others lust. And we must be, in effect, made captive by God himself. When we are his prisoners, then we are really free for the first time. But we must give ourselves to God's will, and he will not make little puppets out of us. He's looking for sons and daughters not robots and slaves."

Mona's eyes filled with tears, and her voice trembled. She pressed her hands against her lips and tried to control herself. "I don't know what to do! I just don't know, Aunt Lenora!"

Lenora had counseled many women, and this one, being of her own blood, was especially precious to her. She prayed silently for a moment or two, letting her eyes close, then she opened them and said, "I think you know too much, Mona. You've heard the gospel all your life, and you've become hardened to it in a way. Here's what I want you to do. Go someplace—doesn't matter where—lock yourself in a room, get out in the middle of the woods where you can holler and nobody will hear you. Stay there, and begin to call on God. Don't give up. God has been seeking you, but now you must seek him."

The cabin on the Buffalo River was set in the most isolated place that Mona could find to rent for a week. "It ain't much. Not for a lady like you," Jack Simms said. He was a little awed by talking to a real live Hollywood actress. "It's just one room, and there ain't no electricity nor even running water. Just drink out of the creek. No bathroom, you understand. You wouldn't like it."

"I'll take it for a week. Could you take me there?"

They bounced over crooked roads, through first-growth fir and pine timber that towered over them, and then he left her, with a week's supply of food.

The sound of the jeep diminished, and she walked outside and took a deep breath. The trees were whispering overhead in the breeze, the sky was blue, and the creek purled beside the little cabin, tinkling as it fell over the stones.

She had never been alone like this in her life, and there was no way out until Simms came back for her.

She went back inside the cabin. She smiled at the rustic simplicity: a bunk bed with a cotton-tick mattress over link springs, a table and three mismatched chairs, a roughly built cabinet, a bookshelf full of tattered, mostly western, novels. Nails served instead of a closet. She had been instructed on how to use the gas lantern, and there was a coal oil lamp with two gallons of coal oil "just in case." An ancient cook stove with a pile of wood in a box beside it challenged her. She had never built a fire in her life, and she set about it at once. It was quite a chore, until she learned to use very small sticks as kindling to build it up. She unpacked her supplies and, since she had not eaten since breakfast, found a frying pan and cooked her first meal: bacon and eggs and black coffee.

She sat down at the table and started to eat, then halted. She bowed her head, saying, "I came here to find you, God, so I'll do everything I know. Thank you for this food and this place. Amen."

At first Mona thought she would lose her mind. The silence pressed in upon her. The sky was too large. She knew there were bears and wolves and coyotes in the vicinity. More than once she wanted to walk the five miles to the neighbor to call Simms.

She was not a solitary person. The hum of human voices, the motions of human bodies, the activities of the world had been her element, as water is element for a fish. During that first day and the next, she kept expecting to hear a voice and was anxious to see something besides the trees and the inside of the little cabin. She walked by the stream and into the woods, never going too far, for she feared getting lost more than anything. Evenings, she cooked her meal and sat on one of the chairs outside the cabin until the sky turned velvet black and stars began to spangle it. Then she went inside and opened the only book she'd brought—a Bible. Lenora had given her a few guides, and she read the Gospels through once, then started again. She went to sleep aware of the sounds outside the little cabin that gradually became her citadel.

After three days, she'd learned to sit and to be silent. She walked in the woods, at the same time seeking God, and she read the Gospels again and again.

On the fifth day, the sun had disappeared over the mountains, and she could barely see to read. She prayed and felt nothing. She read eagerly at first and then plodded on deliberately, stopping to ask God to help her.

Just before total darkness fell she sat outside with the open Bible on her lap. She prayed the same prayer that she had prayed, it seemed, a thousand times since she'd arrived.

"Oh, God, I need you so much! Please help me!"

She expected nothing, but—she felt tears suddenly rise in her eyes, and all of the Gospel events that she'd read began to come to her. She remembered how Jesus touched lepers and gave sight to the blind, how he loved the unlovely, and how women had been drawn to him. She sat for hours thinking of the Lord Jesus Christ, and something in her melted. It was as if a river of ice had thawed. The thick, solid ice broke into smaller chunks, and they were swept down the river, and then the river was free.

Mona knew that God was around her and was in her, and she began to pray this time with faith. "Oh, Lord Jesus, I have sinned against you and against my parents and my family and others. I do repent as you have commanded, and I invite you to come into my being. I will obey you the best I know how, but please save me, Lord Jesus."

Lenora Stuart picked up the phone and said in her businesslike manner, "Colonel Stuart here!"

"Aunt Lenora!"

"Mona, it's you!"

"Yes, it's me, and I've got something to tell you."

Something in Mona's voice, a new element that had been missing, caused Lenora to cry out. "What is it, Mona?"

Mona was holding the telephone in the general store in Jasper. She was unaware that the clerk and several customers were staring at her, listening to every word she said.

"Get my trumpet ready, Aunt Lenora. If God wants me to toot, then I'll toot!"

20

WEDDING BELLS

After Jake and Stephanie's wedding and honeymoon in Morocco, Jake returned to his duties at the *Examiner*. In late July, Stephanie was sent to Cairo after Egypt's President Nasser nationalized the Suez Canal. Tension was high as Great Britain and France prepared for possible military action. Stephanie began developing special news gathering skills because of the prejudice against women in the Arab world.

Jake and Stephanie decided not to decide on anything for a while. He did begin pursuing possibilities for work with International News Service, but there were no guarantees or even the likelihood that he and Stephanie could be assigned as a team. So for the present, he concentrated on working rather than worrying about her safety or about their future. He wrote to her parents:

> I'm sure this seems like the oddest arrangement in the world to you. But you should see her light up when she talks about the work she's doing. She loves it. Our agreement was that I would bring no pressure to bear on her to quit. And when I see how excited and involved she is—and how good at the work—how could I? Yes, I miss her. But she is in my heart in a different way now—with joy, not with pain. And I suppose with all the time apart, we'll remain newlyweds a long time. And we write lots of passionate love letters to pass on to our grandchildren.

Tom met Mona at the airport in Fort Smith. She was wearing a black-and-gray-striped cotton blouse with three-quarter length sleeves and a Peter Pan collar, a matching black and gray striped skirt that flared out slightly from the waist and fell to midcalf, and a pair of ballerina black patent leather shoes. She smiled only briefly, although she put out her hand and took his with a strange, nervous intensity. He pulled her close, scooped her up, and kissed her. Then she relaxed and smiled at him. "I didn't realize you're so strong. Put me down," she said.

"There are still lots of secrets you don't know about me, Mona."

They had no difficulty finding topics of conversation during the long drive. She sat close to him in the truck, resting her head on his shoulder some of the time. Before they arrived at Logan's, Tom asked if she felt too tired to change and come over to the Vine.

"I'm not too tired," she said, "but let me see if Logan has anything planned."

Logan was sitting on the porch whittling. He got up stiffly when they pulled in. "Well, howdy, y'all," he said. "Glad to see you, Tom. How do, Mona. Why, you look just beautiful!"

Mona went to him and gave him a hug and a kiss. "Here I am again, Uncle Logan, just like a bad penny."

"Logan," Tom said, while he was getting Mona's luggage, "why don't you and Mona come for supper at the Vine tonight?" He turned and winked at Mona.

"Why, Tom, that's mighty hospitable of you. Sure you young folks want a old codger like me hangin' around?"

Tom put the suitcases down and took the old man's hand. "Logan, you've been a mighty good friend. Please come to supper."

"All right, all right, we will—if that's what Mona wants to do, that is." He grinned, for he knew very well that Mona wanted to go.

Tom carried Mona's luggage upstairs, then kissed her, saying, "Come about six."

After supper, Logan sat with Granny and the others swapping stories. Mona said, "I've got to talk to you, Tom."

"All right. Let's walk down and see the new pigs. They keep secrets pretty well."

They walked slowly down the path, holding hands, to where the new porkers were rooting at their massive mother. They watched the pigs, then turned and walked away toward a field where several goats grazed. In the twilight, she turned to him and said, "Something's happened to me, Tom, and I wanted to tell you about it."

"What is it?"

"I feel rather foolish saying this, but I don't know any other way to put it." Mona bit her full lower lip for a moment and then noted the half smile on Henderson's face.

Tom felt the turbulence of her spirit as someone might feel strange currents cut across the wind as it blows. For him she had become a white core of light in darkness, a personality of fragrance and will, a stubborn spirit set against the world. She had wanted many things and had been betrayed by her wants. But her spirit seemed to glow in her like live coals, and she was a beautiful and robust woman with a woman's soft depth and a woman's spirit and a woman's fire.

"I found God," Mona said, half laughing, but then she reached out and touched his chest with a gesture that was both pleading and intimate. She began to tell him how she had fallen into such despair and despondency that it had driven her to seek her Aunt Lenora. Her eyes glowed as she spoke, and once her lips trembled as she related how she had called upon God out in the wilderness and how he had answered so completely.

She shook her head, the last sunlight of the day caught the gleam of her hair, and the shadows revealed the strong bone structure and the fine texture of her skin. "So that's one thing I've come to tell you, Tom."

Henderson put his arms around her. His eyes were bright, and he said fervently, "I can't tell you how glad I am to hear that, Mona. It's the best news you could've brought. I'm glad for you."

"There's something else," she said, taking a step away from him.

"What's that?" Henderson watched her face and was amazed at how mobile it was and how he seemed to be able, almost, to see into her thoughts. She was excited, yet with a tremulous quality that might bespeak either fear or eagerness. When she hesitated, he smiled and said, "Go ahead. Let me have it. I can take it."

"All right." Mona could hardly breathe, and she tried to smile. "I've come to tell you that I'm in love with you."

Henderson knew his own feelings, but in the evening tranquillity he could not find a response. He heard one of the goats bleating in the hoarse manner of such animals, and behind him faintly came the squeal of the new piglets. He watched as the air blew Mona's hair around her face. She was watching him intently. Then he knew what to do. It was one of those times that comes to a man infrequently, when he casts aside all of his doubts and uncertainties, and his will seems to coalesce into a determination, with the certainty that it is right. "In that case you'll have to marry me."

Mona smiled, satisfied.

He went to her and folded her in his arms and kissed her.

When he lifted his head, she reached up, brushed his hair back and whispered, "Oh, Tom, I'm so happy!"

His eyes were glistening, and he couldn't speak. He nodded.

They walked along the path in the growing darkness, heedless of the time, and for perhaps the only time in his life, Tom couldn't stop smiling. He held her hand and she felt, as she looked at him, a sense of longing and a knowledge that she had found her way with God and in other ways as well. "It's strange, isn't it," she said, "how different people find God in different ways. Richard came here and found his way through being with other people. I had to go off alone."

It was late when they returned to the house, and Logan had gone home. Tom at once broke the news to everyone there. Granny threw her hands up and cackled, "Well, I swan! I coulda told you this a long time ago, but you young folks never have time to listen to people with sense." The entire group gathered around Tom and Mona, laughing, slapping Tom on the back, and the women embraced Mona.

Mona's heart was high, but she caught one glimpse of Carmen, standing just inside the kitchen door. The woman's face was still, and her back was stiff with anger and grief and jealousy. Mona resisted the impulse to go to her, knowing it would be useless. *Oh, Carmen*, she thought, *if only I could tell you how much I know how you feel, how I've longed for the very things you long for.*

Tom said, "Come on. Let's go tell Logan. He'll probably break out a bottle of his freshly squeezed apple cider for us."

It was supposed to be a small wedding, but with a family the size of the Stuart clan, there was little hope of that. It was held in the same little church where Amos's funeral had been held a year and a half before. Mona's uncle Owen was performing the ceremony for them. The wedding was overdone, as weddings usually are. Tom had watched Mona practice, talk with her bridesmaids, and excitedly go through buying the trousseau. Her wedding dress was whispered over and discussed most of all. It was a fine white silk with a thin white chiffon covering the skirt and bodice. The chiffon made up the long narrow sleeves, which ended in a V on the back of her hand, where small pearls and crystal beadwork created a serpentine design. The bodice was fitted, with a low, scooped

neckline, and pearls and crystal beadwork covered it front
and back. The skirt was long and full with a short train, and
the bottom of the dress was decorated with the same pearl
and crystal beadwork. Her veil would be attached to a small
wreath of flowers on the top of her head, and the sheer netting
would trail down to the middle of her back. She planned to
wear a choker of three strands of pearls, and her shoes were
white satin.

At the rehearsal, Tom said to his future father-in-law, "I
think a bridegroom's nothing but an impediment to these
things. The women ought to get together, do all of this buying and primping and dressmaking, and the men ought to go
off on a fishing trip or a hunting trip or something. Then the
bridegroom ought to be brought in ten minutes before the
ceremony, stuck into place, and made to say his piece. Otherwise he just gets in the way."

Pete grinned at him. "I felt the same way myself, but when
I saw Leslie walk down the aisle—Tom, you'll think she's
worth it."

After what seemed an interminable time, Tom was standing at the front of the church next to Richard, his best man.
The bridesmaids and Maris, the matron of honor, made their
procession. Then, he looked up the aisle and saw Mona on
Pete's arm. Suddenly everything was different. *This is the
woman I love,* he thought, *and I'm a lucky dog to get her!* As she
came toward him, he studied her, having heard much about
the dress. The pearl and crystal beadwork caused it to shim-
mer in the lights as she walked down the aisle.

But it was not the dress as much as the happiness in Mona's
face that gave him the most pleasure. When she was being
given away, Tom had an absurd and irrational impulse to simply step forward, lift her veil, and kiss her hard right on the
mouth. Somehow Mona sensed this. Her eyes sparkled, and
her lips turned up in a sly smile. She shook her head slightly,
and when he came to stand beside her, she squeezed his
hand.

When Owen finally said, "You may kiss the bride," Tom lifted the veil, pulled her forward, and held her tightly, kissing her with evident ardor. He was aware of the applause and the laughter going up. When he released her, she said, "Thank you for going through this for me. It was worth it to me just to see you wear something besides jeans and a T-shirt!" Then they were moving up the aisle.

Filming of *Bride of Quietness* began in September. Adam had been careful to keep Tom involved at every step, including converting the book to a screen play. An experienced screenwriter assisted him, but it was clear that Tom was in control. Henderson was introduced to the curious as just another screenwriter. Adam refused to give out any information about how he'd gotten permission from William Starr to make the film.

The mystery heightened expectations for the movie's release.

21

ROCK BOTTOM

The city of Little Rock, Arkansas, about 150 miles east of the Stuart farm in the Ozarks, was the center of world attention in 1958 in the struggle to end racial discrimination in the United States. The attendance of nine black students at Little Rock Central High School set off one of the first great tests of power between the federal and a state government in the twentieth century. Through the 1957–58 school year, students attended Central High with troops of the U.S. army and the Arkansas national guard, ordered into federal service, maintaining order. In February 1958, the school board petitioned the federal district court in Little Rock for a postponement of its desegregation plan because of the violence and public hostility.

The case ended up in the Supreme Court. Chief Justice Earl Warren called the justices to return to Washington in August to make a determination before the new school year began. Lawyers said that the school board was powerless to deal with the forces in Arkansas opposed to desegregation. Attorney Thurgood Marshall of the NAACP argued for the nine students, and others presented strong arguments against delaying desegregation. On September 12, the court ordered the Little Rock plan for desegregation to proceed immediately. Its opinion was announced as the joint product of all nine justices—an unprecedented way to emphasize the court's unanimity on the racial issue. The court put the blame on Arkansas governor Orval E. Faubus and the state legislature and said that maintaining law and order was not more important than the black students' constitutional rights. The justices also stated that the decision could not be nullified by evasive schemes, foreseeing the next phase of the struggle— Governor Faubus closed Central and the other high schools of Little Rock before they opened. He tried to privatize them, thus making them exempt from the court's order, by getting the school board to lease the schools to a private corporation established by segregationists. The court enjoined the "private" schools from using public school buildings or teachers. President Eisenhower repeatedly called for compliance with what he called the moral command of the Supreme Court.

Stephen Stuart had kept up with news of the ongoing racial turmoil. But it was not in his thoughts as he left the prison carrying a small, shoddily made suitcase he had purchased for three dollars from one of the incoming inmates. He paused and let his eyes run over the expanse of the blue skies and breathed the air deeply. He had been outside in the yard during his imprisonment, but that was different. A sense of relief came over him that made him weak. Many times he had despaired, doubting if he would ever breathe a free breath again. Now he was out, and it frightened him that it was so strange. His knees even felt weak, but he began to walk toward the prison bus that ferried visitors back and forth to the city. He felt reluctant to get on, but, as he took a last look around at the flat-topped buff buildings, a resolution formed in him, and he said under his breath, "I'll never see this place again, so help me!"

R. D. Melton was ill at ease. He sat behind his limed-oak desk and toyed with the onyx pen that was in its onyx holder, not looking at the man across from him. But he had to look, and he put the pen down and spread his hands apart in a helpless gesture. "Well, Steve. I'd like to help, but I really don't see how I can." He felt the steady gray eyes of the man across from him, and they made him shift nervously in his chair. Stephen Stuart had appeared out of nowhere and asked for help to get back into business. The two had been business associates and even friends—at least to the point of playing golf and going out to parties on occasion—but Melton had a strong sense of survival. *Stuart's a loser. He took the count once, and nobody comes back in this business. Too bad, but I'll have to turn him down.*

Stephen sat straight in the chair. He had learned to read people before he went to the penitentiary, and inside it had become second nature to him. Survival meant understanding your enemies and discovering those who could be your friends. Looking across at the well-groomed man in the Brooks Brothers suit, he saw no friend. Melton was the fifth man that he had looked up in Oklahoma City, all of whom he had helped, to some degree, when he was in business. A sense of despair settled over Stuart as he listened to Melton's voice falter each time he looked him in the eye.

Melton glanced at the clock and drummed his fingers on the desk and said, "Maybe we can talk about this later, Stephen. I've got an appointment in ten minutes. Where are you staying?"

"So long, R. D. Thanks for the help." Melton had been one of his last hopes. Stephen wanted to leap across the desk, grab the expensive tie, and smash Melton's face in, but he had acquired more control over himself than that. Instead, he got up and walked out of the room, ignoring the weak voice saying, "Hey now, Steve! Wait a minute—"

As he left the office building, he thought, with a paralyzing sense of urgency, *I've only got eighty-seven dollars left. How can I expect to get started in business on eighty-seven dollars?*

He walked along keeping his head down, his mind exploring possibilities and rejecting them. He had done this many times before his release, but he had thought that though they might have seemed weak inside, when he was out he would be able to manage.

All afternoon Stephen wandered the city, some of the sights bringing a sense of poignancy and some bitterness. He found a park, sat down, and drew his coat up, coughing in the sharp November wind. He thought of his family—some of them had the means to help him. His parents might have the means, but he was too ashamed of what he had put them through to ask. He thought Aunt Lylah, for example, might help. Uncle Amos was gone. Uncle Owen, of course, had no money, nor had Aunt Lenora. Aunt Christie was married to a successful lawyer—he might be interested in a deal. As he sat slumped on the bench he discarded all those possibilities and got up, saying, "I'll make it on my own, or I won't make it at all." His jaw set, he walked off purposefully—although he had little confidence.

His money had shrunk to almost nothing, and with a sense of self-disgust Stephen stepped into a tiny liquor store on Jefferson Street and mumbled, "Pint of vodka. The cheapest you got." He took the bottle, handed over his last five dollar bill, and took the change. Stuffing the bottle in his pocket, he moved outside. He had been drinking every day for the past week. It was almost the end of November, and he had found nothing. He longed for the oblivion of drunkenness, but it was early and he knew he would need the vodka to get to sleep that night. He left Jefferson Street not knowing what to do. The thought came to him with a bitter tang, *I was better off back in the pen than I am now. At least I had a place to sleep—which I won't after tonight, and plenty to eat, which I haven't had lately.*

He wandered the streets, and late that afternoon he decided to swallow his pride and shame and go to his parents' house. He had thought of them often, and he began to walk to a bus stop to catch a bus to their home. He had not eaten anything but a hamburger for the past two days, and his stomach growled, he was coughing, and he longed for a drink. The sun was edging downward, and late afternoon shadows formed as the trees cast their dark images on the ground.

He was startled when a voice said, "Hey! What are you doin' here, fella?"

Stephen turned and saw that an Oklahoma City police car had stopped and two men were getting out. They studied him, and one came up to stand before him, holding his stick with his right hand and tapping it gently into his palm. "I asked you a question, fella. What are you doing here?"

"Nothing. Just walking."

"Just walking, eh? Hey, Al. He says he's just walking."

"I heard him, Fred."

The police officer named Fred said, "This is a residential area. Where do you live?"

"The Baron Hotel."

A brash grin went across the officer's face. "Not a very fancy place. How long you been there? Where you from?"

The big one said, "He's a vagrant. Let's haul him in, Fred."

Fear shot through Stephen. He knew what would happen if he got into trouble again, and he said quickly, "Look, I'm broke all right. Been looking for work and haven't found any, but I haven't done anything wrong."

The officer clearly had the inclination to arrest the shoddily dressed man before him. "Didn't anybody tell you there's a recession on, fella?" he asked. Then he shrugged, saying, "Jail's full already. Get out of this neighborhood. Go on back to where you belong. If we see you around here again, you'll be in the lockup."

"Thanks, Officer."

Relief washed over Stephen as the car door slammed, and the two officers watched as he quickly turned and walked back the way that he had come. Bitterness flooded through him, and he thought, *If I get in trouble again it would kill my parents.*

He drank half of the bottle of vodka before he got back to the hotel. He waited outside until the clerk went to the washroom, then he sneaked in, going up to his second-floor room. He knew he would be asked to leave, and he had nowhere to go.

He reclined on the bed taking sips of the vodka, wishing that it were a quart instead of a pint. The liquor dazed him, but still he was aware of his misery. He sat up on the bed and stared at the floor helplessly, not knowing what to do. He rose and walked to the window and looked out. He finished off the bottle and slumped in the chair. Thoughts came to him, almost dreams. He thought of Mona. Right after he was released, he had gone to see the movie *Bride of Quietness*, which had won numerous awards. He had received letters from both Mona and Tom, and they had come to see him in prison twice.

In the drunken dream that came to him, he could see Henderson's face and hear his voice, "When you hit bottom, come to the Vine, Stephen."

He lurched to the bed and went soundly to sleep then, and when he woke up in the morning coughing, his tongue thick and his head pounding, he knew that he had no choice. He had thought of killing himself several times, but such a thing was not in him. He rose slowly, went over to the dresser, pulled out his clothes, put them in the suitcase, and tried to consider what he could sell to get bus fare to Mountain View. He had but one thing left—he looked down at his wristwatch, a Baume & Mercier gold watch given to him for his graduation by his parents. It had been returned to him when he was released. The inscription on the back said, "To Stephen, our pride and joy, with love from Mom and Dad."

He went downstairs and, getting a hard look from the clerk, said, "I'm clearing out."

He walked across the street to the small dingy building with the three balls hung outside. When he came out, he had a few bills in his hand and a pawn ticket for the watch.

"Maybe I'm crazy, but at least I won't have to look at Oklahoma City."

He made his way to the Greyhound station, found he didn't have enough to get to Mountain View, so he bought a ticket to Fort Smith, and when the bus pulled out, leaving diesel fumes heaving in the air, he slumped in his seat and closed his eyes, with despair so hard in him that he could hardly think.

The bus ride was tiring. He had been coughing for several days but had killed the symptoms with alcohol. Now without it he began coughing so hard that the old woman who sat beside him looked at him with disgust. "You ought to take something for that cough!" she snapped.

"Yes, ma'am, I think you're right."

By the time he had gone a hundred miles he knew that it was more than a cold. His chest was hollow, he coughed constantly, and his head pounded as if someone were driving spikes through it. But he rode on, dozing when he could, and again the thought came to him, *I must be crazy going to that place, but I don't know what else to do.*

22

A PLACE FOR STEPHEN

December came to the Ozarks in one of its more virulent forms. During the last days of November, ice storms tore down power lines, and the roofs of several chicken houses had collapsed. The storms tied up the roads, for there were no snowplows in Arkansas. Snowplows were called for, however, on the first day of December, for heavy snows fell and blanketed the mountains and the valleys with a pristine, sparkling blanket, beautiful, but paralyzing the land.

The University of Arkansas at Fayetteville, about forty miles north of the Stuart farm, called off classes for the first time in its history. The students were ecstatic over this, and there was a frenzy of snowball fights, ice sculptures, and sledding down the steep hills on the campus.

Those at the Vine survived the ice storm and the heavy fall of snow very well, although it was necessary to bring the cattle into the barns to feed them since even the dried brown grass of the pastures was under two feet of snow. Some of the pipes were frozen, which kept the men busy. The older children had gone tobogganing. The women continued the usual cooking, cleaning house, and caring for the children, who were all home from school, and Carmen Rio found it even enjoyable. She was ironing clothes, a big bushel basket at her feet, and looking out the window enjoying the sight of the trees, which had become giant crystal mushrooms. The sun was out, and the snow crystals glittered, hurting her eyes. She

253

squinted but admired the way that the snow made even the fading old barn beautiful, its rounded crown lending it an air of grace. A neighbor had come by with a blade to plow out the driveway, and his big half shepherd, half who-knew-what was running through the snow biting at it and barking a rapid staccato that carried over the otherwise silent landscape.

Hanging a pressed white shirt on a hanger, Carmen picked up another as Enrique came in. One quick look at his face told her that he was unhappy, and she said sharply, "Why don't you go out and play in the snow with the other kids?"

"I don't want to."

Slapping the shirt down on the ironing board, Carmen expertly pressed it, but her mind was on the boy. He was in trouble at school, had not done his homework, had been involved in a fight. She had gone to see the principal, who said, "He's a bright boy, and he was doing so well. I don't know what's come over him." The school was a small one and Enrique and Consuela had not encountered the level of prejudice they might have in a city school. People at the Vine had become accepted in the community as eccentrics, and they were expected to be "different."

Carmen knew very well what was troubling Enrique. "You miss Mr. Henderson, don't you?"

"I guess so. Do you think he'll ever come back and live here?"

"No, I don't think so. Just for visits maybe, like he's been doing. But he always takes you hunting or fishing when he comes."

"But he's hardly ever here." Enrique's voice was unhappy, as was his countenance. He stood on one foot, pulled a knife out of his pocket, and started to carve his initials in the painted door facing.

"Don't do that! You know better!"

"I don't know what to do!"

"Well, do *something!* You're driving me crazy. Go play Monopoly with Consuela."

Giving her a sullen glance, Enrique slouched out of the room. Shaking her head, Carmen felt the pressures build up in her. She had adjusted, after a fashion, to Tom and Mona's marriage. Realistically she had always known that he had never cared for her—not in the way a man cares for a woman—and with that hope gone she was more focused than ever on the children.

She had just finished the last of the ironing when she saw a car come down the road. Moving to the window, she stiffened as she saw that it was the sheriff's car. She knew the sheriff, a rather gruff man named Steele, and wondered what he could want.

She opened the door, and the big red-faced man pulled his hat off. "Lookin' for Mr. Pilcher, ma'am."

Richard and Laurel had gone to Bible school. Morgan Pilcher was in charge. "He's gone to cut wood, Sheriff Steele. My name's Carmen Rio."

"Well, I got a problem here. Any of the menfolk around?"

"No, sir. They're not. Can I be of any help?"

Sheriff Steele was wearing a pair of green corduroy pants and a red and green wool mackinaw. His ears were red from the cold, and his nose was a crimson dot. He stared at her uncertainly, then shook his head. "Well, I don't know as anybody here can help me." He shifted his feet, stomped them to get some of the snow off, then nodded toward the car. "Got a fellow out here who claims to be kin to Mona Stuart. He's either been drinkin' or he's sick. I can't tell which."

"What's his name?"

"He says his name's Stephen Stuart. That's about all I can get out of him. I don't know what to do, miss. He looks like to me he oughta be in the hospital. He ain't got no money—I checked on that—and he's in pretty bad shape."

Carmen thought rapidly, then nodded. "If he's kin to the Stuarts it'll be all right. Bring him in."

"All right. Better put him in a bed, though. He can't sit up."

"We've got a room that's not being used. It's already got bedcovers. Just bring him in." She watched as the sheriff waded back through the snow and heard him say, "Come on, Carl. We'll have to tote him in."

Carmen opened the door for them, then she moved quickly ahead to open a bedroom door. She stripped the covers back and said, "Just put him on the bed."

"You want us to undress him?" the sheriff inquired.

"Just get his coat off, and put him down there." She watched as the men stripped the coat from the unconscious man, whose head lolled back. He had tawny hair, she saw, and a lean face that was very pale except for the twin spots of crimson on his cheeks, which to her spelled fever. The two men, she saw, were accustomed to handling drunks, for they simply stripped the coat off, tossed the man on the bed, then jerked his shoes off without unlacing them.

Turning to her, Steele said, "I'll check back later to talk to Morgan about this. We gotta be sure it's all right. I don't know a thing about this fella. He may be dangerous for all I know."

"I don't think he looks too dangerous right now. It'll be all right, Sheriff Steele," Carmen assured the officer. "I will take care of him. Morgan will be back sometime this afternoon."

"All right, ma'am."

As soon as the men left, Carmen moved over and studied the face of the man in the bed. She put her hand on his forehead, and it seemed blistering.

Hearing him whisper something, she leaned forward and asked, "Can you hear me?"

She leaned closer still, but all she could catch was, "Need to see Mona . . ."

A noise behind her caused her to turn as Granny peered in the door. "Who's that?" she inquired, coming over to look at the sick man.

"Sheriff Steele said his name is Stephen Stuart. He's asking to see Mona."

"Well, he ain't gonna see nobody if that fever gets any worse." Even as she spoke, a series of coughs rent the air, and the thin body seemed racked with pain.

"That sounds like pneumony either comin' on or already got him," Granny said. She went over, put her hand on his forehead, then shook her own head. "He's burnin' up."

"I think we'd better call Dr. Cravens."

"I reckon so, for all that's worth, and you better call Logan Stuart, too. That'd be his kinfolk if he's kin to Miss Mona."

"All right. I'll call them both."

"I'll sit here by him, and when you get back I'll fix him some of my potion. That'll probably do him more good than a doctor."

Dr. Cravens came at once, and while he was there examining his patient, Logan entered the room, followed by Granny. "Hello, Doc," Logan said, coming across to the bed. He bent over the still form. "Why, that's my nephew Stephen!" he exclaimed. He turned to Carmen saying, "How'd he get here?"

"Sheriff Steele brought him. He didn't know what else to do with him. He was asking for Mona."

Cravens finished his examination, straightened up, and put his stethoscope back in his bag. "He needs to be in the hospital."

"Well, I reckon we'll have to do what you say," Logan said. "I'll just—"

"N–no hospital!"

The group standing around the bed were startled. Stephen's eyes were open. Cravens said, "Don't be a fool, man. You're on the verge of pneumonia."

The thin voice whispered again, "No hospital."

Logan leaned over and said, "Now look here, Nephew,

you got to listen to the doctor. He knows best." He tried to persuade Stephen, but the answer remained the same.

Dr. Cravens was a busy man. "Well, so be it." He looked at Logan and said, "He must be a Stuart all right. You're all as stubborn as blue-nosed mules."

Logan laughed but quickly grew serious. "Can I take him to my place, Doc?"

"You don't have anybody to take care of him there, do you?"

"Well, I'm there."

"He's gonna take considerable nursing, Logan, if he won't go to the hospital." The doctor's eyes went over to the two women, and he said, "You two had any experience nursing?"

"I've had aplenty," Granny said quickly, "and I've got some potion that'll do him more good than them pills of yours."

Cravens laughed. "All right, Granny. You may have something there. Medicine won't do a whole lot of good. I'll leave some with you, but mostly he just needs to rest. Do what you can to keep his fever down, and with luck he may make it."

Carmen was looking down at the prone figure and saw the glazed eyes fixed on her. "Mona," he said, "I've come back."

"I'm not Mona."

But the sick man was in a delirium. He insisted on calling her Mona, and after Cravens left, Logan sat and watched as Stephen clung to the notion that Carmen was his sister. "Can't understand it," Logan muttered. "You don't look anything like Mona. Not nothin' at all."

"No, I don't!" Carmen said rather abruptly.

She left the room, and Logan asked with surprise, "What's the matter, Granny? Did I say something wrong?"

"Course you did! Men are allus sayin' somethin' wrong, and you're a man. Why don't you git, Logan? Go out and kill three chickens, on account of we're gonna need lots of chicken soup for this man."

Logan grinned, got up, and said, "I can do that. You do the doctorin', and I'll do the chicken killin'."

Stephen had a bad night. His fever rose, and Carmen and Granny took turns doing what they could to bring it down. It was nearly dawn when Carmen came in from checking on the children and taking a short rest. She found Granny with her old black Bible open in her lap over her faded wool dress. She was humming, and Carmen picked up the words. "There's not a friend like the lowly Jesus, no not one, no not one."

The old woman turned around, and her eyes were as sharp and clear as a blackbird's, despite her age. "Did you get a little sleep, honey?"

"Yes." Carmen came over and pulled up a cane-bottomed chair and sat down beside the older woman. "You go get some rest now."

"Ain't a bit tired! It's almost daylight anyhow. No sense goin' to bed with the sun comin' up." She rocked back and forth in her rocking chair, singing again in a louder voice, "There's not a friend like the lowly Jesus, no not one, no not one."

She studied the face of the sleeping man, and she said, "I do believe his fever's gone down." She watched as Carmen went and put her hand on his forehead. "Ain't it so?"

"I believe it has, but he's got that horrible cough. You'd think he'd be torn in two by now."

"He's gonna be all right, honey. The Lord done told me so."

Carmen was accustomed to Granny's direct words from God. At first she had laughed at the old woman, but, having been around her considerably, she saw goodness and compassion that she could not deny. She herself had only a nominal religion, but she knew that Granny's kind was red-hot, boiling over, and ready to spill out at any time.

As if she read the young woman's thoughts, Granny said, "You're gonna be saved one of these days."

"Did the Lord tell you that?" Carmen smiled.

"Well, I ain't claimin' I heard no voice like Moses did on the mountain—but I been prayin' for you, child, and I believe God that you're gonna be converted."

"What does that mean? Converted?"

"Well, I'll tell you how it is. I was saved when I was fourteen years old. I was out hoein' cabbage when I got saved," she pronounced, and her laugh was low and filled with good humor. "I jist called on Jesus, and there wasn't nobody there to hinder me. Right down at the old home place.

"You asked about being converted," Granny returned to Carmen's question. "You don't know what that means at all?"

"No. I heard it on the radio, and I've heard Tom talk about it, and you."

"Well, you've had two children. When they come they was jist little babies not able to do nothin' for theyselves. You had to feed 'em and take care of 'em and clothe 'em. You know what being born in the flesh means. Well, Jesus said in John chapter three," Granny nodded emphatically, "you must be born *again*. It puzzled the fella he said it to, just like it puzzles you, feller by the name o' Nicodemus. He said, 'How can a man be born again?'" Carmen was leaning forward listening intently. "Jesus said you're born once in the flesh, and you have a father and a mother on earth, but there's something else that can happen to you, and that's when you have a change in your heart, and something new comes into you, and it's the Lord Jesus is who it is."

Granny quoted Scriptures and told stories of how friends and relatives of hers were converted and how they were baptized and had gone on with God. She said gently, putting her hand on the younger woman's, "I know this sounds turrible strange and odd to somebody who ain't been used to hearin' it, but all it means, child, is that when you get ready to go to

God, you just call on Jesus like I did out in the cabbage patch.
And then he comes into your heart."

"How could he do that? He lived two thousand years
ago."

"Why, child, he's alive just like you're alive. Just like I am,
and I can't tell you how, but I know you've had something
like it. Ain't there times," she said wistfully, "when that little
old sweet girl of yours comes right into your heart. You know
what that's like."

"Yes," Carmen whispered, "I know what that's like all
right."

"Well, that's sort of in a way like what happens when Jesus
comes in. You just know he's there, and he said, 'I will never
leave thee, nor forsake thee,' and then—Lookie! I think he's
wakin' up."

The two women instantly turned their attention to the
patient, who was stirring and, indeed, was struggling to sit
up.

"Here now," Granny said sternly. "Settle yourself down
there."

"Where–where is this place?" Stephen's voice was thick
and his eyes, though clear, were bewildered.

Carmen said, "Are you thirsty?" She helped him to sit up,
and Granny poured a glass of water, which she fed to him. He
almost choked on the water, still coughing a great deal.

"Where am I?" he whispered.

"Why, you're at the Vine. You were brought here by the
sheriff," Carmen said. For a moment Stephen could not put
it all together, then it all came back to him, and he nodded.
"Yes," he said huskily.

"Could you eat something?" Granny asked.

"Guess I could."

"I'll go get some soup," Granny said. "I made up enough
soup to heal a regiment."

"Where did you come from?" Carmen asked the young
man.

"Oklahoma City." His voice was cracked and hoarse, and he coughed so hard that Carmen reached over and held his shoulders.

Granny came back with a bowl of chicken soup on a tray. "Here, you feed him this," she said, putting the tray down on the table beside the bed. Then she sat and watched as Carmen spoon-fed the warm broth to the weak man. Granny asked, "You were sure hungry. When is the last time you ate?"

"Not for some time."

"Well, a man never did know how to take keer of hisself," she said, shaking her head in despair. "You menfolks would be in bad shape without us women."

Stephen finished the soup, and sleep returned quickly. He simply closed his eyes and relaxed back on the pillow.

Alarmed, Carmen said, "Granny, what's wrong with him?"

"He just reached the end of his rope. Come to plumb rock bottom, child. Seen 'em do that a lot, but he ate something, and the fever's going away. He'll be all right. You'll see."

Mona came into the room, her eyes wide with concern. She saw Stephen sitting in a rocker beside the window, and as he turned to face her, she saw that he was thin and gaunt. "Stephen!" she cried and ran over. He started to get up, but she put her arms around him and held him down. "Don't get up," she said. "We came as soon as Uncle Logan called."

"Well, Sis," Stephen said, a faint smile on his pale lips, "I'm still alive. I wasn't sure I would be."

Tom came in behind Mona. He grinned at the seated man. "You look like you've been pulled backward through a knot-hole, Stephen," he said. He put his hand out and was shocked at the frail grip of the other. "How are you feeling?"

"Well, I'm able to sit up while they change my bed," Stephen answered laconically.

"We've all been worried sick about you," Mona said.

"Dad's ready to take his belt to you. We learned you were released early, but we didn't know where in the world you went. Why didn't you go home? Why didn't you call?"

"Well, like the doctor says, all of us Stuarts are stubborn as blue-nosed mules."

Tom dragged two chairs across where he and Mona could face Stephen and said, "Sheriff Steele told Logan he found you out on the road coming from Fort Smith, afoot in a snowstorm."

"Ran out of money, Tom. There weren't any buses running anyway." He smiled for the first time, saying wryly, "I know what a country mile means now. The fellow that told me that the Vine was just a few miles down the road didn't have much sense of distance. It's a good thing the sheriff came along. I think I'd have frozen if he hadn't."

"You're fever's all gone, Granny says," Mona spoke up. "But you're still weak. I can tell."

"Weak as a kitten," Stephen agreed cheerfully. He looked at the two of them and said, "As soon as I got out I saw *Bride of Quietness*. Best film I ever saw."

Mona flushed with pleasure and reached over and took the thin hand. "Any actress would have looked good in that role."

"That's not so," Tom argued. "But I was pleased with it."

Mona wanted to ask more about Stephen's adventures, if they could be called that, but she did not think he wanted to be questioned. They sat talking until Carmen came in with a covered dish. She turned to go when she saw Tom and Mona were still there, but Tom called out, "Wait! Carmen, don't deprive the man of his dinner."

Stephen watched Carmen's face flush. He had been ill but he was still quick-witted. He saw the look she gave Henderson, and he knew. *She feels something for the fellow*, he thought. Looking at his sister, he wondered if she knew it, then decided that she did.

"Sit down, Carmen, and tell us about your patient."

"No, let me tell you about *her*," Stephen said moving over to the table and taking the tray from her. "She's about the best nurse a man ever had. I don't know how many nights she sat up caring for me like I was a baby."

"Granny did most of it," Carmen said, embarrassed.

But Stephen was effusive in his praise, and when she left the room, he shook his head. "Sure is a fine woman. Been through some hard times, I expect, like everybody here."

The visit went on for some time, and after Tom and Mona left, Carmen came back to get the dishes. Stephen asked, "Have you known Tom and Mona a long time?"

"I guess so." The answer was guarded. She looked up and said, "Why do you ask?"

"Oh, no reason. What kind of a man is Henderson? He's my brother-in-law, but I don't know anything about him."

A light came into Carmen's eyes. "He's the best man I've ever known," she said. "He helped me and my kids out when nobody else cared. He's—" She broke off suddenly and left the room, carrying the tray, and Stephen stared after her.

She had a bad case. Too bad. She'll have to get over that, he thought.

It was two days later when he spoke of it again. He and Carmen were getting to know each other. He learned her story, and she learned his. He found it easier to tell her of his incarceration after he found out that her husband had been involved in crime. He listened as she told her story, and he blurted out, "I get the impression that you have feelings for Tom."

"Don't say that!" Carmen said sharply. She looked up, and he saw her eyes were filled with unshed tears. She looked away, and he said softly, "I'm sorry, Carmen. Anybody would like Tom. He's that kind of a man."

"I have no right to like him now. He has a wife, and he's the kind of man that will stick to her no matter what."

"That's good to hear. I'd hate to think of my sister married to any other kind."

They talked for a long time, and she spoke of her fears for her children and for her future. They were sitting close together, looking out the window from time to time at the snow that was at last beginning to melt. The sadness in the young woman touched Stephen. He had not felt compassion for anyone for a long time. She seemed as thoroughly alone in the world as if there were no other thing alive on the planet. All her search for color and warmth, for the comfort of a husband's closeness, had ended with a great solitariness. She had a curtain of reserve that she drew about her, but Stephen felt that behind that curtain was a woman of great vitality and imagination. She had pride, too, that could sweep her violently and send up a blaze in her eyes. He sought for some way to tell her of his feeling and said, "I think you'll be all right. You're too pretty a woman, and too fine, not to find someone who'll care for you."

Shocked by his words, Carmen looked up. The tears made her eyes seem larger and darker, and her black hair, as black as the darkest night, framed her pale face. "Do you think so?" she whispered.

He reached over, took her hand, and held it. It was strong, stronger than his own now, and he put his other hand over it, saying, "Sure, you'll come out all right."

Carmen thought about that for a moment, then she pulled her hand back gently and her words were toneless. "Things never come out all right."

"Don't believe that," he said quickly. "You've got children. You need to have hope for them."

"Do you have hope?"

Her question caught Stephen off guard. "Not much," he said finally, "but I wouldn't have come here if I didn't have a little. I made an absolute, utter wreck out of my life. I had everything, Carmen. Everything. But I threw it all away. Now, I guess I'm looking for something to hold onto."

"Like what?" she inquired curiously.

"I don't know, but I know that life has to mean something; at least it seems to for some people."

Carmen thought of Granny and nodded slowly. "For some people, but not for me."

Again he spoke quickly, "I don't like to hear you talk like that. You're young and pretty, and for some man you'll have everything." He saw her face change as he spoke and was unable to identify the change. His words pleased her, but still there was a caution in her, and he thought, *She's been so hurt and cut up she's afraid to trust anybody. And why should she trust me—a failure and an ex-con.* He watched as she rose and left the room, then he sat back in his chair thinking for a long time about her and about her children. He was surprised that he had the capacity to think of someone else instead of pitying himself, and this pleased him and made him feel more alive than he had for a long time.

"Well, I'll tell you, missy," Logan Stuart said, smiling at Carmen. "If you ever decide to go into the nursing business, you can take over my case."

Carmen liked Logan. He was a cheerful old man who had lived a full life and was now a widower but was not bitter. The two of them had something in common—being alone. She laughed, saying, "There's nothing wrong with you. You're healthy as a horse."

"Even horses get sick," Logan said, winking at her. "Is Stephen up?"

"He's playing checkers with Enrique." She thought for a moment, then nodded, a pleased expression in her eyes. "They get along very well. Stephen has a way with him, and Consuela, too. Just like . . ."

Logan knew she had almost said, "Just like Tom," but he knew also why she broke off her speech. "Reckon I'll go in and see him," he said. "Before I leave maybe you'll let me have some of that raisin pie."

"How do you know I've got any?"

"You always have some stashed away."

"All right. I do have one piece left. I hate to waste it on you, though."

Logan grinned, then went to Stephen's room, where he found a checker game in full progress.

"I'll take on the winner," he said.

"That's me," Enrique grinned. "I've won the last two games."

Stephen winked at the older man, "Won 'em fair and square, too."

Logan leaned back and watched the two players with pleasure. Enrique's face glowed with excitement, and he slammed the checkers down every time he jumped a man, making the board bounce. When he won the game, he jumped around and said, "I win! Three times in a row!"

"Well, we'll try again later," Stephen said. "You run along while I talk to Mr. Stuart."

When the boy was out of the room, Logan said, "You're lookin' good, Stephen."

"I'm feeling better. I'm going to try and get out a little bit tomorrow my nurse says."

"Listen to your nurse. That woman knows a heap. Got a head full of sense—and pretty as a speckled pup."

"Yes, she's pretty, and more than pretty."

Logan had thought to tease Stephen, but he was pleased with the answer anyway.

"Yes," Stephen continued, "she is an attractive woman, but it's more than that. I admire the way she's stuck with her kids instead of just throwing up her hands."

"You get along good with that boy, don't you?"

"I guess I do. I've never been around kids much, but it's been easy with Enrique. Maybe," he said with a shrug of his shoulders, "because I was weak as a sick kitten. He came in here and sat down and we'd talk. It was like he was the older one," he said with a grin.

"I think he misses Tom," Logan said. "He was always taking the boy hunting or fishing."

"He's already been after me about that," Stephen said, "but I haven't been hunting or fishing since I was a kid—summers when you and Clint and Dad and I went—remember?"

"Sure I do. Anytime you want to go fishin' I gotta pond full of bluegills and bass. That pecan orchard out there is full up with squirrels that oughta be shot and et. Bring the boy over. We'll have a good time."

Logan left, repeating his invitation, and almost at once Consuela came in and sat down across from Stephen. Her lips were pulled tightly together in a line, and her face was discontented.

"What's wrong, Consuela?" Stephen asked.

"Nothing."

"Come on now. I know better than that. Where's that smile?"

"I don't have any smiles."

"I bet you smile for your friends." Stephen was less comfortable with Consuela than with Enrique. He couldn't play dolls with her, but he had discovered that she, too, liked to play board games, especially Monopoly, and they'd had several bloodthirsty contests in which her dark eyes had flashed with competitive spirit. Stephen said, "Tell me about your friends at school."

"I don't have any friends." Consuela's lips trembled and she said, "They make fun of me because I'm different."

Shocked by the girl's vulnerability, Stephen said quietly, "You want to tell me about it? Come over here and sit beside me." He was surprised when she came at once and sat down in the chair beside him. He put his arm around her and squeezed her and said, "Now, tell me all about it. Sometimes it's good to say things out loud."

Consuela began to speak. "I don't have any friends. The girls all get together and they leave me out. Some of them call me a Spick. I told them I'm not a Spick. I'm Cuban." Her shoulders began to shake, and Stephen had not the slightest idea of what to say to a brokenhearted eight-year-old girl.

"Well," he said, "I don't have any friends either. So maybe you and I can be friends."

Instantly Consuela turned and said, "You're always playing with Enrique, but you never pay any attention to me."

"That's because I'm a little bit embarrassed around young ladies. I know how to get along with boys, but I'm not so good with girls."

"I bet you are," Consuela said.

"I'll get better, so maybe we can be best friends." Carmen had told him this expression was current among kids at school, and the effect on Consuela was amazing.

"Yes," she said, "me and you. You'll be my best friend."

"Okay. How about if best friends have a game of Monopoly?"

Carmen had come to the door and stopped. Neither Stephen or Consuela had seen her, and she witnessed the scene silently. As the two began to set up the board, she bit her lip and shook her head. Stephen had managed to break through the barrier to Consuela that she herself had difficulty with. Carmen went in, greeted them, and sat and watched as they played, and she noted how Consuela blossomed with Stephen's attention. A smile came to Carmen's lips then, and her eyes grew soft as she watched them.

23

A STAR TO STEER BY

By mid-December, most of the snow had melted away. Stephen had become strong enough to move around comfortably outside, and he even made several relatively long walks into the woods. On Saturday morning, he ventured out accompanied by Enrique and Consuela. The children showed him their favorite hideouts, the creek, the tracks of various kinds of animals. When they returned, Carmen scolded them—all three. "You should not make Mr. Stuart walk so far. I ought to take a switch off the peach tree to you!"

"It's all right, Carmen," Stephen said, quickly moving to put his hands on the children's shoulders. The three were bundled up in heavy clothes, and Stephen's cheeks were flushed, and his eyes were bright from the exercise. "They had to show me the creek where Enrique caught the big bass last summer."

Carmen tried to appear strict. "You let them do anything with you, Stephen! You spoil them to death!"

"No, I don't. I just let them do what they want to, and that way they're real good."

She could not keep from laughing. She slapped at his arm and shook her head in mock disgust. "Go on in and help Granny. You promised to help her peel potatoes."

"Don't forget, Stephen, I mean Mr. Stuart," Enrique piped up. "You promised to let us take you for a ride on the horse this afternoon."

"He is not riding any horse! Not today!"

"Aw, Mom. He wants to," Enrique whined.

"I don't care what he wants, it's not good for him. Now, you go do your homework, and Consuela, you go clean up your room. It looks like a pigsty."

As the children scurried off, Stephen pulled off his coat and hung it on the peg beside the front door. "We had a great time," he said. "I wish you had been with us."

"I'm glad you did."

He started for the kitchen but turned and smiled. He had a good smile. "Maybe you can ride the horse with me," he suggested.

Carmen frowned and shook her head. "I've never been on a horse in my life. I don't have any riding clothes."

"Wear those nice jeans. They fit you real well," he said. "They're just as good as anything, and wear that blue shirt I like. You may have to hold me on the horse. I haven't ridden in a long time."

"All right." Carmen smiled. "Tomorrow we'll do it."

"No, today."

She could refuse him nothing, it seemed. "All right, Stephen, today."

"Good." He went over and took her hand, and she looked up with surprise. "I don't want much," he said blandly, "just my own way."

Carmen giggled. It was something that had come over her lately. Stephen had a quick wit that flashed out and always amused her. She pulled her hand back and said, "Get along with you now and peel those potatoes."

Moving into the kitchen, Stephen picked up a paring knife, sat down on a stool, fished a potato out of a bucket, and began peeling it.

"Watch what you're doin'! You're cuttin' them peelin's too thick! They're supposed to be thin!" Granny said sharply.

Granny was one of the most fascinating persons he had ever encountered, and he could listen to her tell stories by the hour, mostly stories of her childhood. Apparently she had a photographic memory and never forgot anything. Her relationship with Jesus Christ, he had quickly found, was the most important thing in her life, and he had already committed himself to going to church with her. As he peeled potatoes, he began to question her about what went on in her church. "Do people shout at your church?"

"Not like they used to. Oh, when I was a girl I seen 'em shout. Methodist people. There was a preacher called Sam Perry. He was a Wesleyan Methodist, and he would preach sanctification. He preached on snuff one time, and nearly everybody threw their snuff away, and the people would shout. Oh, they would shout, Stephen!" Then she shook her head sadly, saying, "The church ain't strong as it used to be in that line. Kind of drifted back. All the churches have gone off. People had church back when I was growin' up. They don't live the good life like they used to. Too high-minded."

The two talked until all the potatoes were peeled, and Granny said, "I got me a feelin' about you, Stephen boy. I think God's going to get you good one of these days."

Stephen stared at the old woman. She was thin and worn, but her eyes were bright as diamonds. "Well, Granny, I think it would take God himself to do anything with me."

In the afternoon, Carmen came to Stephen, who was reading in his room. "Well, are we going to ride that horse or not?"

Stephen grinned and got up. "We'll be like Dale and Roy," he said, pulling his coat out of the closet and slipping into it.

"Put your hat on. The one with earmuffs. You'll freeze out there."

"Yes, ma'am," Stephen said mockingly.

Enrique and Consuela were jumping up and down, and they all made their way out to the barn, where one of the young men, Tiny Jeeter, brought the old mare out. She was fat and beyond anything more than a short gallop. "How do I get on?" Carmen said.

"Just get on the chopping block," Enrique said. Carmen stood on it, balanced precariously. "Just take the reins, then throw your leg over her back."

Awkwardly, Carmen did, and then Tiny set Enrique and Consuela behind her.

"Not room for me. You ride a spell, and then I'll try it," Stephen said.

He watched, laughing at the three bumping along as the mare plodded around the corral, led by Tiny. When that grew tiresome, Carmen said, "You now, Stephen."

She slipped off the horse, and carefully Stephen got up on the block and then straddled the horse, with the children in front. He took the reins from Tiny and said, "Get up, horse!" The children squealed, and Enrique was allowed to hold the reins.

After the children had their ride, Consuela said, "Now you, Mama. You and Stephen."

Stephen slid off and lifted Consuela down, while Enrique got down himself.

Stephen winked and said, "How about it, Dale?"

"All right, Roy," Carmen said. She climbed the chopping block, straddled the horse, and Stephen mounted behind her. "You do the steering," Stephen said cheerfully. "I'll do the kicking." He kicked the mare in the flanks sharply, and she broke out into a fairly brisk canter. Carmen squealed and began to slip from side to side. "Here, you're going to fall off of this critter!" Stephen reached around her waist and locked his hands in front, holding her tightly. The horse continued her speed, but Stephen did not notice it, for even though he and Carmen wore heavy winter coats, he became aware that he was holding a very shapely woman in his arms. He could not let go for fear of her falling—and he was not inclined to do so anyway.

Carmen was likewise aware of Stephen's arms around her. She hadn't been intimate with anyone since her husband had died, and Stephen's closeness and his warm breath on her cheek were both alarming and exciting. Stephen said in a tight voice, "I guess you better slow this mare down."

"All right." Carmen pulled awkwardly at the reins, and the mare settled to a walk. Carmen expected Stephen to release his grip, but he still held her close. "You can let go now," she said.

"I will in a minute."

Carmen waited, and when his embrace if anything grew tighter, she said, "You're hugging me."

"I think so."

"Well—don't do it."

"I can't help it," Stephen said. Her hair was in his face, and it smelled sweet of shampoo. "I think I'm having a relapse," he whispered in her ear. "I have to hold onto my nurse, or I'll fall off this horse and hurt myself."

Carmen did not know what to do. She whispered, "You must stop! The children will see."

"Well, all right then," Stephen said. As they rode back, he said innocently, "You know, I've just discovered I really like horseback riding. We'll have to do it more often."

In the evening, Stephen helped Enrique with his schoolwork while Carmen and some of the others cleaned up from supper. Then he read to Consuela—and she read to him—until Carmen came to take the children for their baths. Consuela said, "Come and say good night when I'm ready for bed, Stephen."

Later when he went to their room, he wrestled with Enrique a little, laughed at him, and then moved over to Consuela's bed. She got up on her knees and put her arms around his neck. She was very light and seemed so fragile to him, and she whispered, "I love you, Stephen," in his ear. It moved him greatly. He kissed her on the cheek, and said, "Good night, sweetheart."

Stephen sat talking with Morgan about the Vine's book-work—with the end of the year approaching, Morgan was getting things in order for taxes. Stephen offered to show him some bookkeeping shortcuts. Morgan grinned, knowing why Stephen had been in prison. Stephen smiled himself. "Don't worry. These are *legal* shortcuts." After Morgan turned in, Stephen went into the kitchen. It was nearly eleven o'clock, and everyone else had gone to bed, too. Taking a quart bottle of milk out of the refrigerator, he poured himself a glass, and when Carmen came in from the hall, he said, "Come and join me."

She got a glass, and he poured it full of milk. They stood drinking it, and she said, "I'm as wide awake as an owl."

"So am I. Let's fix some coffee and stay up and watch TV."

"There's nothing on at this time of night."

"It doesn't matter. I don't want to go to bed. I might miss something."

He fixed a pot of coffee, then the two of them went in and sat down on the couch in front of the small black and white TV. The movie turned out to be something called *Horrors of Dracula*. When it had been on for ten minutes, Carmen laughed. "It's hard to be afraid of that Dracula. He looks so silly!"

"You're right, he's about as scary as a bowl of oatmeal." They watched the movie, laughing and poking fun at it.

Stephen started to speak, but he heard a sound and cocked his head. "What's that?" he said.

"The chickens!" Carmen said with alarm. "Something's after them!" She got up and started out the door, and he said, "Wait a minute! Get your coat on!" He got their coats, and the two of them moved out into the darkness. They heard a dog barking in the distance. There was as yet no moon so it was very dark and their eyes were not accustomed to it. "Can you see your way?" Stephen asked.

"I can't see a thing."

"Here, take my hand." He reached out, and she took his hand, and the two made their way toward the chicken roost. Suddenly she stopped and squeezed his hand hard. "Look!" she said.

By staring hard, Stephen saw a large gray fox trot across the yard. The fox appeared unhurried, and there was a chicken in its mouth.

"Why, you varmint! I'll get a shotgun and break you of that habit."

"He'll be gone by the time you get back."

"I never saw a fox take a chicken before."

"They've been doing it since Tom sold his hounds. We ought to have a big wire fence around the chicken house."

They stood silently in the cold air, and Carmen said, "Look at the stars. That one over there."

"I think that's Arcturus."

"Is it? It must be nice to know all their names."

"I don't know the names of many. I know sailors steer by that one sometimes."

They stood looking up at the stars, and her hand was still in his. He murmured quietly, "I envy those sailors. All they have to do is look up at the stars, find one to steer by, and then they know where to go."

"That would be nice."

Her voice was soft, and he turned. His eyes had adjusted to the darkness and he was able to make out her features. "You'll find your way, Carmen," he said gently.

"I don't know, Stephen. I'm like a ship that doesn't have any star to steer by. I just float from one day to the next. I don't have any goal."

"I guess we're mostly like that, ships without stars."

From far off they heard the cry of a coyote, always a lonesome sound to Stephen. "I feel about like he sounds. All alone and don't know what to do."

"Your family's not like that."

"No, they're not. You take Uncle Logan. He knows exactly

where he's going. He's going to heaven, and I think he's a little bit anxious to get there."

"That's the way it is with Granny. She talks about heaven like it's, well, like it's Fort Smith or someplace so close by that one day she just might move over there. It doesn't bother her a bit to think about dying—but it bothers me."

"I know. It bothers me, too."

"You believe in God, don't you?"

"Yes, I do, but not like my parents. I don't know what I believe, but what they've got, I need."

Carmen was silent for a long time. The air was cold, and her hand was warm in his. "So do I," she whispered finally.

He bent closer to see into her face. "I wish things were better for you, Carmen." She did not speak, and he kissed her. It was brief, and then he put his arms around her, pressing her cheek against his shoulder. "We'll make it," he said. "Somehow we'll make it."

Carmen rested in his arms. She did not know what was in his heart, but she knew what was in hers. She was lonely and needed exactly what he gave her, the warmth of his arms, his lips, a word of encouragement, and the approval she longed for. She looked up at him and said, "Let's pray to God right now. We both know what we need to do. Let's just do it!"

Stephen smiled at her. He took her hands, and they both knelt before God, finding the perfect star to steer by.

THE CIRCLE IS UNBROKEN

T he Stuart family's most precious tradition was the reunion on Christmas at the Delight Hotel. It was not the food, the gaily wrapped packages, or the Christmas tree; it was the family itself that gave meaning to it. They lived scattered all over America, but when December came and Christmas drew near, they all began to speak about the reunion. It was a fixed point in their lives.

Peter and Leslie came happily in 1958, happy over what God had been doing in the lives of their children. Their son-in-law, Tom, was writing another book. The movie *Bride of Quietness* had received both critical and popular acclaim. It did for Mona what she had hoped *The Soldier* would do— brought her offers of some good parts in good movies. But, at thirty-five, Mona decided to leave Hollywood a success. She had new and different goals. In September, Tom had taken a teaching position at his old college in Kentucky, and Mona was working there as a teaching assistant in the drama department while she finished her college degree.

Peter and Leslie were in their room at the old homestead speaking of this. Leslie went over and put her arm around Peter as he stood by the window. They looked out at the snow, which was falling again, and she said, "It's nice to have a white Christmas."

"It would be nicer if Stephen would come to the reunion."

"I don't think he will," Leslie said quietly. "He was polite and nice about it, but he says he just can't do it."

"*Why* can't he do it? What's such a big deal about coming to his own family reunion?"

"You ought to know, Pete. He's the only failure. He sees his sister who's a successful movie star, he sees his cousins doing well in business, his uncles' and aunts' successes at what they do. And he's ashamed of what he did to us and of being what he calls an 'ex-con.' That's a lot to overcome."

"That's foolish!"

"It's exactly," she said sprightly, "the sort of thing *you* would do if you were in his place! He's very like you in that respect."

"Is he? Well, I wish he were more like you." They stood in a half embrace, and Leslie said heavily, "He's got to make his own decision, Pete. No one can make it for him. I just thank God that he is out of prison and doing better than he has been. That's enough for me—for now."

Jake had driven Rose and Lenora down from Chicago. Stephanie was in Germany. She had been in Lebanon covering the crisis there from July to October, had taken a brief vacation at home with Jake, then in November was sent to Berlin, where tensions were building with the Soviet Union. "I just got a letter. She's starting with the Associated Press the first of the year," he told Jerry as soon as they met at the Delight. "She's thrilled because this is the first job she's gotten on her own merit rather than on your dad's influence. And," he continued, smiling, "since the AP is based in New York, she and I will at least be on the same continent more often—I hope."

Laurel and Richard and Johnny had come with Jake, too, and were staying on at the Vine until it was time to go back to school in January. Johnny, at eight, was growing like a weed. Richard had adopted him as soon as he and Laurel were married. When Johnny asked about his father, they told him he had died, but they discussed between themselves at what point they should tell him—*if* they should tell him—

that his parents had not been married. Mona spoke of this to
Adam, who sought out Richard.

"I don't know if you're aware that I was born out of wedlock," Adam said. Richard was startled—it had never crossed
his mind and he had never heard anyone in the family men-
tion it. "I think the sooner your boy knows the truth the
better. Otherwise when he does find out—and he will—he
may feel lied to, even if you've just omitted a fact."

"Yes," said Richard, "we've pretty much decided we do
have to tell him, but when is the time right? He's not concerned about anything like that now."

"I think maybe that's the best time. He can sort of get used
to the idea before it becomes important. I was older when I
found out about my father, and I went into a tailspin for a
while." Richard didn't comment—he didn't want to pry and
ask for details. Adam continued, "I was about Johnny's age
when my mother married my real father—your uncle Jesse."
Adam smiled. "I loved Jesse, and he loved me, but he never
adopted me even though I called him Dad. Aside from all the
Stuart pride, I think you've done a good thing for Johnny by
giving him your name. You and Laurel have to decide what's
best to tell him, but I thought I'd give you my ideas as one
who's been through it."

"Thanks, Adam. You've given me a lot to think about. And
you've set me wondering—what other family secrets am I
missing out on?"

"Well, you know your mother practically raised me, don't
you?"

"I always had the impression that she'd had a lot to do with
you, that she met my dad while she was your nanny."

"Yeah. I remember some of it. Your dad was sort of wild
back then," Adam said.

"I've heard that. What do you remember?"

"Maybe you should ask him about it."

"Another family secret, I guess," Richard said, smiling.

Bobby didn't come to the reunion because he had a concert date. Jerry and Bonnie were deeply concerned about his lifestyle. But they had a lot to be happy about in Laurel and Richard. They had given them a wedding, "since," Jerry told Bonnie, "we didn't have to pay for a wedding for Stephanie."

"Well, I finally get a grandchild out of it at least," Bonnie sighed. "But they live so far away, it's not fair—I hardly get to spoil Johnny at all. I suppose it's a good thing I stopped counting on having my grandchildren around." She had gone to work as a volunteer for the Salvation Army in Los Angeles, so she and Lenora had to compare notes about operations in their respective cities.

Mona and Tom, too, were staying at the Vine instead of the crowded hotel. Mona was excited to see how Stephen had improved in health and how his whole attitude had changed. She whispered to Tom, "There's something about this place. It makes people different."

"It's not just this place," Tom said. "Have you seen the way he looks at Carmen?"

"Yes. You noticed that, did you?"

"I'm a sensitive writer. We notice things like that," he said solemnly. Stephen was sitting beside a table cracking walnuts with Carmen, who picked them out with a pick and agile fingers. Granny was there also, and she was telling the children a story about how to cure snake bite.

Without preamble, Mona went over and stood before Stephen. "Won't you please come to the reunion?" she said. "Everyone wants you to be there."

Stephen shifted uneasily. "Maybe next year, Sis. It's too soon."

Mona said, "It's your decision, Stephen. You know they'll all come over here to see you, anyway."

"I'll think about it."

As soon as the door closed, Stephen said to Granny, "I wish they wouldn't keep bugging me about the reunion."

"You orta go. You're just stubborn," Granny said firmly. She put the cup of nuts down on the table, gave him a withering look, then stomped out.

Her behavior irritated Stephen, and he got up and walked around the room several times nervously. Truthfully, he wanted to go to the reunion, but he could not face the looks of pity he was sure they'd all give him. He could not stand pity.

"Stephen?" Carmen came into the room. She said quietly, "You ought to go to the reunion."

Staring at her with an expression of disbelief, Stephen said angrily, "Don't you start on me, Carmen! I'm not going!"

"No one can make you go, but you talk to me about how I need to face up to things. Well, what about you?"

"It wouldn't prove anything if I went."

"It wouldn't prove they love you—you already know that. But it would prove that you are a man who has some toughness in him." He stared at her, and she saw anger and frustration in his eyes. "You're a Stuart, and you ought to be proud of that. If I had a family like you do, you wouldn't catch me running away from them, no matter what I'd done."

"You don't understand, Carmen. They'll feel sorry for me."

"What's wrong with that? When Enrique knocked all the hide off his knee, didn't you feel sorry for him?"

"That's—that's different!"

"It's not different at all. When we hurt ourselves or do something foolish or stupid, you don't think it's good for others to feel pity and compassion?" She argued without anger, and there was a gentleness in her voice that wore him down. He had been staring out the window trying to ignore her, but she touched his arm and said, "Please, will you do it for me, Stephen?"

He turned and saw that her lips were trembling. "Why does it mean so much to you?" he asked quietly.

"Because—I don't want to see you hurt. I want to see you be the man that you can be."

Stephen looked into her face and found an answer that he had been searching for. He took a deep breath, then said, "If I go, will you go with me—and bring the kids?"

Her answer was all ready for him. She knew she would be frightened to be thrust into a setting where she was the only outsider, but she lifted her chin and said, "Yes, we will all go. Now go get ready. I'll get the children ready.

Jerry finally came across Gavin, in the lobby of the hotel. "Man, what a fertile bunch we Stuarts are!" said Gavin.

"Guess we're in on the postwar baby boom, all right," Jerry chuckled, "though you couldn't tell it in my branch of the family."

"Well, give it time, Nephew. Say, Phil's boys went to one of Bobby's concerts. They were hoping he'd be here. They tell me he's as good as Elvis!"

"We'll see if Elvis's popularity outlasts his stint in the army."

They filled each other in on family news. Gavin said, "I didn't think Nolan was ever going to finish medical school. I keep trying to get him interested in flying just so I'll have something to talk to him about."

Jerry laughed with him, then said, "Speaking of flying, Gavin, I've gotten involved with something an old flyboy like you might be interested in. Have you ever heard of Wycliffe Bible Translators?"

"No, can't say I have. They fly?"

"Well," said Jerry, "they're missionaries and they need pilots to fly them in and out of remote places—bush pilots."

Gavin looked interested. "You think they'd want old duffers like us?"

"Bonnie and I are going to South America for three months. She's going to work in one of their offices, and I'm going to fly missionaries and supplies in and out of the jungle. You and Heather want to come?"

"Sure," Gavin said. "At least I do. I don't know about Heather and the jungle." He looked thoughtful. "Do they take decent care of the planes, or are they crashes waiting to happen?"

"No. You'd be impressed. They're very professional."

Jerry saw a gleam of excitement in Gavin's eyes that hadn't been there in a long time. "Maybe Phil would be interested, too—but his kids are still too young to have their old man risk his life, like those young men who got killed in Ecuador a couple years ago," Gavin said. "Come on. Let's go talk to Heather and see what she thinks about it. Let's get Bonnie to talk to her, too. Would you and me get to work together? Wouldn't that be like old times!"

Lylah had flown in to Fort Smith with Adam and Maris and Suzanne and Samuel. "I don't know if it was easier when I was younger or when they were!" she told Lenora. Lylah's health had bounced back some. "I work less, have made some new friends—old ladies like me. We gossip and eat and talk about our grandkids. But we've been talking about finding some sort of project to work on. I bet you'd have some ideas about that?"

Lenora smiled. "I think I might be able to make some suggestions. How about visiting folks in the hospital or in the old folks' home? Or maybe some juvenile delinquents need grannies? Or you could work with Bonnie at the army's home for unwed mothers. Is that enough, or should I keep going?"

"I think that's enough to think about. Do you think I'd have to tell them I was an unwed mother? But maybe they'd like to know it isn't the end of their lives. And Bonnie and I haven't spent much time together in years. That would be nice. But do you know she and Jerry are going to be what they call short-term missionaries, in South America?"

"No. Really? That's wonderful! I hadn't heard that. It must

have something to do with airplanes if Jerry is going. Tell me about it."

The big meal was ready, and the family gathered in the large dining room of the Delight. Tourists had discovered the Ozarks, and Merle had had six rooms added on the previous spring and had moved a wall to enlarge the dining room. "Still," he told Arlene, "there are so many Stuarts this year that next time we might have to prop the dining room doors open and run tables out into the lobby!"

Jerry sat in the place at the table that had always been Amos's. Last year they'd left that chair empty, but Rose told her son it was time that he took it. Johnny sat next to his grandma Bonnie and enjoyed all the attention. Jake sat next to Richard and talked about Stephanie. "She says being a woman in this line of work has some advantages. Sometimes she can get stories from people because she doesn't seem as threatening as a man might. But I think it's because men like to talk to pretty women."

Logan had invited Granny to come and they sat with Violet and Dent and Clint and Carol and all their kids, Logan's beloved grandchildren. "I'm sure glad Richard and Laurel will be here a while," he said. "I've missed 'em."

"I don't know how you could miss anybody with a mess of relations like this!" Granny chuckled.

Owen rose, and as he did everyone in the dining room thought the same thing, that Amos was missing. Always it had been Amos, the oldest, who stood and made the opening remarks and called for Owen to ask the blessing. The mantle had fallen on Owen, who said, "We all still miss Amos, don't we? I know I do. But I'm proud of our family, as he was. Our family has worked to bring about good for our country, some in the military, some in various kinds of ministry, some—" He stopped abruptly and straightened, his eyes open wide with a mild shock.

Everyone turned, and it was Leslie who whispered, "Stephen!"

Stephen came through the entryway. His right arm was holding Carmen, and his left hand clutched Consuela's hand. Enrique stood beside his mother smiling, looking not at all frightened.

A quiet fell over the dining room for just a second, and then Stephen said, "We'd like to join you—if we could."

Pete was already on his feet. "I've got a place saved for you over here—all of you. Come over here, Son." As the four made their way to Pete's table, every Stuart, every in-law, cousin, uncle, aunt, all had to go shake Stephen's hand and pound him on the back. Most of them managed to kiss Carmen and shake hands with Enrique and wheedle a kiss out of Consuela. There was a hubbub of laughter and talking, and when Stephen looked around at Carmen he saw tears running down her cheeks. His own eyes felt misty, and he said huskily, "Well, they'll get tired of this pawing at us sooner or later."

Carmen held his arm tightly. "I don't mind," she whispered, diamonds in her eyes.

When order was restored and people had been persuaded to get back to their places, Stephen said, "There's something I want you all to know. Carmen and I have both given our lives to Jesus Christ, and we want to serve him the rest of our lives."

Owen looked at them fondly. He closed his eyes and began to thank God not only for the food, but for the family. As Owen prayed, Stephen found Carmen's hand. He squeezed it, and she squeezed back fiercely.

Peter and Leslie made no pretense of bowing their heads. They were both staring at their son, and Leslie whispered in a voice trembling with emotion, "He's going to be all right, Pete!"

Pete put his arm around his wife and said, "Yes, the circle is unbroken."

EPILOGUE: THE LEGACY

The events of the fifties shaped the events of following decades. That's how history works.

Stalin died in 1953. The colorful Nikita Khrushchev eventually gained the ascendency over his rivals. Krushchev's anti-Stalin rhetoric was blamed for encouraging Soviet satellites to revolt. One of the lasting images of the fifties is that of Soviet tanks rolling through the city streets of Eastern Europe—Berlin in 1953, Poland and Hungary in 1956—putting down civilian uprisings against Communist regimes. By the late fifties, like a gushing wound, as many as twenty thousand refugees a day were fleeing from East to West Berlin. This flow was dramatically stopped when Soviet-controlled East Berlin erected the Berlin Wall in 1961.

The "space race" and the "arms race" lasted until the end of the Cold War. Sputnik I and II, the first earth-orbiting satellites, were launched in 1957 by the Soviets and created a sense of national crisis—the U.S. seemed to be falling behind its adversary. The psychological impact was enormous. Sputnik drastically changed American plans in politics, budget-making, education, military buildup. Fear that the Russians had the capability to launch a nuclear attack on the United States was growing, evidenced by more elaborate plans for civil defense developed in the late fifties.

The Civil Rights movement continued gaining ground. The fights over desegregation in the fifties continued into the sixties, from the nonviolence promoted by the Rev. Martin Luther King Jr., student sit-ins at lunch counters, and growing black pride, to the rioting in Watts, Newark, and Detroit in the mid-1960s and the assassinations of black leaders like Malcom X and King.

Television had begun to make its mark. It was Joseph McCarthy's televised investigations of the army in 1954 that shined public light on his tactics and brought about the downfall of this man who through beguiling fabrications had driven people from their jobs, had aroused public condemnation against them, and had destroyed their reputations.

Some of the fifties fads endured—*American Bandstand,* Silly Putty, Slinky. The Barbie doll appeared late in the decade to become an icon selling in the millions, and clothing manufacturers could hardly keep up with the demand.

And the Stuarts endured. Their legacy was the adequacy of Jesus Christ in all times, whether of war or of peace, joy or sorrow. Some of the family found their peace through community, like Richard and Stephen, some through solitude, like Mona. They came by varied routes to personal acceptance of the family's fundamental creed: Christ is the answer.

Five Missionaries Slain in Ecuador
by S. Stuart Taylor
QUITO, ECUADOR
10 January 1956 (INS)

Five American missionaries were killed on January 8 by members of a tribe of Auca Indians they were trying to evangelize. The information so far is that the missionaries had made contact several times with the Auca, at the Curaray River in northeastern Ecuador, but on this occasion something went terribly wrong, and five young men are dead, leaving behind widows and young children.

Bulganin: "Imperialists" Trying to Divide Soviet Union
by S. Stuart Taylor
WARSAW, POLAND
21 July 1956 (INS)

Premier Nikolai Bulganin of the Soviet Union spoke in Warsaw today claiming that foreign imperialists were making use of political and economic difficulties in Poland to divide the Soviet Union. The political difficulty he referred to was the so-called Poznan revolt on June 28, which put an end to the pretense of popular support for the Communist regime. Fifty thousand laborers in Poznan staged a strike and held a procession demanding bread, free elections, and the departure of the Russians.

Israeli Attack No Surprise to British and French
by S. Stuart Taylor
CAIRO, EGYPT
30 October 1956 (INS)

Yesterday's invasion of Egypt by Israel seems to have been a complete surprise only to the U.S. It now appears that both France and Great Britain had some foreknowledge. Tensions have been building since Egypt took full control of the canal in July and has steadfastly refused to yield to American, French, and British efforts to establish an international agency to operate it. The Egyptians

289

insist that they are willing and able to do it.

Anglo-French Forces Capture Port Said in Bid to Take Suez

by S. Stuart Taylor
CAIRO, EGYPT
6 November 1956 (INS)

Today, British and French forces landed at and captured Port Said and Port Fuad in Egypt, following the bombings begun on October 31. Many here in Cairo view the Anglo-French action as an effort to destroy President Nasser as well as to gain control of the Suez Canal, which is critical to oil transport to Western Europe and the United States. Israeli troops are said to be within thirteen miles of the canal.

U.S. Outstanding in Track and Field in Melbourne

by S. Stuart Taylor
MELBOURNE, AUSTRALIA
8 December 1956 (INS)

The 1956 Summer Olympics were officially closed today by Avery Brundage, president of the International Olympic Committee. Attendance at the games is estimated at over two million. The United States won sixteen gold medals in track and field, including Bob Richards in the pole vault, retaining his Olympic title. In swimming, although the Australians won most of the gold medals, the close competition with the U.S. kept fans cheering and applauding. Among notable team competitions, the U.S. still has never lost an Olympic tournament basketball game, winning the final 89–55 over the Soviet Union, with Bill Russell and Bo Jeangerard scoring 13 and 16 points, respectively.

Tightened Border Controls Block Hungarian Refugees

by S. Stuart Taylor
VIENNA, AUSTRIA
1 February 1957 (INS)

The controls at the Hungarian border with Austria have been severely tightened in the last few days. Through interpreters, many Hungarian refugees here tell of fleeing for their lives in the middle of the night and making treacherous frontier crossings. Among them are students who took part in the spontaneous revolt that began last October and lasted until the Soviets took military action in November against an essentially civilian uprising. The Intergovernmental Committee for European Migration, assisted by the United States Escapee program and voluntary agencies, is gaining momentum in assisting refugees to emigrate from Austria and resettle. Estimates put the number of refugees at 178,000. Though the border closing has slowed the flow into Austria to a trickle, refugees continue to flee to Yugoslavia.

Hammarskjöld Concludes Talks with Nasser
by S. Stuart Taylor
CAIRO, EGYPT
26 March 1957 (INS)

UN Secretary General Dag Hammarskjöld today concluded seven days of talks with Egyptian president Gamal Abdel Nasser concerning operation of the Suez Canal. Talks were certainly helped by the withdrawal of Israeli forces from Egypt and the Gaza Strip earlier this month. The canal has been blocked by Egypt with sunken ships, which are being cleared by a UN salvage fleet. The Suez

matter is expected to increase Nasser's prestige in the Arab world as a champion of Arab nationalism.

Arkansas Governor Uses National Guard against Negro Students
by S. Stuart Taylor
LITTLE ROCK, ARK.
4 September 1957 (INS)

Yesterday, the governor of Arkansas, Orval E. Faubus, surrounded Central High School in Little Rock with 270 national guard troops and state police armed with billy clubs and rifles. Nine Negro students were thus barred from entering for the fall term. Faubus claimed he was acting to prevent public disorder; critics charge that the governor is intent on at least delaying if not voiding U.S. Supreme Court ordered integration.

Mob Violence in Little Rock
by S. Stuart Taylor
LITTLE ROCK, ARK.
23 September 1957 (INS)

Governor Orval Faubus, in compliance with a federal court injunction, withdrew national guard troops from Central High School in Little Rock, and an outbreak of violence ensued when eight Negro students attempted to enter today. Four adult Negroes walked up the street toward the school in a diversionary tactic. The waiting mob attacked, beating and kicking them, while the Negro students entered the school. When the crowd discovered the students had entered, they shrieked and howled; women wept and screamed. Three reporters on the scene from *Life* magazine were also beaten. Some white students left the school, cheered by the mob. The howling mob outside and attacks from white students inside resulted in the Negro students being taken out of the school by police a few hours later.

Ike Orders Army to Little Rock
by S. Stuart Taylor
LITTLE ROCK, ARK.
24 September 1957 (INS)

President Eisenhower today ordered U.S. Army airborne troops to Little Rock to restore order after yesterday's violence at Central High School. The nine students finally started school. The president stated that the federal troops would not leave until Faubus complied with court orders to enforce integration.

Further Attacks on Vice-President
by S. Stuart Taylor
WITH THE VICE-PRESIDENT
CARACAS, VENEZUELA
13 May 1958 (INS)

Vice-President Richard M. Nixon's goodwill tour of Latin America was further beset by strife as Mr. Nixon's limousine today was attacked by a mob. We are told that President Eisenhower has dispatched a thousand marines to Caribbean bases and has challenged the Venezuelan government's ability to protect the vice-president. Today's attack follows the one in Lima, Peru, a few days ago, in which university students threw eggs, stones, and epithets at Mr. Nixon. He was spat upon and shouted down though he tried unsuccessfully to win over his attackers by argument. Some sources attribute these attacks to

Communist instigation, but others cite the effect of the U.S. recession on Latin America and on general U.S. indifference to Latin American concerns.

New French Premier de Gaulle Tours Algeria
by S. Stuart Taylor
BÔNE, ALGERIA
6 June 1958 (INS)

New French premier Charles de Gaulle returned to Paris today after a three-day visit to troubled Algeria, in which he announced that all Algerians, including Moslems of both sexes, would be completely French, forming one electorate. While Premier de Gaulle was received with cheers, the FLN *(Front de la Liberation Nationale)* is not expected to give up the call for independence. The FLN is the voice of the Moslems in rebellion and was responsible last year for the massacre of 302 villagers at Melouza, as well as for an ongoing campaign of bombings and violent attacks in Algeria and in France.

The inability to resolve French problems in Algeria was the primary factor in

bringing de Gaulle to power, ending the fourth republic. De Gaulle was the leader of Free France in World War II. He accepted leadership June 1 on the condition that he, not the French assembly, would have full power to reform France's constitution.

Alaska Wins Statehood at Last
by S. Stuart Taylor
WASHINGTON, D.C.
7 July 1958 (INS)

Today Alaska, the territory dubbed "Seward's Folly," became the forty-ninth state of the Union and the first noncontiguous state. The U.S. thought so little of the region after purchasing it from Russia that for seventeen years the territory had no government at all. It wasn't until gold was discovered in the Klondike River, just across the Alaska-Canadian border in 1896, that Americans took an interest in Alaska. At the behest of some of the sixty thousand Americans who went looking for gold, congressional representatives back home finally began writing some legislation for Alaska.

The admission of Alaska opens the door for another noncontiguous territory, Hawaii, which has also sought statehood for many years.

Marines Land in Lebanon
by S. Stuart Taylor
BEIRUT, LEBANON
15 July 1958 (INS)

Marine units attached to the U.S. Sixth Fleet, on duty in the Mediterranean Sea, have landed in Lebanon in response to the Lebanese government's request to the U.S. for protection. Lebanese president Camille Chamoun has long come under criticism from Arab nations for his more and more open alignment with the U.S. Rebellion broke out in April. UN observers did not substantiate Chamoun's charge that massive military intervention by the new UAR (United Arab Republic, formerly Egypt and Syria) was taking place, so the Lebanese government appealed to the U.S. for military aid on the grounds that the country is being threatened by foreign intervention.

At this time no predictions are forthcoming as to how long the U.S. troops will be here.

Khrushchev in Talks with Ike
by S. Stuart Taylor
CAMP DAVID, MD.
27 September 1959 (AP)

Today is the last day of the history-making visit of Russian premier Nikita S. Khrushchev to the United States. President Eisenhower and the Soviet leader are holding talks at Camp David, focusing on disarmament. President Eisenhower has been invited to visit the Soviet Union next year. Mr. Khrushchev also withdrew his ultimatum that the Allies get out of Berlin. Sources say the talks have gone much better than expected in light of the Soviet premier's behavior earlier in the trip.

Highlights of Mr. Khrushchev's antics include the mocking "gift" of a model of the Soviet's latest space success, a lunar rocket launched recently. In a speech to the UN, Khrushchev was outrageous, boastful, and condescending, proposing the elimination of all weapons—nuclear and conventional—in four years.

His transcontinental tour in the company of UN ambassador Henry Cabot

Lodge was also not without incident. Mr. Khrushchev was upset that he wasn't permitted to go to Disneyland, for security reasons.

The administration hopes that these talks are the beginning of a new spirit in Soviet-American relations.

Ike Concluding "Personal Diplomacy" Tour in Paris Talks

by S. Stuart Taylor
WITH THE PRESIDENT
PARIS, FRANCE
19 December 1959 (AP)

President Eisenhower begins talks today with French, British, and West German leaders. The president is nearing the end of his 22,000-mile goodwill tour of eleven nations in Europe, Africa, the Middle East, and Asia. The president announced he will suggest a series of summit meetings between the Western powers and will urge that Premier Khrushchev of the Soviet Union be invited.

The president stated before the tour that he believes in personal diplomacy—that his goal was to promote international understanding that the U.S. wants "to search out methods by which peace in the world can be assured with justice for everybody."

It appears by his enthusiastic welcome in India as the "prince of peace" and the warm receptions he received elsewhere that perhaps that goal was in some measure achieved. But will the tour result in concrete progress in international relations? The president has one more year in office to find out.